Spirit of the Amaroq
A Story of Salvation

James Charles

ISBN: 978-1984198617

Credits
Cover Artist: Designs by Ms G
Editor: Sherry Derr-Wille

Dedication

As Always, for Linda

"Your task is not to seek for love, but merely to seek and find all the
barriers within yourself that you have built against it,"
Rumi.

Chapter One

Sorrow comes to all, and it often comes with bitter agony.
Abraham Lincoln

Before sunrise in his basement gym, he curls weights, pumps out fifty pushups, crunches fifty sit-ups, jumps rope for ten minutes, and punches a boxer's speed bag. Pastor Jack Douglas, at thirty-three years of age, keeps the body God has given him healthy by eating well and maintaining a rigid physical regimen. He had played various sports in high school and boxed in college.

He flips off the light, sprints up the basement stairs and makes his way outside. Shirtless, because the late spring humidity hasn't decreased much during the night, he runs through his suburban Puckett, Georgia neighborhood as the sun rises over Savannah to the northeast.

"Good morning, Pastor," a man dressed in a robe hollers while stooping down to pick up the morning paper off his lawn.

"Good morning, Bob," Jack says zipping by.

Two blocks later, dripping in sweat, Jack spies a middle-aged woman getting into her sedan. "Looking good, Pastor," she calls out, winking.

"Good morning to you too, Joan." He notices her eyes lingering on him far too long.

He jogs down the street, circles around, and two miles later makes his way back to his modest two-story home.

Inside, he towels off then runs up the stairs to a bedroom. Cracking open the door, he sees his eight-year old daughter, Rebecca, still fast asleep. He tiptoes over to her bedside, sits and brushes back a sandy-blond strand of hair from her face. He leans down, kisses her forehead. "Good morning, champ," he whispers.

She yawns, opens her eyes. "Hi, Daddy."

"Today's your big day. Ready to knock 'em dead? I'll be there right after my last appointment."

"I'm nervous."

"Nervous? Nonsense. It's just like a practice game."

"What if I freeze?"

"Look, you're the best soccer goalie I've ever seen. Just like we practiced. Keep your eye focused like a laser on the ball. I've never seen someone as quick as you. I see you on the Olympic team someday." He jerks to one side pretending to jab at her. She blocks his hands. "See?" he teases.

"Daddy," she protests, furrowing her brow.

He leans in, tickling her. "Let's go get Aaron and wake Mommy up."

She follows him into another bedroom across the hall where his six-year-old son, Aaron begins to stir. Rubbing the sleep from his eyes, he sits up.

Pressing his index finger to his lips, Jack signals with his other hand to follow them. They creep into the master bedroom and jump onto the bed, smothering Janette. She moans, trying to pull the pillow over her head. Jack snatches it away and leans in for a kiss. Meanwhile, Rebecca and Aaron tickle their mother.

"Stop. Y'all're monsters," she says, wincing.

"The Lord has commanded thee to rise," Jack says. "His work is to be done."

She yawns. "Tell the Lord I need a day off. Even He took a day off."

"So shall ye have the Sabbath."

"Always the preacher." She stretches.

"You guys get ready for school." Jack nods to the children. They scurry off. "Close the door, Aaron," he shouts after him.

Aaron doubles back and closes the door.

Jack lies down next to his wife.

"Eww. You're sweaty."

"Yeah?" He climbs atop her. "Joan gawked at me again."

She chuckles. "Three quarters of the ladies in your congregation

2

only show up to gawk at you on Sundays."

"I thought my services were full because of my sermons. I'm crushed."

"All right. All right. Don't forget vanity and pride are sins."

"Ha, ha," he says. "Now who's preaching, miss newly promoted deputy city manager?"

"Enough already." She pushes him off. "I have a meeting with the Governor's secretary at nine." Pulling her nightshirt off over her head, she tosses it at him where it lands on his face. He pulls it off and watches her head for the shower, her shoulder-length brown hair bouncing from side to side.

~ * ~

Jack makes the children's lunches in the kitchen. Aaron crunches on cereal; Rebecca reads a book for school.

"Stop it." Rebecca sneers at Aaron.

"You stop it," Aaron says back at her.

"What?" Jack snaps at them.

"He's kicking me under the table."

"She started it."

"You started it." She kicks him.

"Well, I'm finishing it." Jack drops their sandwiches onto the table. "Pack your own lunches."

Aaron sticks his tongue out at Rebecca and stuffs his sandwich in his pack.

Janette enters wearing a tan-colored cotton sateen two-button jacket and pencil skirt. Jack's wandering eyes trail her moves as she carries a briefcase and sets it on the counter. He winks at her.

"What?" She grimaces at him and glances at the children who pay them no attention. She pours a glass of orange juice. "I'll meet you at the game after the budget meeting?"

"Yes. I'll leave the shelter at three." He pours himself a glass of milk. "I still think they should've named it after you."

"Don't be ridiculous, Jack. You do that for dead people." They sit with the children at the table.

"I'm just saying. If it weren't for you, the Puckett Women's Shelter wouldn't exist." He sips his milk. "Hey, champ," he says to Rebecca. "We can take the team out for pizza after the game if you like."

"What if we lose?"

"Win or lose. We celebrate."

Rebecca frowns. Raising an eyebrow, Jack purses his lips and nods, teasing her.

After they finish their breakfast, Jack reaches out his hands to Rebecca on one side and Aaron on the other. Janette completes the hand-holding circle. "Lord," Jack says, bowing his head, "we enter this day knowing you watch over us, you are all-loving, merciful and gracious. We ask you to bless us this day o' Lord. In Jesus' name. Amen."

"Amen," the others say in unison.

Motioning to the children, Jack says, "Let's go. Brush your teeth."

Rebecca stows her book in her backpack and runs upstairs following Aaron. Janette rises and organizes papers in her briefcase while Jack clears the table and rinses the dishes.

~ * ~

At the front door, Jack kisses and hugs his children. They run off and climb into Janette's minivan.

Janette gives Jack a long and enduring kiss. "See you tonight," she says after pulling back. "Love you."

"Love you too."

Standing at the door, he watches her settle into the driver's seat. The children wave at him as Janette backs out of the driveway.

Jack hurries upstairs and jumps into the shower. While soaping up, he hears a low boom then the shower door rattles. He figures it must be a military jet from Moody Air Force Base west of Brunswick that flew over and caused a sonic boom, as they had many times in the past.

He dresses in slacks, a dress shirt and loafers, grabs his notebook with his sermon and departs the house a few minutes later.

At the main intersection not far from his house where he waits at a red light to turn left, a police car zips by, its siren screaming. Other cars pull to the side to let the police car pass. When clear, Jack makes his turn, heading in the opposite direction.

Jack drives through Puckett, a town similar to others in the South with historic city centers erected after the Civil War. Sherman's Army destroyed much of Puckett on his march to the sea.

He pulls into a one-story church and parks in a large lot. Built with glass, metal, and Georgian granite stone in a circular design, the Puckett Christ Our Savior Church was meant to signify God cradling his faithful. The main worship hall, or nave, has a wide ceiling built of metal and glass allowing the sun, like God's love, to shine in from above. The altar stands in the middle in a semi-circle, so the congregation can feel embraced by God's presence.

Entering his office, Jack greets the church secretary, "Good morning, Millie."

"Good morning, Pastor," she says. A retired school teacher, Millie works for nominal wages to serve the church and keep busy. "Carl is running late at the shelter, so he said you can meet him there at eleven. The shipment for the pantry will arrive then."

"Thanks."

She goes into an adjoining office as he sits, scanning the mail on his desk.

A moment later he sets the mail aside, opens his notebook and reviews his sermon. He circles a passage: "The Lord our God is merciful to the penitent." He opens his leather-bound Bible, finds a section he has marked, and jots it down in his notebook: Ephesians 2:4, "But God, who is rich in mercy, for his great love with which he loved us." And, Psalms 145:9, "The Lord is good to all: and his tender mercies are all over his works."

Jack hears car doors slamming closed outside in the parking lot. *Odd, I don't have any appointments until afternoon.* He turns back to his sermon.

Millie backs into his office. "Pastor?"

He looks up. "Yes, Millie?"

"The, ah, Sheriff..." she says, her voice trailing off.

He stands from his desk, peers out the window to see the sheriff and a deputy making their way into the church. Jack leads Millie into the hall past the altar where Sheriff Bennett and his deputy enter, meeting him halfway. "Mitch," Jack says to Bennett, a tall, middle-age man with a barrel chest. "You look like you've come to arrest a fugitive." He smiles.

"Jack. We, ah," his voice cracks, "well, ah, we have a situation." The deputy behind him stands statuesque, looking down at the floor.

"What is it, Mitch?" Jack's handsome smile droops into a frown.

"I think you should sit down."

"Mitch? What's going on?" He continues to stand.

Bennett puts his hand on Jack's shoulder, squeezing it to the point where his knuckles turn white. "There's been an accident."

"What are you talking about?" Jack says, his voice rising.

"It's Janette."

Millie gasps, holding her hand to her mouth.

"Janette?" In almost staccato-like fashion Jack says, "An accident? What? Where is she? In the hospital?" He pushes past Bennett, knocking Bennett's hand off his shoulder heading for the door.

Bennett hustles after him, followed by the others. He grabs Jack by an arm, spins him around. "Jack, listen." Still holding his arm, Bennett says, "Janette's not at the hospital."

"What're you saying, Mitch?"

Bennett chokes up. "The children, Jack."

"The children?" His face tenses. "They're in school."

Bennett inhales deeply then exhales quickly. "No."

Jack's eyes twitch back and forth, examining Bennett's tightening face. "She dropped them off. They drove away to school. At the school. I saw them drive off to school."

"No. Not at the school."

Jack shakes loose from Bennet's grip. "I gotta go to them." He bolts for the door, racing for his car. The men dash after him followed by Millie. Bennett catches up, blocking Jack's access to the car door.

"Mitch, what're you doing?" He tries to get past him. "I have to see my family."

"I can't let you do that, Jack."

6

"I *have* to see them. They need me." Jack tries to dodge around Bennett, but Bennett continues to block him, his deputy hovering as if ready to pounce. Jack's adrenaline surges to the point that he could put his boxing skills to work. He doesn't care about them being police officers, congregants, and friends. He'd punch them if they try to keep him from his family.

Millie sobs, tears stream down her cheeks. Jack surveys the men. At last, Bennett says, "I don't know, Jack. I don't think that's a good idea."

"You gotta let me go or I go myself. I know the route they took." His eyes dart from the sheriff to the deputy who holds him at bay as if he were a psycho killer cornered, holding a dripping knife in his hand in a back alley at the scene of a crime.

Bennett sighs. "Okay. Okay. But, you listen to me. You do what I tell you and don't interfere with the investigation."

Everyone holds their pose for the longest time. At last, Jack pushes through the huddle heading for the sheriff's cruiser. Bennett glances at his deputy then scurries after Jack. Millie hangs back as Jack climbs into the back of the cruiser and sits. Bennett crawls in beside him. The deputy drives them off.

The cruiser turns onto the double-lane main highway that runs through the suburban sections of town.

A few miles down the road another cruiser blocks their way where a deputy diverts motorists to turn down a side street. He waves the Sheriff on through. A couple hundred yards later near an overpass, they pull up to fire trucks blocking the road. The highway has been closed in both directions.

Jack climbs from the cruiser, spots the coroner's van next to a fire truck. Beyond that, he sees the smoldering remains of a tractor-trailer gasoline tanker on its side under the overpass. The cab, darkened by the fire and smashed, but intact, detached and rolled several yards away from the tanker. Jack figures the truck crossed the open median into on-coming traffic, struck a vehicle, the tanker-trailer crashed into the overpass piling, exploded and flipped onto its side.

Bennett and his deputy stand next to Jack. The tanker spilled the flaming gasoline all over the highway. The pavement still smokes from the foam the fireman sprayed to extinguish the fire. The scene looks as if an airstrike decimated the highway. A crater in the highway under the overpass had formed from the blast next to the tanker. The overpass above had been damaged and blackened by the fire as well.

Jack sees the burned-out and smashed shell of Janette's minivan flipped over onto its side next to the tanker. He realizes the truck struck her van before the tanker-trailer slammed into the overpass piling where it exploded. He starts to walk in that direction, slipping and sliding across the sticky blackened substance beneath his feet, but picks up his pace to a slow jog. Bennett and his deputy trot after him, but not before Jack finds white sheets covering the seats in the van. They catch up and restrain him. "No, Jack," Bennett says. "You don't want to see this."

Struggling to break free he shouts, "I want to see my family!"

Firefighters hosing off the pavement, the coroner and his assistant taking pictures of the van, dressed in protective booties, watch on as Bennett says, "I can't let you do that. It's not the way you want to remember them."

Not only stronger than all of them, but with his adrenaline exploding, Jack breaks free, falls to his knees and pulls the sheet off the driver's seat. Before the men can get to him he crawls over to the rear passenger seat, reaches in and rips the sheet off the backseat. His wife has been decapitated and all three have been burned beyond recognition. Still strapped in their seats, they hang sideways in their seatbelts.

Three more deputies rush over to assist. Together, all four deputies latch onto Jack who fights to break free. They drag him away from the van. The coroner hustles over, covers the bodies as Jack sits on the roadway, his legs outstretched and his pants soaked from the gasoline. The deputies struggle to get a firm grip on him because he keeps pushing them away.

"My family," Jack sobs, spittle dribbling out.

Holding onto Jack, they subdue and carry him over to a first responder's vehicle. "Can you give him something?" Bennett says to a paramedic.

The paramedic frowns but nods. He prepares a sedative while the men tussle with Jack. "I gotta go to them," Jack says, crying. "I mean, I gotta help them. Can't you see that? I gotta be with them. Come on, Mitch."

Soon after the paramedic injects the sedative, Jack releases his grip and becomes dead weight. The deputies have crumpled his clean, pressed dress shirt. Several buttons are torn off. His hair mussed, he mumbles indecipherable words and phrases as the paramedic straps him to a gurney. They load him up and drive off.

Chapter Two

Deep in earth my love is lying,
And I must weep alone.
Edgar Allen Poe

He lies in the fetal position in the middle of his bed wearing only tight-fitting boxer briefs clutching a pillow, half of it covering his face. Jack raises his eyes slightly as his mother, a well-groomed and proper Southern Belle wearing a loose-fitting, black Southern-style summer dress, pushes back the half-opened bedroom door, peering in. "Jack?" she says.

His eyes follow her as she enters and sits on the edge of the bed next to him. He doesn't move or acknowledge her presence.

Leaning over, kissing his head, she whispers, "I'm here, son."

She brushes his unkempt sandy hair from his face, glances around the darkened room, the hot morning sun streaking in through a crack in the curtains. Stroking his hair, he doesn't stir, but stares over the pillow past her, his nose just below the edge, breathing in through the pillow.

"What can I do, honey? Tell me what to do."

After a long pause, he whispers through the pillow, still staring past her, "I can smell her, Mother. The pillow. I can smell her on the pillow."

"I know, baby. I know." She caresses his head.

After a couple minutes, still brushing his head, she says, "I know how hard this is. We'll get through this with our faith in the Lord. He will help you, all of us, through this. We have to be strong. Have faith in God. It's our faith that sustains us in the darkest times. You know that better than anyone, Jack."

His eyes dart up and seem to burrow right through her. "Why has He forsaken me? Me of all people?"

"No. No, He has not. He has not forsaken you."

He pulls out a recent photo of his family from in between the pillow and his chest, handing it to her.

She glances at it, looks back at him and starts to place it onto the bed, but he pushes it back at her. His face tightens. "Look at them, Mother. You look at them." He pushes it right up to within an inch of her face and holds it there. His voice cracking, he says, "Look at them long and hard. Look at Rebecca. Look at Aaron. You look at those faces. Look at those beautiful smiling little faces."

"I…" Her hand holding the picture trembles, but he holds it against her attempt to push back. "Jack, please. Stop. You're frightening me."

He relents, snatches the photo from her, tucking it just between his chest and the pillow again.

She quivers.

"Get out, Mother." His eyes dart away from her. "I don't want to see anyone." He stares past her again.

"Jack, I…" She hesitates, looks him over. "I understand. You're in shock. Grieving. It will be okay. With God's love, with prayer…"

"Go, Mother."

Frozen, she doesn't move.

"Get out."

She shudders, stands up, backs away, and out the door.

~ * ~

He stands in the shower for the longest time, letting the water cascade over his face and roll off his body. How long? He has no idea, except the water has cooled.

Jack turns the water off, steadies himself with his hand against the wall. *How am I going to get through this day? How can I face all those people? People I've counseled in their own grief? People I've reassured that God would look out for them? Love them? Be faithful to them? Give them strength? Guide them in their grief?*

He stares at the drain as water from his body drips onto the floor.

Dragging himself into the bedroom, he stops in his tracks and looks at his wife's pillow on the bed next to the upside-down family photo. He stares for the longest time while holding the towel at his side. A tear falls from his eye, landing on his cheek. Then a tear from his other eye lands on his other cheek. Then another. Then another and another until tears stream down his face. *I've got to pull myself together to say goodbye to my family. I have to.*

He wipes the tears from his face with the towel and tosses it onto a chair. He drags himself over to the bureau, pulls out pants, a dress shirt, and socks. He puts on underwear, sits on the bed, unable to continue, staring at his clothes. He hasn't dressed in five days. He looks at his shoes below him. *Do I put on the shoes first? No, I have to pull on the socks first. Just pull on the socks. So why can't I pull on the socks?*

At last, he lifts one sock off the bed, cradles it in his hand, examining it. A minute goes by before he pulls it on a foot. He looks at the other sock all by itself. All alone. Without its partner. *I have to put the other sock on, right? I have to, because it belongs with the other one, okay? How can I not reunite them? How can I put on one sock and not the other? It just doesn't seem right.*

At last he picks up the other sock, examining it too. *Put the other sock on. You have the power to put the other sock on, or not. Put the sock on.*

He puts the sock on. *There. How difficult was that? You had power over the sock. You controlled the sock's destiny. That's all there was to it. How difficult was that?*

Now the pants, right? He pulls on his pants, then his shoes, one at a time, just like the socks. He looks his shirt over for a time before putting it on, carefully threading each arm one at a time, buttoning and tucking it into his pants.

He shuffles into the bathroom, looks at himself in the mirror. He hasn't shaved in five days either, since that morning. *Did I forget to shave? Have I forgotten how to shave?* He scrutinizes the stubble for the longest time, rubbing it. He doesn't shave.

Back in the bedroom, he stands staring in his closet at his ties and jackets. He hears someone knocking on the opened bedroom door behind him but doesn't turn to look. He continues to stare into his closet.

"You about ready, son?" he hears his father say.

Jack glances over at him, peeking in. His father enters wearing a dark-blue, double-breasted Brooks Brother three-piece suit with a watch chain dangling from the watch pocket. His father looks like an older version of Jack in his mid-fifties, albeit heavier from fine dining. Jack doesn't answer but turns his head back to examine his suits in the closet staring at him.

"We're going to be late," his father says, edging closer.

Late? What is late? It's not as if my wife and kids are waiting for me. Waiting to see me. They are gone now. Forever.

He watches his father pull up next to him.

Glancing at Jack then into the closet, his father says, "Oh. Well, let's see. Let's try this one." He reaches into the closet and pulls a tie off the rack. "This will work." He ties the tie around his own neck then places it over his son's head, pulling it tight up to Jack's neck and adjusting it. He chooses a jacket off a hanger, holding it up for Jack. "Here ya go."

Jack looks down at his arms. Now his arms won't move. *Move arms. What is going on?* After a moment, his arms seem to rise by themselves. His father slips the jacket over Jack's floating arms.

Jack stands there unable to make his legs work now. It seems to him he's losing control to command his body. At times, his mind is blank; no thoughts, no emotions, just void as he stares at nothing.

His father puts his hand on Jack's shoulder. "I know, son. I know. We have to be strong. The Lord will see us through this. He loves you, you know that, Jack."

Jack looks over at his father with a blank stare.

"Come on, son." He guides Jack out the door, holding onto Jack's shoulder.

~ * ~

A Black Lincoln Continental Town Car pulls up to Jack's church. The driver exits and opens the rear passenger door, but no one gets out.

Grace, Jack's older sister, scrambles out of the front passenger door and her father exits out of the other rear passenger door. Grace hurries around to the door where the driver stands. She reaches in, takes Jack's hand, helping him out.

Arm-in-arm, they lead Jack inside.

There, they amble toward the altar past a packed, sniffling congregation. Jack doesn't see anyone, or hear their weeping. He doesn't even realize where they have taken him. It seems he's in a black hole, being slowly crushed by gravity. He does see, however, a beautiful flower-adorned adult casket and two smaller ones coming into view.

Grace and his father stop with him at a seat in the front row where they attempt to steer him into to it, but he resists, pushing past them. They hold off but trail him as he goes up to Janette's casket where he rubs it once along the side. He stands there for the longest moment until his body falls over onto it. Grace places her palm on his shoulder, his arms now hanging over the casket on either side.

After a minute, they pry him from his embrace. He shuffles over to one of the smaller caskets, rubs it, and does the same with the third. They help him to his seat.

Pastor Douglas, Jack's father, ascends into the pulpit as Jesus did for the Sermon on the Mount. "Let us pray," he says. He leads the congregation in prayer, but Jack hears nothing, staring at the three boxes perched in front of him. He does look up, however, at his father when he hears him say, "We are all part of God's plan. He has a plan for all of us."

Jack averts his eyes back toward his children's caskets. His father speaks for a couple more minutes, Jack tuning him out. At one point Jack thinks he hears singing, *Praise be to God in the Highest*, but he tunes that out too. He has no idea about the passage of time anymore. He is stuck. *Has time warped?* In a sense, it seems he saw Janette and the children off to school only this morning. In another, it seems as if a thousand years have passed. He knows, however, because he not only has a degree in Theology but Cosmology, that time and space is one and the same, the space/time continuum. The passage of time is nothing more than a tool of measurement, man's tool, measuring his passage through space. If you are one year old on Pluto, you are about two hundred and forty-eight years old on Earth. However, there is only one moment in time, and that is the NOW moment. Man records consecutive NOW moments into a tool called time, much like a page in a book.

"Amen," his father says, ending the ceremony.

"Amen," the congregation echoes.

The ceremony ends about forty minutes after it began. Grace touches Jack on his arm bringing him back to Earth. He glances up at her standing over him like an angel in the clouds. Grace, his mother, and father, help him stand as pall-bearers, too many to count, lift the three caskets and carry them past him down the aisle.

~ * ~

At the cemetery, Jack's father says a few more words, none of which Jack hears. Grace helps Jack to his feet. She escorts him to the caskets resting above the communal grave that will forever cradle his family in the Earth until it is enveloped by the sun as a red giant in a billion years. He hugs Janette one more time, just as he had in the church. "My love." He kisses her casket. He bows, places both hands on Rebecca's casket and kisses it too. "Goodbye, Champ. I love you so much." He repeats the gesture at Aaron's casket and recalls a quote from Hamlet, whispering, "Good night, sweet prince: And flights of angels sing thee to thy rest."

They escort Jack arm-in-arm once more and walk him toward the Town Car. A man in his thirties, dressed in a crumpled shirt, a crooked tie, blue jeans, sporting long hair and a bushy mustache, intercepts them. He has an arm in a sling and bandages about his burned face and arms. "Pastor Douglas?" he says to Jack, his voice cracking.

Jack cocks his head.

"I'm so sorry...fer your loss." He shifts on his feet, his face tightening. "I was...well, I mean...it was an accident, you see. I been driving, for ah...oh...about twelve hours straight, right? I had to be in Jacksonville later that morning. Was running behind, ya know, that morning. I was running late."

Jack says nothing, squinting, trying to understand.

"I mean...I don't know what happened. You see, I musta took my eyes off the road, ur, I mean they might have closed for a second. Just a second ya see. What I'm trying to say is…"

Jack taps the man on the bicep of his uninjured arm. The man flinches. "I understand," Jack says. "I forgive you, sir." The man steps aside to allow Jack and his family to pass.

They help Jack into the Town Car and drive off.

Chapter Three

The World is the mirror of myself dying.
Henry Miller

He sits down at his kitchen table and sifts through legal documents dressed only in his underwear. His wet hair is brushed across his head and beads of water, a result of not toweling off from the shower, adorn his shoulders, chest, and washboard abs. A scrubby sandy-brown beard has filled in about his face. The mid-morning sun shines in through the open kitchen window. He scans a bank statement: *Deposit: one hundred twenty-nine thousand dollars. Balance total: two hundred forty-nine thousand dollars.* He sets it aside and hears a soft "peep."

Jack looks up to see a song sparrow sitting on the sill at the open window looking at him. It has a brown upper part, dark streaks on its back, and a white underbelly with a dark spot in the middle of its breast. He studies it.

The bird hops down onto the counter under the window. It chirps then flies over to him, landing on the cross-bar of Janette's chair. It looks at him while singing a melodious song comprised of quick, isolated notes in a crisp and clear rhythm. It repeats the song a few times.

Jack hears a knock at the front door. The bird stops singing, cocks its head. Keys rattle in the lock and the front door opens. "Jack?" his mother calls out.

"Jack?" his father says from the living room. "You here?"

The bird flutters back over to the window sill. Jack watches it raise and lower its head in rapid succession three or four times and chirp. Someone closes the front door. The bird flies off.

His parents enter the kitchen dressed as always, in attire for a Sunday sermon. "Jack, honey," his mother says setting her purse on the table then kissing him on the top of his head. "We're just checking in on ya. It's been five weeks, since, well, the accident."

Jack says nothing, watching her as she walks around to face him.

"Yes, well, son," his father says. "We want to see how you're getting along."

Jack watches his mother scan a pile of dirty dishes in the sink, hand towels crumpled and thrown on the counter, and a pizza box with half the pizza still in it.

"What's all this?" his father says picking up legal forms off the table.

"I'm taking some time off."

"Well sure, we understand, that's to be expected, but this says a deed of sale."

"I sold the house. Below market value. Just to get it done quickly. Still made a nice profit."

"Below market? Why?"

"Sold the car. Sold everything."

His mother frowns, looks at her husband to say more, but cuts in and says, "Jack, we know this is hard, but you have to move on. People carry on. You made it through the shock and grieving process, now the healing period begins. You know that."

"Have I?" He glares at her, shuffles the legal papers and stuffs them in a large manila envelope, closing the clasp. "Made it through? Well, I *am* moving on, mother." He looks over at his father. "I'm resigning from the ministry."

"Jack, you've built so much here. Six years. You can't just quit. People are depending on you."

Jack stands, half-naked as he is, and says, "You can assign a new pastor to the ministry. The city will get a new deputy city manager. The people will carry on, like they always do."

"A Doctorate in Theology, a coveted assignment here in Puckett, close to your ancestral home in Savannah, you just can't give this all up."

"Sure, I can." He assesses their reactions, his mother pursing her lips in disapproval, his father narrowing his eyes. "Look, I truly thank both of you for all you've done for me. I can't stay here with the past haunting me. I have to get away and reassess."

"Reassess? You mean turn your back on God and His plans for you?"

"His *plans* for me?" Jack glares at his father. "His plans?"

His father glances at his wife then looks back at Jack. "We can get you some help. I know the best in the field."

"Mental health field?"

"Well, yes. You know better than anyone, being not only a man of God but one of science."

"No thanks, Father. I'm not mentally ill."

"Well, of course not. You know? Some counseling?"

"Counseling? As you might recall, I have my certificate in family counseling." He turns, heads to the living room, his parents following.

"What will you do, son?" his father says. "Where will you go?"

Jack stops at the foot of the stairs, turns to him. "I don't know. I don't know." He climbs the stairs, leaving them standing there looking after him.

~ * ~

Jack ambles up one aisle and down another at a sporting goods store pushing a shopping cart with a large camping backpack in it. He picks out survival gear, other camping items, and heads to the checkout. There, he waits in line. A television blares down at him from up on the wall with news about tornados that have wreaked havoc throughout the Midwest plains. It seems to him televisions are all over the place and one cannot avoid them. They're even at the gas pumps.

A reporter interviews a couple about a tornado that destroyed their neighborhood, killing several people. The man, with one arm around his wife and the other around his daughter, who holds the family cat, says, "God was watching out for us. I thank God that He saved us."

"Your neighbor wasn't so fortunate," the reporter says.

"We feel so terrible about that," the woman says. "Our thoughts and prayers are with his family."

"Sir," the cashier says, interrupting Jack's viewing.

Jack looks down from the television at the cashier. He pulls up to unload his items.

Chapter Four

Absence and death are the same—only in death there is no suffering.
Theodore Roosevelt

Still unshaven, his hair growing wild, Jack hikes along Highway 25 north of Statesboro shouldering his pack. Two water bottles dangle from rings on its sides. *Go west. Keep moving. Wherever I end up, so be it. I have to just go, go somewhere, anywhere but Georgia to sort things out. This is not about finding myself, purpose, or even about finding God. Heck, I thought I'd found Him before. It's about moving. Keep on moving. If I stayed, I wouldn't move. Not as in move to another house, another church. I wouldn't move my body. Move my mind. Move my soul, if I have one anymore.*

A big rig honks, bringing him out of his stupor. Jack continues walking as the rig pulls over ahead of him. As he approaches, the driver leans out the passenger window. "Where ya headin'?"

Jack stops below him near the door. "Nowhere." He squints up at the man in the hot summer sun.

"Nowhere?" The man chuckles. "Never heard that one before. You wanna lift?"

Jack looks him over, takes a swig from his canteen. "Reckon so."

The man opens the door, Jack climbs in.

"Name's Graham. Bill Graham." He sticks out his hand.

Bill Graham? Jack raises an eyebrow and shakes his hand, saying, "Jack Douglas." He stows his pack behind the seat in the large cab.

The driver shifts into gear. "Yeah. Bill Graham. I get that look a lot. My mama was saved by him." The rig pulls out onto the highway. The driver is in his fifties and wears a khaki Wrangler work shirt with its sleeves ripped off at the shoulders reminding Jack of Larry the Cable Guy. He looks

21

over at Jack. "I'm goin' as far as Columbia."

"Oh, well, I'm going out west, northwest somewhere, I guess."

"I should drop you in Augusta then."

Jack nods. They sit in silence, except for the rush of wind past the open window, the hum of the engine and the sound of the rig's tires buzzing on the pavement.

"Ya on vacation?"

"No."

Graham glances over at him. "I don't mean to pry."

Jack doesn't respond but looks out at the scenic Georgia countryside passing him by.

Graham says, "Just on an adventure then?"

Jack takes a long time to answer. "My wife and two children were recently killed in an accident."

"Oh, shit. I'm sorry. I'm so sorry, Jack."

Jack says nothing but stares ahead at the highway rushing toward him.

After a long stretch of silence, Graham looks over at Jack then back at the road. "My mother died last January. She was eighty-nine. Heavy smoker, alcoholic. Until, well, Billy saved her. Didn't partake in any vice after that."

Jack glances at him but says nothing. He understands the trucker is lonely for conversation and is just being polite, but he picked up the wrong guy.

At the outskirts of Augusta, the rig pulls over. Jack grabs his pack from behind the seat, climbs down from the cab. "Thanks, Billy. Get some rest."

"Sure thing, Jack. You take care of yerself. And, I'm really sorry fer yer loss."

Jack doesn't answer but closes the door. Billy Graham drives off into the afternoon sun.

He hikes into Augusta in the evening after sundown and finds a greasy diner on the edge of town. He enters and sits at the counter near the register.

An attractive waitress in a tight-fitting uniform bounces over to him, the top of her breasts showing. "Hi, honey," she says in a southern twang. "What can I get ya to drink?"

"Milk please. Thank you."

"Sure thing." She gives him a warm smile and pours his milk. "You fixin' for a hearty meal?" She chews gum while still smiling at him.

"Yes, ma'am. The chicken and dumplings." He points at an advertisement of their special on the wall behind the counter.

"My. Ya sure is a proper one." She scribbles his order on a pad, tears the slip off and hangs it on the cook's wheel. She moves on to another customer to refill his coffee.

A middle-age man enters the diner, dressed in dirty, torn clothes. He has a filthy long beard and hair. He saunters up to the counter near Jack. The cute waitress returns the carafe to its heating pad and goes over to the man. "Can I help ya, sir?" she says, crinkling her nose.

The man fingers through loose change in his palm. "I'd like a burger, maybe some fries."

"Ya might be better off goin' to fast food for that," she says chomping on her gum. "Cheaper deal, for the money."

"That shit'll kill ya."

She raises an eyebrow. "Burger, fries, comes with a drink. But it's eight ninety-five. Plus tax."

Jack watches as the man jiggles his change, clearly not enough for what he wants. "Here," Jack says to the girl. He pulls a wad of cash from his pocket, peels off a ten dollar bill and hands it to her. "On me," he says to the man.

The man narrows his eyes at Jack who stuffs the wad of cash back into his pocket.

"I'll place the order," the waitress says to the man. "Wait outside."

A few minutes later the girl serves Jack. "That was a very nice thing ya did…" she says, raising her eyebrows, her voice trailing off, indicating she's waiting for his name.

"Jack," he says.

"Of course it is," she says, smiling again, stretching her hand out for a shake. "Of course it is."

He studies her hand for a moment but shakes it.

She takes longer than usual to release her hand from his, letting it slide slowly from his palm. "Ya sure got pretty hazel-green eyes, Jack." She winks at him.

He nods, barely, presses his lips together.

"Well, just give me a holler if you need anything else."

"Is there a motel nearby?"

"Just down the street. Take a left at the first intersection."

"Thank you, ma'am."

She smiles at him again then delivers an order to a patron at a booth behind him.

Jack is no fool. He realizes she's flirting with him, like the church ladies. He thinks it's very sweet, and she's very cute, but romance, certainly casual sex, is the furthest thing from his mind. In fact, he had only ever made love to his wife.

He pays his tab, gives her a generous tip. She frowns when he bids farewell.

He makes his way down the street in search of the motel. Turning at the intersection, he sees the neon motel sign in the distance.

Something strikes the back of his head. He topples over onto the sidewalk. His vision blurry, he rubs the back of his head but manages to see the homeless man from the diner riffling through his pockets. Another homeless man stands next to him holding a stick.

The man from the diner pulls the wad of cash from Jack's pocket. "I got it," he says. "Let's go."

Just as the diner-man with the cash begins to walk away, Jack trips him. The man falls down with a thud, but holds onto the cash.

Jack releases his arms from his pack, jumps up. The man with the stick stands back, shaking. "Just give me back my money and I'll let you go," Jack says.

The diner-man with the cash stands. "Looks like yer outnumbered, mista."

"Look, I really don't want to hurt you. Neither of you." He scans the other man with the stick.

The diner-man with the cash sneers. "Hurt us?"

"Please. Just give me the cash and you can go."

"Give me that," the diner-man with the cash says to his friend with the stick. He grabs the stick and swings it at Jack. Jack ducks, pivots and grabs the stick from him. He tosses the stick far away.

The stick-man charges Jack, throwing a punch. Jack puts those boxing skills to use, ducks from the incoming blow and pops the man in the face, knocking him down.

The diner-man with the cash lunges for Jack. Jack dodges him too, turns, and punches him in the face, causing blood to spurt out of his nose. The diner-man swings around. Jack doesn't want to hurt him anymore so he grabs him by his arm, flinging him to the ground. Jack reaches down and grabs the cash from the man's hand. Both men lie there, cowering, looking up at him. Jack peels off a twenty-dollar bill, throws it onto the diner-man's chest. "I would've just given you some if you had kindly asked."

Jack lifts his pack, shoulders it, and walks up the sidewalk.

Inside his dark and dingy motel room, Jack drops the pack next to the bed and sits on its edge. He draws in a deep breath, exhales, eyeballing one of those cheap, generic, abstract pictures of a beach on the wall. He rubs the back of his head where he had been struck by the stick.

He finds the ice machine outside the room down the hall, fills his ice bucket, and goes back to his room. He wraps some ice in a towel and sits on his bed, pressing it against the small lump on the back of his head.

Several minutes later, he dumps the ice into the bathroom sink.

At his bed he opens his pack, pulling out his running shoes, gym shorts, and athletic socks placing them on a chair. He sits on the edge of the bed, takes out his family photo, the one he had shoved into his mother's face. He places it on his lap, his family smiling up at him. He extracts from his pack his leather-bound Bible, holding it in his hands for the longest time, examining it. At last, he opens and flips through the pages, but closes and stares at it again. A tear wells up in his eye and drips onto the Bible. He wipes it away with the tip of his finger. He sets the Bible aside, pulls up onto the bed holding the photo, switches off the lamp, and curls up, embracing the extra pillow in the darkness.

Chapter Five

Everyone can master a grief but he that has it.
William Shakespeare

Sunlight streams in through the thin motel curtains striking his face. Jack stirs to discover he's slept in his clothes; the family photo and his Bible on the bed next to him. He gets up, strips, urinates in the bathroom, and while washing his hands, examines his thickening beard in the mirror.

He returns to the bedroom, sits on the edge of the bed, staring at the photo. *I have to keep at my routine. I can't turn into a moping blob. I have to keep at it. Keep moving.* He gets up, does pushups and sit-ups by locking the tops of his feet under the bed. He pulls on his running shorts, athletic socks, and running shoes. He places the do-not-disturb sign on the outside door handle and slips the motel card-key in his sock.

Because it is already a hot summer morning, he jogs shirtless up one street and down the next. Augusta begins to stir with people on their way to work. Jack has to stop at an intersection as a school bus passes, taking the kids to summer school, he figures. He scans the faces of the young children in their seats glancing back at him.

He jogs on. A mile later he passes a supermarket parking lot. He notices two middle-aged women getting out of their car as he zips by. One of them whistles at him and calls out, "Hey, handsome."

He hears the other woman say to her, "Blanche, shame on you."

It hadn't bothered him before. Joan from the neighborhood did it many times in a subtle way, and the women at the church ogled at him. Now, it began to bother him. Times changed, he realized, where men routinely received this type of so-called cat-calling more openly. *Perhaps I should wear my T-shirt from this point on.*

He continues on for a couple more miles until he circles back to the motel. He showers, dresses, packs, and checks out.

He purchases a breakfast sandwich and milk at a coffee shop, tops off his water bottles, and hikes on.

~ * ~

Jack hikes most of the morning until an open-bed pickup truck with five Mexican migrants stop to give him a lift on Highway 78. They are all young, in their twenties. He gives them fist-bumps, since that's how the kids do it. These young boys had already fit in with other American youth in many ways. "Where you going?" the one with a Braves cap asks in perfect English, albeit with an accent.

"Out west. You?"

"Gainesville. We do landscaping. For the rich." He smiles.

Jack nods. *Makes sense*. He readjusts the aviator sunglasses he bought at the sporting goods store in Puckett.

In Gainesville, Jack hops off the truck, fist-bumps the boys again, shoulders his pack, and heads north on Highway 23.

By early evening, he hikes into Cornelia and finds a motel. After a shower and a light supper at a nearby restaurant, he meanders back to the motel, stopping in the lobby where they have a small library with free books. Most are trashy romance novels, but he finds an old paperback of *Blood Meridian or the Evening Redness in the West* by Cormac McCarthy. It looks interesting so he picks it up and retires to his room where he reads in bed until falling asleep.

~ * ~

The next morning, he repeats his exercise routine and heads north on 23 into the Appalachians.

Later that day near the North Carolina border, he pulls off the road and sets up camp for the night. He extends a bedroll then unpacks a sleeping bag. Eating a sandwich he bought along the way, he sits on his bag with his back against a tree, admiring the solitude.

He continues reading McCarthy's book. He supposes he chose quite the story. He knows all too well of the evil, the violence in the world, however this book took it to the extreme. The main character, the kid, wow, he didn't seem to have any redeeming characteristics. Nonetheless, Jack reads on.

After sundown, his eyes grow heavy, so he curls up in his bag drifting off to sleep in the sticky summer heat alone, under the stars.

~ * ~

Hot, smelly air blows onto his face, waking him at daybreak. He opens his eyes to see an enormous Black Appalachian bear hovering over him. He doesn't move, closes his eyes to a crack as the bear licks his lips. Using its snout, it nudges Jack's head.

A moment later the bear moves on, figuring he's dead, Jack reasons. He cracks his eyes open to see the bear sniffing at his pack about five feet away from him. His torso exposed because it had been a warm night, he wonders if he should jump up or just stay still until it moves on.

The bear nudges the pack, pawing at it, its huge claws scraping against it now. *Is it worth my life? Darn, I have no life. What does it matter?* He sits up in a jolt and yanks the bag off his legs. "Arrrrr," he screams at the bear, flailing his arms and standing on his tiptoes.

The bear turns around, jumps on its hind legs. Displaying its teeth and growling back at him, the bear is as tall as Jack. It must weigh about five-hundred pounds.

Standing his ground, he waves his arms yelling at it some more. It growls at him again and leans forward. Jack makes a half-step lunge at it. The bear drops to its feet, turns and scampers off down the trail. He watches until it disappears from sight.

His adrenaline surging, he feels victorious. He looks up at the sky, makes a fist, shaking it at the clouds. "What else you got?"

The clouds don't answer him.

He opens his pack, pulls out a breakfast bar, peels it open, and chomps off a bit. "Steal my food, will ya?" he says in the direction the bear went.

After finishing his breakfast bar and washing it down with water, he packs up and hikes back to the highway.

In Mountain City, he tosses out his trash before entering a general store. Inside, he grabs a hand-held basket then selects some items to get him through a couple days. A man with two small children, perhaps five or six years old, enters the store. "Now, hold on to your brother," the man says to the girl, perhaps a year or two older than the boy. She obeys her father, taking her brother's hand. They bypass Jack in the aisle. He watches them pass. He turns his head to look down at his basket, staring at its contents for a moment. He feels light-headed, almost as if he's going to pass out from a loss of blood. It's as if his heart has stopped beating, or perhaps it has disappeared. He places his hand onto the shelf to regain his equilibrium.

"You okay, mister?" the clerk calls out from behind the counter.

"Huh?" Jack says looking over at him. "Yeah. Yeah, I'm fine." He approaches the register and places his items on the counter. The clerk rings him up.

Outside, he sits on the steps, stuffing his supplies in his pack when the two small children exit the store with their father. Jack keeps his head lowered, not looking at them as they pass. They climb into their minivan and drive off.

"Is this how it's going to be?" he says looking over the treetops at the sky.

The sky doesn't answer him.

Shouldering his pack, he starts out again. His mind kicks into overdrive. *I have to keep going. Perhaps I should find a place like this to live. Find a place with no kids. A place with no people. I have just stared down a bear. I could live in the wild like Tarzan now that I have dominion over the animals. I don't need people. Nobody depends on me anymore, so why should I care about being around people, or care about people at all? Sure, I will need to get supplies and other items from time-to-time, but I could find a place and build a shack and live nowhere, off the grid. People do it all the time. I have enough money for a long time. I have the money from the sale of the house. I have all the investment funds back in the bank in Puckett to draw on. I have all of Jeanette's money that she made. I have all the children's funds. Yeah, the children's funds, for college.* He shakes his head. *Janette. I've got to get her off my mind. God, I miss her so much. Yeah, that's what I'll do. Get off the grid and wander for some time. The heck with everything. I don't need anyone or anything anymore.*

Chapter Six

Alone, no one can hurt you.
Lakota

For the next two weeks after a few camps, hiking, no rides because he didn't want to get to know anyone, Jack checks into a motel in Knoxville. The receptionist wrinkles her nose at him.

In his room, he unpacks and sorts his dirty laundry. *Wow, my clothes smell. I guess I do too and that's why the receptionist scowled at me. Although, hanging out with myself for the past couple weeks, having bathed only a couple of times, so be it. This must be similar to how cowboys in the old dirty west lived and in the western I'm reading.* He shrugs it off.

Standing in the shower, he lets the hot water roll off him for a time. He soaps up and scrubs areas he never knew he had. In front of the mirror, he examines his thickening beard. *Perhaps I'll become a lumberjack.* He had always kept his hair well-trimmed and short, but it now grew in all over the place.

Lying in bed, he continues reading the paperback book he bought. After a couple of Chapters, he tires of the violence and abhorrent disregard for life. *I hope I can get through this.*

He sets the paperback aside and picks up his Bible. Randomly opening it, it falls upon Deuteronomy 31:6. He reads it out loud, "Be strong and courageous. For it is the Lord your God who goes with you. He will not leave you or forsake you."

Closing the Bible, he glances at his family photo resting on the nightstand. Placing the Bible next to the picture, he grabs the extra pillow, curls up into the fetal position and stares at his family, all but ghosts now. He falls asleep with the light on.

At checkout the next morning, Jack picks up two postcards in the lobby, fills one out for Grace, and another one for his parents. He disconnected his cellphone and discarded it before leaving Puckett. He writes the same on each card: "On the road. Everything fine. Love, Jack." He buys two stamps at checkout and drops the cards in the mailbox.

~ * ~

Over the course of the next few weeks, Jack hikes, snaking his way through Kentucky, Illinois, Iowa, and in South Dakota, he hikes a trail where he camps along the Missouri River. He buys fishing tackle and catches both large and smallmouth bass for many of his meals. He avoids people as much as possible, enjoying being alone and camping with nature.

However, at a truck stop near Crow Creek, South Dakota while grabbing supplies off a shelf on an aisle near the register, a young man with long hair and torn jeans at his knees pulls out a gun, pointing it at the cashier and shouting, "Empty it all in the bag." He holds up a paper bag.

Jack stands back, surveying the scene. A middle-aged couple stands near the young cashier, a boy not out of his teens. The cashier's hands tremble as he opens the register and fumbles with the money.

"Come on," the bandit yells, looking over at the couple. He scans the activity outside the window behind the cashier.

While dropping some cash into the bag the bandit holds, the cashier scatters several bills on the floor and bends down to pick them up. The bandit reaches across the counter and strikes the cashier on the back of his head with the gun. He falls to the floor. The bandit reaches into the till, grabbing a handful of cash.

That's it. I can't take this any longer. Jack grabs a can of beans off the shelf and throws it, striking the bandit in the shoulder.

The bandit turns as Jack rushes forward. The bandit lifts the handgun in Jack's direction squeezing off a shot. Jack dives onto the floor avoiding the bullet, rolls, and spins round, knocking the legs out from under the bandit. The bandit goes down. Jack snatches the handgun from the bandit, tossing it down the aisle. Jack jumps up, grabs the bandit's T-shirt in the ball of his hand and lifts him up. The bandit takes a swing at him, but Jack moves his head, punches the bandit squarely in the jaw, knocking him out. The bandit's body droops, so Jack lets it fall to the floor.

The cashier stands up. Jack says, "Get something to tie him up." To the couple behind him he says, "Please call the police."

The cashier nods then runs down an aisle returning with some rope as the bandit begins to stir. Jack hog-ties the bandit.

"Those were some moves, sir," the man with his wife behind Jack says. Jack glances at him but doesn't respond. *This is like the characters in* Blood Meridian or the Evening Redness in the West. *Well, sort of.*

Jack waits to give the police a report. He's dismissed a couple hours later. He finds his way back to the path along the river heading upstream away from civilization.

~ *~

By the time he reaches Bismarck, he hasn't had human contact for about a week. It has been serene. *After all I've been through, and with the incident at the truck stop, I want to live without human contact forevermore.*

However, he checks into another cost-effective motel to undertake his usual ritual of spending a day or two washing his clothes and resupplying.

That night he brings himself around to completing *Blood Meridian or the Evening Redness in the West*. Jack finds one quote in the epigraph that pops out, giving him pause. How apropos he muses, that this book found him. He remembers the quote from a philosophy class years ago. However, like most of the young and immature in college, he had given it little thought at the time.

> *It is not to be thought that the life of darkness is sunk in misery and lost as if in sorrowing. There is no sorrowing. For sorrow is a thing that is swallowed up in death, and death and dying are the very life of the darkness.* Jakob Böhme

Jack sets the book aside after finishing it. He lies there, staring at the ceiling until he falls asleep with the light on.

~ * ~

At a diner in Bismarck, Jack sits, eating dinner, his bangs hanging in his eyes. He tries to tuck them behind his ears, but they aren't quite long enough to do that yet. They fall back into his eyes. A middle-aged waitress saunters by. "More milk, sir?"

"No. Thank you." She strolls off. He chews on a chicken leg, stripping it to the bone. After eating fish for many days, the chicken is a welcomed change in diet.

While paying at the register, he notices an advertisement on a bulletin board: *Men wanted to work on the oil rigs near Williston, North Dakota at the Bakken shale basin oil fields. No experience necessary. Will train.*

He studies the handbill for a moment. *I have depleted much of my on-hand cash. Although I'd be around people, could I do this so as not to dip into my bank funds for a while? Oil rigging? Might take my mind off my past. Why not?* Jack tears the handbill from the board. He folds and stuffs it in his Wrangler Jeans' pocket.

~ * ~

A few days later in the early evening, Jack hikes up to the North Star Oil company field office near Williston. He sees lights burning through the windows and notices someone working inside.

Inside the office, he sets his pack near the door, approaches the secretary at the desk. "Here for a job?" she says.

"Yes, ma'am. Yes, I am."

She looks him over, scanning his tight-fitting jeans. "Ya sure look the part." One of her eyebrows rises.

"Pardon me, ma'am?"

"You'll do just fine. Here ya go. Fill these out." She hands him forms and a pen.

"Thank you, ma'am."

"You can sit over there." She signals with her head toward some chairs against the wall. He notices her eyes lingering on him when he sits in a chair. She smiles then looks down at papers on her desk.

A few minutes later he hands the forms back to her. She scans them. "You don't have a current address?"

"No, ma'am."

"Where ya stayin'?"

"I haven't found a place yet. Just got in."

"No vehicle?"

He shakes his head.

She taps the tip of her pencil on her lips, examining him. "Wait here." She stands and heads into an office in the back. He waits at her desk, scanning the large industrial trailer-office.

A couple minutes later she emerges with a man, perhaps in his sixties, beer belly and bald. "This is the manager, Curly Reynolds," she says.

Of course, he is. "Sir," Jack says extending his hand.

Curly sticks an unlit cigar in his mouth. Shaking Jack's hand, he says, "We can put you up at the man-camp. Sally can get you set up."

"Thank you, sir."

"Call me, Curly."

"Yes, sir. Curly, sir."

He turns and disappears into the back office.

Sally drives him in her pickup about a mile down the road, past pumping oil rigs scattered across the barren North Dakota landscape. She's in her forties, perhaps, and has a weathered face and faux blond hair. He can see her brown roots. She isn't unattractive for her age, but looks as though she's lived in these parts battling the below-zero wind-chill for quite some time and has scrapped all her life.

Sally parks. Jack grabs his pack from the truck bed and follows her into the main hall of the man-camp. "North Star's been around for some time," she says. "One of the oldest operations up here."

Jack figures as much, seeing how the camp building looks dated, a one-story structure built of cinderblocks.

"This is the dining facility," Sally says, "the rec room with pool tables over there, a television and housing-keeping here." Jack scans the dining room with thirty-odd tables. A dozen scattered oil-riggers eat their dinner. A cook works in a small attached kitchen, and several refrigerated units display sandwiches.

Jack follows Sally into an office. "Oh, and we have a full workout gym just off the main room, over there," she says pointing outside the office door. Jack looks in that direction. She finds a clipboard and a key on a keyboard on the wall. She hands Jack the key then scribbles some information onto a form clipped to the board.

She leads him out of the office down a long corridor, much like a hospital ward. "New roughnecks share a room with one other crewmember," she says. "You're gonna be paired up with a derrickhand. Since you don't have a truck and you'll keep the same hours, he can give you a ride for now. It's not far, but stick close to this kid like glue. He's quiet, smart and dependable. Been here several months. As you might guess, there's a high turnover in this business. It's a tough profession. Takes some steel balls, but you look like you have a pair."

He glances over at her, frowns.

She stops at a door and knocks. A young man, no more than nineteen opens it. She pushes her way in. "Sanders, this is Douglas. He's yer new roughneck. Make 'im feel at home, teach 'im the ropes. He doesn't have a truck, so give 'im a lift." She pinches Sanders on his cheek. "Yer such a cutie."

Sanders, a lean, average-height kid with sandy blond hair and blue eyes, blushes.

"Orientation is at eight, sharp," she says to Jack. "Chow opens at five-thirty." Sally winks at Jack, turns on a dime and high-tails it out.

"You can bunk there," Sanders says, pointing to a bed in a nook.

Jack notices another bed in another nook on the other side, in-between the bathroom. A kitchenette with a table stands near the door.

"Name's Chris," Sanders says, extending his hand.

"Jack." They shake. Jack drops his pack on his bed, examines the room and thinks this arrangement could work, for now.

"You have any experience?"

"None."

"That's how they like it. So they can train you the way they want.

Most guys come in with an attitude, especially the ones who have experience. They think they know it all. Want to do it their own way. They usually require workers with trucks, but they're desperate and short. Last roughneck we had quit days ago with no prospects on the horizon. Been working seven days a week since."

Jack sits on his bed, taking his shoes off.

"There's a towel in the closet, right there."

Jack nods.

"Look," Sanders says, "orientation usually ends at five, but our shift, which will be your shift, is twelve on and twelve off. Starts at eight. Walk on over to rig sixteen-B and you can observe for a couple hours. Meet the crew. It's just a mile down the road the way you came in."

Jack nods again as Sanders pulls up onto his bed where he flips through a men's fitness magazine. Jack grabs a towel from the closet, a clean pair of underwear from his pack, and goes into the shower.

The kid seems helpful. He showers, towels off, and pulls on his underwear. At his bed he places a T-shirt and a clean pair of jeans and socks for the morning on his nightstand. He notices Sanders still flipping through his magazine. Jack doesn't have anything to read, so he pulls his Bible from his pack and reads from a passage that falls upon him, James 5:11: *Behold, we consider those blessed who remained steadfast. You have heard of the steadfastness of Job, and you have seen the purpose of the Lord, how the Lord is compassionate and merciful.*

Jack contemplates this. He has preached sermons related to this passage. He understands its context and how it applies to his situation. *Yet, how much must one endure? Will I have to go through another trial? Why am I, of all people, on trial to begin with?*

Sanders clicks out his light. Jack places his Bible on his nightstand and turns out his light. He stares at the ceiling thinking about that passage trying to put his past out of his head and behind him.

Chapter Seven

An active body and mind has no time for pain.
Siddhartha

The only one working out in the gym the next morning, Jack finishes, grabs his towel, wipes his face, his neck, and on the way to his room, passes a large, flabby man with a nasty scar above his eye. The man scowls at Jack, so Jack lowers his head, averting his eyes.

He opens his door as Sanders dresses. "Morning," Sanders says.

"Good morning." Jack's a well-mannered man, yet he tries to stay detached.

"I wondered where you went. A workout? Impressive." Sanders pulls his boots on.

Jack removes his sweaty T-shirt and tosses it onto his bed. "Done with the bathroom?"

"Yeah," Sanders says, looking over at him then away.

Jack sits, pulls his shoes and socks off. He grabs a fresh towel from the closet.

"I'll see ya after five then?" Sanders says, departing.

"Sure."

Jack showers, dresses, eats breakfast, and waits in the main hall for orientation. Six new roughnecks assemble to wait with him.

"All right, listen up," says a little rounded man with white hair on the sides of his balding head. "Follow me."

They follow him to a classroom down the hall where the man flips on the lights. "Take one of these and have a seat." As they file into the room, the man hands them each a large paperback book stacked near the door, much like a textbook.

Jack takes a seat, looking through the book while the others trickle in. The book describes oil-rigging and exhibits diagrams of oil rigs.

"Name's Rodriguez. Y'all are mine for the next four days. You listen and learn, and most importantly, follow orders, you live. Leave the bullshit at the door. We don't want independence here. We want muscle machines that know what to do and when to do it. Work as a team. The North Star way. I don't give a shit who you are, where you come from, or yer Betty-Sue back home. Hell, I don't give a crap about how yer mommy nursed ya and cradled ya in her arms when you cried. Y'all understand?"

Most men mumble. Jack doesn't.

"All right then," Rodriguez says.

They spend the first day learning oil-rigging one-o-one. First up, Jack learns the positions. The rig manager is the main rig supervisor responsible for all the rig operations, drill activities, and equipment. He normally has experience in all the other positions below him, because he was promoted over the years. Next up, the driller, similar to the rig manager, helps supervise the crew. He operates the rig's hoisting equipment, manages the rig floor, driller's console, brakes, monitors, throttles, clutches, and other gauges. Third in order, the derrickhand, who manages the uppermost section of the drilling string as it's lowered into the wellbore. The derrickhand works most of the time on the so-called monkey-board, a platform up in the rig's derrick. Next, the motorhand, is responsible for keeping the engines that power the drilling equipment working smoothly. He also trains the roughnecks, maintains and lubricates the machinery, assesses tongs that help connect and disconnect the drill and spinning chain, works with the rig boilers, tests the equipment, and orders tools and replacement parts. Last, the roughneck is an entry-level unskilled position responsible for taking care of the equipment, including its cleaning, maintenance, painting, rust removal, and other peripheral tasks associated with the rig such as keeping the deck clean and clear of hazards. He also moves equipment around the rig and connects sections of the pipe for the well.

In the afternoon, the men huddle around a mock rig behind the camp, while Rodriguez meanders around, pointing out the various components and quizzing his roughnecks.

After class, Jack makes his way down the highway to rig sixteen-

B. He stops at the fence surrounding the rig and waits. He sees Sanders up on the monkey-board pointing at him while talking with a man at the bottom of the rig. The man looks back at Jack then approaches. "Douglas?" the man says.

"Yes, sir."

He opens the gate, lets Jack in, closing the gate behind him. "Pullen," the man says extending his hand. "Rig manager. Call me Nick."

Pullen appears to be in his forties perhaps, Jack reckons. Jack shakes his hand.

They walk over to the edge of the rig platform. Pullen, a large man with a swagger who reminds Jack of John Wayne, points to Sanders. "Sanders you know, driller's Peterson, motorhand is Ryan, as in Private."

Jack nods.

"No, that's what we call him," Pullen says cracking a smile. "We call him private."

"I see," Jack says.

Pullen looks him over. "Private Ryan?" He rolls his eyes. "Forget it. Hey, you look older than the average roughneck."

"Second career," Jack says.

"Well, I don't give a shit. You look like you can do the job. Physically, I mean. You ain't got any mental problems? I mean, we don't have any time for that shit."

That's the second person who suggested I might have mental issues. "No. No mental incapacity."

"Incapacity?" Pullen raises an eyebrow. "Yeah, well. Damn right if you fixin' to be on this crew."

Jack looks at Pullen as he examines him. "The other guy," Pullen continues, "Collins, is a temp roughneck on loan from an idle rig under repairs, who you'll replace. Come on."

Jack follows him onto the rig.

"Ryan, Douglas," Pullen says, introducing them.

Ryan, a wiry kid with greasy hair and in his mid-twenties, offers his hand. "Hey."

Jack shakes his hand.

"Peterson," says a large man about Jack's age. They shake.

Jack hangs back, observing until the shift ends at eight. The night crew arrives and takes charge. Sanders climbs down from the derrick to walk with Jack to his truck. They get in, Sanders driving back to camp. "Whaddaya think?" Sanders says looking over at Jack.

"Honest tough work."

"Yeah. Most guys come and go. The ones who stay, like Pullen, have made it a career."

Jack looks over at him then out the window at the passing rigs.

"I'm just sticking around for a while," Sanders says. "Just saving a bunch of money. Figuring things out. Want to go to school. Maybe engineering or something."

Sanders pulls into the lot. They climb out and enter the hall. Sanders cleans up, going into the mudroom where workers take off their muddy boots. Jack grabs a tray of food in the dining facility and sits by himself.

Sanders meanders over with a tray and sits with Jack a few minutes later. While eating, Sanders looks up at Jack. "Where ya from?"

Jack hesitates, but says, "Georgia. Near Savannah."

"No kidding? I'm from a small town north of Jacksonville." He chuckles. "Small town. Yeah, really small." He looks down at his plate.

Jack looks up from his meal then back down again. *The kid is just trying to be friendly. Just try to engage, okay*? Looking up, he at last says, "Why do you say that? A small town."

"Oh, I dunno." He shrugs. "It's just that, well, no real jobs there, I guess." He looks down at his plate again as he swirls his beans around with his fork.

Jack takes some time before he says, "There had to be something, in Jacksonville. Why all the way out here?"

Sanders' turn now, taking a moment to answer, "Ah, saw an ad online. Sounded adventurous. Wanted to get away." He frowns. "Yeah, get far away."

Jack glances up at Sanders who now toys with his mashed potatoes. Jack leaves it at that. He looks over at Curly entering the hall. Curly catches Jack's eye and strolls over. "Pastor Douglas," he says.

Jack freezes, squinting up at Curly while holding his fork above his food. "Can we talk?"

Jack says. "Over there?" He motions with his fork, sets it onto his plate, glances at Sanders, and gets up. He leads Curly over to the side of the room.

"Background check came in," Curly says.

Jack notices that flabby, burly-looking man with the scar above his eye sitting nearby looking up at him when Curly says that. Jack looks back at Curly, whispers, "*Was*, a pastor."

"I'm sorry..." he stops himself in mid-sentence, whispers back to Jack, "fer yer loss. Look, I just want to be sure that yer, ah, emotionally stable and all. I get it. It was awful and I'm deeply sorry, but I gotta protect my operation. We can't have any loose cannons, mentally, on the rigs. Men's lives depend on roughnecks to do their jobs, pay close attention to their tasks."

"I won't be a problem, sir."

Curly studies him, hesitates, and rolls an unlit cigar around in his mouth. "Well, I dunno."

Jack's eyes bore through him. "I can do the job, sir."

Curly sighs. "We're really short-handed, but you slip up, just once..." He pulls his cigar out and says, "Stop with the sir shit, Douglas. Look," he says, glancing at that scarred man. "You'll need to loosen up. A little at least." He shifts, continuing to whisper, "Guys 'round these parts are, sorry 'bout the language, but this is the shit you'll hear, mother-fuckin', shit-kickin' sons of bitches. They come lookin' for a quick buck and a fuck. It's a hard-scrabble profession, riggin', and they can be yer best friend, especially on yer crew, or assholes. If you act too different, they'll smell blood." He examines him. "You look like a strong, tough-guy, Douglas. At odds with what most would stereotype as a preacher. With yer educational background, you should be smart, but we don't need smart asses. Guys too smart fer their own good and all. Guys who know too much."

"I understand," Jack says. "I just want to make some cash, mind my own business, and be on my way in a few months." He looks Curly over as well. "I can *do* the job."

"Awright. You mess up, yer out."

"Thank you, sir. I mean, Curly, sir."

"Okay then." He sticks the unlit cigar back into his mouth, chomps on it and turns to leave.

"Oh," Jack says.

Curly turns back to him.

"Please keep my former profession to yourself."

Curly nods then exits the hall. Jack returns to his table, picks up his tray, drops it at the trashcan then heads to his room.

In his room, he gets ready to turn in. Sanders enters a minute later and goes about his business getting ready for bed. Neither says a word to the other. They retire for the evening.

Chapter Eight

Nothing will work unless you do.
Maya Angelou

Jack finished orientation and joined the crew. A quick study, he jumps right into the action, taking initiative with clearing, cleaning, painting, and maintenance. He gets dirty, follows orders, keeps quiet, only doing his job.

"You're a hell of a worker, Douglas," Pullen says at the end of his first week on the job. "Most roughnecks don't know what the fuck they're doing and need repeat instructions to get it right."

Standing on the platform in front of the pumping rig, Jack squints at him from the sun, wiping his oily hands on a rag.

"Don't say much, do ya? What the hell you do before riggin'?"

"A job that didn't pan out," Jack says.

"Tight lipped, huh? Well, that's yer business. Just keep up the good work." He pats Jack on his shoulder. Jack goes back to cleaning a part.

~ * ~

For the next few weeks, Jack works his shifts, twelve on and twelve off five days a week. The rig has three crews that rotate a few days on, a couple days off. They never have the same two days off each week. He can have a Tuesday and Wednesday one week, then a Friday and Saturday the next. On Jack's days off, he washes his clothes, buys supplies at the small convenience store at camp, or goes with Sanders into Williston for other items as needed. He only eats at camp while the others, excluding Sanders, go into town to dine at cowboy joints, beer halls, or to hit the clubs to play the courting game with girls.

Getting up at five in the morning, hitting the gym, working the rig until eight in the evening, in bed after dinner by nine, ten, he doesn't have time to think about much of anything, certainly nothing about his past or his loss.

When in town, Jack drops postcards to his family, again only writing short notes such as: "In North Dakota. Everything fine. Love, Jack." At camp on his days off he reads books he picks up at the bookstore in town, reading in his room for the most part.

~ * ~

Five months fly by. Jack saves up a lot of money. Williston has a branch to Jack's bank, so he deposits most of his pay into his account. The winter months in North Dakota, along the Canadian border, settle in and are brutal, the temperatures below zero many times, and the wind-chill much below that. Although a southern boy, Jack had experienced some cold storms over the years, but not a winter like this.

Returning from a workout on his day off, Jack enters his room and notices a laptop on Sanders' bed. Catching a glimpse of the screen as he passes, he sees what appears to be pornographic content. Looking away just as fast, he figures Sanders is a young kid who needs a release. In fact, he and Sanders have never talked at great length to one another about much of anything. He's a good kid, driving Jack back and forth to work and to town for supplies, but they keep to themselves, only small-talking. It feels as if he has a younger brother, despite Sanders looking after him.

He hears water running in the sink in the bathroom. Sanders comes out dressed in only his skivvies. "Oh," Sanders says. "I didn't think you'd be back this early."

"Sorry," Jack says, tending to his gear, minding his own business.

Sanders hurries over to his bed and closes the laptop.

~ * ~

Sitting on a couch in the rec room while waiting for his laundry to dry, Jack reads a worn-out paperback copy of *Moby Dick* he found in the rec-room library. He'd read it in high school but has nothing else to read so he's reading it again. He rediscovers the many themes in the book, such as revenge, man in the natural world, fate, and free will. It compels him to contemplate the recurring debates on religious extremism and hypocrisy. He pauses more than once to think about these themes.

Sanders, who also waits in the rec room for his laundry to finish, sits at a nearby table with his laptop, engaged in an online engineering course. Jack, looking up from his book, realizes Sanders *is* like the younger brother he never had. Despite his best efforts, Jack recognizes he has a new friend, a friend he will have to leave at some point. It seems to Jack he has turned the tables, in that he will have to leave someone, opposite of what happened to him.

His rig-mate, Ryan, dressed in jeans, a silver polyester big-tooled floral western shirt and cowboy boots, and Peterson, wearing an outfitter's patriotic horse border print shirt, boots, and jeans, stroll in. They each sport cowboy hats. "You boys wanna hit the town?" Peterson says.

Jack says, "Oh, no. No, thanks."

"You haven't really been into town since ya got here," Ryan says. "Have ya?"

"For supplies."

"Supplies?" Peterson hoots. "Well, goddamn," he says slapping his cowboy hat against Jack's shoulder. "We can hit up Rusty's Steakhouse for a real fixin' unlike the shit they got here."

"Then the Horse Stampede," Ryan says. "They got dancing and real purdy ladies."

Jack doesn't say anything.

"What the hell's with you, Douglas?" Peterson says. He looks over at Sanders working on his course trying to remain inconspicuous. "You fellas'er like an old married couple hanging 'round the homestead."

"Maybe they are," Ryan says, winking at Jack.

"C'mon," Peterson says to Jack. "My treat. This time, partner."

He has avoided this as long as he could, but Jack thinks back to what Curly told him.

"Come on, ladies," Peterson says slapping Jack's shoulder with his hat again.

I shouldn't do this. I really shouldn't go with them. "Well, I don't know."

"Come on," Ryan says. "Gotta live a little."

"Well, I guess. If you rednecks insist."

"Rednecks?" Peterson chuckles, his Sam Elliot-style mustache flopping about his face. "That's the first time I think I heard you crack a joke. Never seen you smile either."

Jack only looks up at him.

"Well, hell," Peterson says. "Let's go. Sanders, you too."

Sanders frowns at Jack who shrugs back at him.

Jack hops in with Sanders. Ryan rides with Peterson. Sanders follows Peterson's truck into town.

At Rusty's Steakhouse and BBQ, the boys wait for a table because on a Friday night the venue is packed full of oil riggers and their families.

Several minutes later Jack's crew sits at a table. Jack scans the menu.

A middle-aged waitress saunters over. "Peterson, you crazy cowboy," she says. "You back again?"

"Darn tootin'," he says. "Brought some fresh meat." He elbows Jack who grimaces, rubbing his side.

"My," she says smiling at Jack. "Aren't you a prize?" She looks over at Sanders. "Well, you're a cutie." He blushes as she winks at him. "Whaddaya rascals have?"

The boys order, Jack having a large porterhouse steak, potatoes, and greens. For dessert, something he almost never has, Jack splits with the men the house specialty, a fresh-baked cherry pie topped with whipped cream. "Good, huh?" Peterson says to Jack.

"Don't normally indulge like this."

"Indulge?" He chuckles in a gruff voice. "Ya sure is a peculiar one, Douglas. Aw, you gotta live it up a little. That's why we gonna hit the Horse Stampede to work it off on the dance floor."

Jack looks away while rubbing his belly.

"You are a commin'?" Ryan says. "It's the best part of the evening."

Jack looks at Sanders who winces.

"I swear yer like an old married couple," Peterson says. "You need each other's permission or something?" He winks at Jack.

"I don't know," Jack says.

"Come on," Ryan says, poking Sanders. "You have the day off tomorrow and might get lucky."

Jack's eyebrows rise but he lowers them quickly. "Well, I guess just for a little while."

"Now that's the right attitude," Peterson says. "Gotta let off a little steam. Hey, whadda they say? All work and no play makes Jack a dull boy?" He elbows Jack in his ribs again and cackles.

"You're a real cut-up, Peterson," Jack says, rubbing his ribs once more.

"A cut-up. That's it. I knew I'd break that 'ole sour-puss of yours. What the hell happened to you anyway? Yer mommy spanked ya too hard?" He giggles.

~ * ~

The crew pulls up to the Horse Stampede. The dance hall covers half a city block. At least a hundred vehicles occupy the parking lot. Jack follows them in.

He and Sanders, dressed in T-shirts, jeans and sneakers, stand out as most of the patrons are dressed like Ryan and Peterson. A large bar stretches from one side of the back wall to the other. The boys meander through dozens of tables and a hundred chairs near the door and cross a large dance floor to arrive at the bar that hosts many patrons ordering or standing around drinking. "Whaddaya have?" Peterson says to Jack.

Jack figures he better take Curly's advice again and play along. "Beer. Whatever you're having."

Peterson glances at Sanders. "Same," Sanders says.

Peterson orders. Ryan orders his own then turns to drool over the assorted lady-folk, looking for action. A couple minutes later, Peterson hands Jack his beer. Jack takes a sip while standing with the boys at the bar, watching the people play. It seems like an alien world to him, a world he had never really known. Of course, in high school, later in college, he went to a few venues with his friends, yet he never had any reason to engage in the ritual he saw playing out in front of him. He had met and courted Janette in high school. Although they graduated from different colleges, they weren't far apart, so they saw one another almost every weekend.

"Hey, Peterson, you some bitch," says the man with the flabby belly and scar above his eye. He pulls up to them.

"O'Reilly, you piece of crap," Peterson says, slapping him on his shoulder.

"Likewise," O'Reilly says. Jack notices his paunch and bad teeth.

"My crew, you know Ryan. This is Sanders and Douglas."

Jack extends his hand for a shake, but O'Reilly ignores him, turns and spanks a waitress carrying a tray full of drinks as she passes, almost spilling them. "Dammit, O'Reilly," she says, scurrying past. "I'll have yer ass thrown outta here again." She makes her way over to a nearby table where she unloads her order.

O'Reilly jabs Peterson in the side. "I think she likes me."

"Right, dog-face," Peterson says.

O'Reilly scampers off to harass some gorgeous girls at the end of the bar. Jack stands with the guys watching as one of the girls slaps O'Reilly. "Ouch," Peterson says. He grimaces at Jack, laughing.

The girls, dressed in western-themed cowgirl blouses, shorts, and cowgirl boots, mosey over to Jack and the boys. The taller one, an authentic blond, stands a little too close to Jack for his liking. Stunning, her arm keeps brushing against him as she sways to the music. The other girl, a cute brunette, stands next to Sanders, winking at him while sipping on a straw, her pink lipstick leaving its mark.

Jack looks past the girl next to him, but she must have thought he was checking her out because she catches his glance, smiles and says, "Name's Cara." She extends her hand.

He reaches out to shake her hand, but she turns her hand over, palm down. Taken aback, but trying to be polite, he shakes it, turning it vertical. "Jack. Nice to meet you." Like the waitress in the diner months ago, she too lets her hand slide slowly out of his. He ignores her flirting, looks away.

Honky Tonk Badonkadonk, by Trace Adkins comes on over the sound system. In a flash, Cara turns, sets her drink on the bar. Smiling at Jack she says, "I love this song. Let's dance." She grabs his hand.

Taken off guard, Jack holds back, but Peterson steps up and takes possession of Jack's drink. He says to Jack, pushing him toward the dance floor, "Git yer ass out there, Douglas. That's an order."

Cara drags Jack to the dance floor. The other girl does the same with Sanders who also protests but gives in after she drags him half-way there.

Oh great. A line dance. Jack has to watch Cara to remember the moves. *It's been years since I have line-danced with....Janette. Had I almost forgotten her name?* He loses his step.

"Little rusty?" Cara says, bringing him out of his trance. He shakes Janette out of his thoughts, concentrating on the moves. He has two left feet but manages not to trip over himself.

After the dance ends, they return to the bar. "I thank you, kindly," Cara says in a country-twang leaning forward, kissing him on the cheek then sipping her umbrella drink.

Blushing, Jack cracks a forced, friendly smile then sips his drink as well. *I have to get out of here.* He sets his half-empty beer glass on the bar and looks around. He sees Sanders and his dance partner heading back from the floor. O'Reilly passes Sanders, bumps into him, knocking him off balance.

Sanders says to O'Reilly, "I'm sorry."

"Yer sorry? Ya better be, twerp." O'Reilly pushes Sanders backward into a group of men standing behind him. He doesn't topple over but catches himself before he does.

Jack rushes forward to assist. "You okay?" he says over his shoulder to Sanders while keeping an eye on O'Reilly.

"Guess so."

The girl with Sanders takes him by the arm, scowls at O'Reilly, and leads Sanders back to the bar.

"Watch yerself, pretty boy," O'Reilly says, sticking his finger into Jack's chest.

Jack ignores him returning to the bar. *I haven't seen behavior like this since high school. I knew it was a bad idea to come here. This is why I would be better off alone, in the woods. I don't need this. I don't need these people. I don't need any people for that matter.*

"Can we go?" Sanders says to Jack.

"You read my mind. Let me go to the restroom, and I'll be right out." Jack scurries into the restroom. Sanders heads for the door.

Exiting the restroom, Jack spots Sanders near the front door whispering into the ear of the girl he danced with. She nods, gives him a hug and a kiss on his cheek.

Out of nowhere, O'Reilly lunges forward, grabs Sanders and spins him around. He throws a punch, hitting Sanders in the face, toppling him over onto the floor. Jack pushes through the crowd of dancers and pulls O'Reilly off before he can get in another lick. O'Reilly lunges for Jack, but Jack dodges him as he had with the homeless man. Jack can smell beer on his breath. "I don't want to hurt you," Jack says.

"Hurt me?" He sneers at Jack, throwing a punch. Jack blocks the blow, turns, and lays a punch squarely onto O'Reilly's face. O'Reilly stumbles backward, shakes it off, lunging for Jack. Jack dodges him once more, striking him yet again. O'Reilly staggers but comes for Jack. Jack hits him one more time. O'Reilly falls to the floor, blood spurting from his nose.

Another man lunges for Jack. "Attack my motorman, will ya?"

Jack dodges him as well, but the man turns around, coming at him again, throwing a punch. Jack steps aside, clocks him too, knocking him down. Yet another man gets into the fray. At last Peterson and Ryan run over. Before long, everyone's fighting one another for no reason except a good ass-kicking. The entire dancehall erupts into a brawl. *This must have been how the Wild West was won. Blood Meridian, indeed.*

He spots Sanders rubbing his face and crawling for the front door. Jack knocks down another rigger who runs at him, dodges a couple others, slipping past yet another, and makes it to the door. He and Sanders run out and jump into the truck.

Down the road they pass several police cars coming up the road with lights flashing and sirens screaming.

"What happened?" Jack says.

"Nothing. I was just telling the girl I wasn't interest…well, I mean I was saying I had a girl back home. That's all. Then outta nowhere O'Reilly attacked me. It's a good thing you came along when you did."

Chapter Nine

Sorrow is a precious treasure, shown only to friends.
African Proverb

Jack works out in the gym as the sun rises the next morning. Coming from the gym, he hears Curly hollering in the main hallway. "Get everyone up. Report here immediately."

Jack wipes the sweat from his face with a towel. "Douglas," Curly says, "wait here."

Jack stands against the wall as the riggers not on shift trickle into the room, Sanders as well, dressed in his boxers and a T-shirt. A few minutes later after most of them had assembled, Curly says, "Anyone with a day off, forget it. We need you to report to the office at seven-thirty."

"What's up, Curly?" one of the men says.

"A fuckin' disaster, that's what's up. Seems there was a brawl at the Stampede last night, and as of last count sixteen of our guys have been arrested and are in the clink. Our lawyers are working on bailing them out, but seeing how it's a fuckin' Saturday, this is a fuckin' mess."

Jack looks over at Sanders who glances back at him. Jack scans the room but doesn't see Ryan or Peterson.

The riggers return to their rooms, shower, grab some quick chow, and head to the office, Jack riding with Sanders.

Outside the office, Jack waits with Sanders as the other riggers pull in. Curly exits the office carrying a clipboard. He says, "We're gonna pair you up as best we can. We might have to shut down a couple rigs for a day until we're back at full strength." He rattles off some rig numbers and names. "Sixteen-B off-line. Douglas and Sanders pair up with Johnson and Guerrero on rig twelve-A."

That means Ryan and Peterson sit in jail. Jack puts the blame for all of this squarely on O'Reilly.

Sanders and Jack drive over to rig twelve-A. There, they meet up with Motorman Johnson and Rig Manager Guerrero.

Near the end of their shift, Curly drives up to inspect operations. Jack stands with Guerrero as Curly says, "Lawyers were able to get some guys released, but Judge Blackbear won't miss Sunday services tomorrow with the misses and can't hear bail on the others until the afternoon."

Sunday services. Seems like another lifetime.

"So," Curly continues, "I need you boys to work another day on this rig."

Jack catches Curly's glance. *Does he suspect what had happened? Was he told how it started?*

~ * ~

After their shift the following day, Jack sits with Sanders in the dining facility with many others eating dinner. He notes O'Reilly, sporting a bruised face and cuts with dried blood, enter and head down the hall to his room.

Jack knows this means trouble. O'Reilly had not only been rejected by that girl but must have gathered, at least in a juvenile way, that Sanders had stolen her from him, although Sanders said he wasn't interested in her, for whatever reason. None of his business. In addition, O'Reilly would be further agitated by the fact he had a court date and would probably receive a fine or something. Jack can't worry about O'Reilly's troubles. Although, he knows they will have to avoid him. Certainly, Jack would not go back into town to hang out like that again.

In the rec room after dinner, Jack picks up *The Call of the Wild*, by Jack London. An American classic, he'd read it in school as well. *I have nothing else to read, so why not?* He heads back to his room.

~ * ~

By Monday afternoon all of the jailbirds have returned. Needless to say, this episode caused the company millions in lost production. Curly and the other bosses had a conniption, rightly so. However, the bosses apparently did not know this event had been triggered by O'Reilly, Jack, or Sanders, so they all escaped the company's wrath.

Jack and his crew arrive on-site at rig Sixteen-B before eight o'clock the following day. The chain on the gate has been cut. Someone cut and draped it around the gate so as to appear from afar that it's still intact. Pullen removes the chain, opens the gate. The crew preps the rig for reactivation while Pullen makes a call to company HQ.

Everything seems to be on schedule as the rig once again begins its operation pumping oil on cue. Sanders works up on the derrick, Peterson supervises the drilling, Ryan attends to the machinery, and Pullen stands off to the side of the platform entering notes onto a clipboard. Jack inventories the equipment, laying out items for cleaning and servicing.

A couple minutes later Jack hears a loud clank, glances up to see Sanders on the derrick ducking from a wire that snaps off the Traveling Block. The other end of the wire flies through the air at the speed of light. Jack jumps to the floor, Ryan is protected behind the driller's shack, but Peterson stands on the platform looking up just as the wire slices through the air decapitating him.

Peterson's headless body falls over, landing onto the platform with a thud. Ryan shuts down the rig by hitting an emergency off-switch as Pullen races over. In haste, Jack removes his jacket placing it over Peterson's corpse as blood oozes from its neck. "Give me your jacket," he shouts at Ryan. Sanders climbs down.

Ryan's face turns ashen. He struggles not to vomit. Jack pulls Ryan's jacket off him and jumps down from the platform. Peterson's head rolled off the platform and landed in the mud. Using Ryan's jacket, Jack covers Peterson's head. Pullen calls the police on his cell then company HQ.

The police and Curly arrive in short order. They take statements and secure the area for investigators. The remaining crew waits until the coroner removes the remains. The crew removes their hats, standing as the coroner and his assistant load Peterson into the van.

In Sanders' truck during the short ride back to camp, they ride in silence, Jack reminded of that other tragic day.

~ * ~

Curly brought in a replacement, and the next day the rig returns to full operation. Peterson's remains were shipped back to Indiana to his family. During their briefing that morning, Pullen says, "Investigators confirmed the wire had been cut so it would snap. It was sabotage. They're not certain who did it, or for what reason."

Jack glances over at Sanders who looks back at him.

"If anybody knows something," Pullen continues. "Speak up."

No one does.

~ * ~

In the dining facility that night, Jack sits with Sanders eating dinner, mostly in silence. Jack struggles to keep his mind off this event. It has also caused him to relive his most recent history back in Georgia. He's sure Sanders is as contemplative as he is.

"You think it was O'Reilly?" Sanders says.

Jack looks up at him after swirling his mashed potatoes around on his plate. "Not easy to prove."

"Should we tell the police?"

"Perhaps, but anonymously." He considers that. "Might be the best way to not cause any more trouble." For some reason trouble has found him, perhaps followed him. *It might be time for me to move on.*

Jack spots O'Reilly slinking over to them. "I got my eye on you, PASTOR." He holds up his index and middle fingers, first pointing at his own eyes, then at Jack's, like a child.

Jack freezes.

"That's right," O'Reilly continues. "The Internet knows all. Yer whore wifey and evil seed were struck down by the Lord, huh? Musta sucked as a man of God, just like ya suck at riggin'."

The vein in Jack's neck bulges. It takes all his inner strength to suppress the rage building in him.

"And you," O'Reilly says, bending down and whispering close to

Sanders. "You's a little faggot, huh?"

Sanders' eyes grow wide looking at O'Reilly.

"Yer little fake girlfriend the other night couldn't keep her mouth shut. Told a friend who told a friend. Ya better watch yer ass, fag. Might get what ya want." He puckers his lips, makes a slicing motion with his finger across his neck and saunters off.

Jack's eyes trail O'Reilly's departure. *I have to get out of here for sure now. That's it.* He gets up, carries his tray to the trash can where he dumps the paper plate and plastic utensils into the trash and places the tray on top. He heads to his room.

In his room, Jack prepares to turn in for the night. He strips down to his underwear and crawls into bed. He picks up *The Call of the Wild* from his nightstand and opens it to where he left off.

Sanders enters. Jack glances up at him but looks back down at his book, continuing to read. Sanders strips down and crawls into bed, turning out his light.

A couple minutes later Jack hears Sanders sigh, perhaps sniffle. Jack puts his book down onto his lap. "You okay, kid?"

"I can't stay here."

"Yeah, me neither."

A long pause then Sanders says, "I'm sorry about your family, Jack. If that's true."

Jack hesitates but says, "It's true."

Another long pause. "I've dealt with guys like O'Reilly all my life. Why are people such assholes?"

"Because they feel inadequate, or threatened."

Silence.

At last, Sanders continues, "I thought I could make a fresh start out here. Where no one knows me."

Yeah, me too. Jack glances at the book in his lap, contemplating it.

"My father threw me out of the house."

"I'm sorry."

A long silence.

Sanders says, just above a whisper, "Jack?"

"Yes?"

"I've never acted on anything. I mean, I'm a virgin. With, well, you know. Anyone."

Jack doesn't respond.

"I'm nineteen years old. How pathetic is that?"

"Look, kid, it's not pathetic. You should be in love with the one you want to be with. What matters is that you lead a good life, be kind to others. Who or what you are is nobody's business but your own." He pauses, looks down at his book again. "Hey, I'm reading *The Call of the Wild*. I'm thinking of heading up there. To Alaska. I don't know what I'll do there, but I've always wanted to see it. I might just live in the bush for some time. Start a business or something. You want to tag along?"

"Oh, I don't think so. You don't want someone like me tagging along."

"I don't care about that. Besides, you can't stay here." Jack waits for him to answer, but he doesn't. "Come on. We'll give Curly notice and get out of here."

"Well, I don't know. I mean, if you're sure?"

"I'm sure."

"Well, okay." Sanders pauses. "Okay, *I will*. Thanks, Jack. Thanks. Goodnight."

"Goodnight, kid." Jack looks down at *The Call of the Wild* in his lap once more. *Alaska. Why not? I feel this allure, a pull, as if it's summoning me.* He sets the book on the nightstand and turns out his light.

Chapter Ten

Vengeance is in my heart, death in my hand, blood and revenge are hammering in my head.

William Shakespeare, *Titus Andronicus*

The next morning at the rig, Jack stands with Sanders next to Pullen. "So, two weeks okay?" Jack says to Pullen.

"It has to be," Pullen says.

"It's just time for us to go." Jack looks over at Sanders.

"You two are a hell of a couple fine workers. Most dedicated and attentive ones I've seen during twenty years of riggin'." He groans. "Gonna be hard, but I understand. It's the nature of this business."

They go about their duties and work their shift.

~ * ~

A few days later, Jack awakes as usual at five o'clock. He gears up for the gym. They've done their best to avoid O'Reilly plus almost everyone, for that matter, not on their crew.

Sanders stirs. "A few more days," he says smiling. He has a glow about him Jack hasn't seen before. Sanders unlocks his footlocker and pulls out a lockbox. He unlocks it and shows Jack a large sum of cash. "I withdrew my account yesterday. I've got about forty-thousand here. For the business we'll start in Alaska. Whatever that'll be."

"Sure, kid. We'll think of something."

Sanders returns the cash to the box, the box to the locker and locks it as Jack departs for the gym.

~ * ~

Returning from his two-mile run fully charged Jack happens upon the guy from across the hall, Flores, coming out of his room for breakfast. "What the hell you two doing in there?"

"What's that?" Jack says, pulling his key from his shorts.

"In your room, making all that noise?"

Jack narrows his eyes at him but turns and opens the door. He freezes in horror, his mouth dropping open. Flores, standing behind him says, "What the fuck?"

The room is in disarray, Sanders' bed ajar, the chair and small table against the window overturned, and the microwave has been knocked off the kitchenette where it rests on the floor upside down. Sanders' lifeless body hangs by a belt noose from the water pipe that runs across the ceiling where the old-style sprinklers are affixed.

Jack rushes over, grabs the chair, stands up and yanks on the belt noose around Sanders' neck. It won't budge, so Jack has to lift Sanders up slightly to undo the belt.

Flores runs for help while Jack lowers Sanders' body to the floor. He feels for a pulse then starts CPR. Men gather behind Jack who thumps Sanders' chest and continues CPR. He blows into Sanders' mouth, but Sanders' face is blue. "Breathe. Breathe."

Flores rushes in, followed by the housekeeper, Perkins, who carries a defibrillator. Perkins rips open Sanders' shirt and attaches the electrodes to his chest. The machine flashes: SHOCK. "Clear," Perkins yells.

The machine whines and shocks Sanders' heart. His torso jumps off the floor. The machine again reads: SHOCK. "Clear," Perkins shouts. The defibrillator whines again, thumps Sanders' chest. "Nothing," Perkins says.

"Again," Jack hollers.

Perkins tries it again. Nothing. He sits back on his heels.

Jack looks at Perkins who shakes his head. Jack again tries CPR and blows into Sanders' lungs. Nothing. He tries yet again. On his knees, hovering over Sanders, his arms straddling the kid, he once more feels for a pulse. Nothing. He places his palm on Sanders' blue face, rubbing the kid's cheek. With Jack's eyes narrowing, his face tightening, he looks up at Perkins. "This was murder."

Perkins, with a blank stare, his mouth hanging open, looks back at him. Jack stands, scanning the faces of the men gathered there. He pushes his way past them and heads down the hall.

Several doors down the hallway, he pounds on a door.

"Awright, awright," a voice calls out from behind the door.

The door opens a crack, so Jack pushes his way in. "You did this, didn't you?" The door swings closed behind him.

"Your boyfriend?" O'Reilly chuckles. "Fuck you, Pastor." He thumps Jack's chest with his palms pushing him back. "One less fag in the world. Don't you Christians hate fags anyway?"

Jack stares him down, his face as tight as can be. He could just strangle him, but using all his will-power and summoning his faith, holds off, almost feeling sorry for the fool.

"Get the fuck outta here." O'Reilly pushes Jack back further. "You can't prove a fuckin' thing. Ya go to the police and yer next."

"We'll see about that," Jack says turning to leave.

O'Reilly throws a punch hitting Jack in the kidneys. Jack goes down, hard. O'Reilly kicks him, but Jack manages to block some of the kicks. He rolls away then gets up.

O'Reilly comes at him. Jack steps out of his way, spins around, punches O'Reilly in the face, knocking him back. O'Reilly comes at him again, but Jack punches him three times in rapid succession. O'Reilly falls backward onto the floor.

Jack again tries to leave, but O'Reilly sticks out his foot, tripping him.

Jack spins around on the floor as O'Reilly jumps on him and throws a punch, hitting Jack in the face.

Jack blocks the next in-coming blow and manages to throw O'Reilly off him. Jack rolls over on top of O'Reilly and delivers several rapid blows. O'Reilly tries to block the punches, yet Jack keeps at it, hitting him over and over again. Blood from Jack's mouth drips onto O'Reilly's chest.

Someone bangs on the door and yells, "Hey. Open the goddamn

door."

Jack doesn't let up. He delivers more hard-hitting blows. O'Reilly's face, a bloody mess, turns to pulp, his arms falling to his side. Jack has broken O'Reilly's nose, his jaw, one of his cheek bones, and caused an orbital fracture of the eye socket. O'Reilly's eye pops out and hangs on the outside of his face by its optical nerve.

Keys rattle in the lock at the door. It opens and several men rush in. Jack gets in a few more licks before they pull him off, including one that squashes O'Reilly's dangling eye. O'Reilly is unconscious, perhaps dead. They drag Jack out the door and into the hallway where they hold him against the wall, his head hanging low.

A couple riggers carry O'Reilly past them, load him onto the bed of a truck outside and speed off.

~ * ~

Jack sits in the dining facility as Perkins washes Jack's bloody hands with antiseptic wipes. Jack looks down at the table showing no emotion. Perkins hands him wipes, gathers his kit and departs.

Curly arrives with the police in tow. They inspect Jack's room while Jack waits at the table.

A couple minutes later Curly approaches Jack. "Goddammit, Douglas. I knew you were fuckin' trouble." He looks around to see if anyone is in ear-shot, lowers his voice and says, "We didn't tell the police about O'Reilly. I don't think he'll talk to them either, if he recovers. The boys're taking him to the hospital now. I don't need any trouble like that. Listen, pack yer shit and get the fuck out. Stop at the office and pick up yer pay."

"What about Sanders' body?"

"He didn't leave any contact information for next of kin."

"He didn't have any. Can you tell the coroner to release him to me?"

Curly sighs and nods. "Sure." He storms off.

Jack watches the coroner roll Sanders away on a gurney in a body-bag.

After the police clear his room, Jack packs his belongings. Just before exiting, he stops at Sanders' footlocker, pries it open with his jackknife and pulls out the lockbox. He pries that open too, takes out the cash, stuffing it in his pack. He departs.

~ * ~

He sits in the waiting room of a funeral home staring at the floor below him. A few minutes later the director comes out of a back room. He hands Jack an urn Jack had chosen, one that's waterproof and airtight. He follows the director to the counter. The director shows him the final bill. Jack digs in his pack, pulls out Sanders' cash. He peels off a few thousand and hands them to the director. He repacks the rest, grabs the urn, and walks out.

Outside on the porch, he places his pack down against the railing and holds the urn in both hands examining it. It's a stainless-steel metallic silver oblong one with a hook on its top, much like one of his water bottles. "Enough," he says looking up at the clouds. "Enough."

The clouds don't answer him.

He clips the urn to his pack next to a water bottle, shoulders his pack, and walks up the highway.

Chapter Eleven

The wind is your only friend when you walk alone.
Native American

Jack heads west along US-2 in Montana. More than one trucker offers him a ride, but he turns them all down.

In Culbertson, he stocks up with supplies and picks up a map. He traces the Missouri River along the map and sticks it in his pocket. He continues on until he reaches Brockton, where he turns and heads along the riverbank. He finds an isolated place to set up camp for the night.

He had bought a pup-tent in Culbertson, so he sets it up, that way he can sleep with his pack inside next to him. Good thing, because it rained during the night.

He awakes the next morning and crawls from his tent. He stretches and observes a beaver waddling along the riverbank near him. He stands, still watching it gather twigs for its home. It seems that his presence doesn't alarm the beaver, so he sits on a log, studying it. Jack admires its instinct, or know-how in constructing a shelter that should protect it from the elements, or dangers of the world. He knows, however, how dangers lurk around every corner. No matter what the beaver does to protect its family, life's uncertainty, its randomness, will most likely intervene destroying its best laid plans.

Jack washes his hands in the ice-cold river. He tore up his knuckles badly from the fight with O'Reilly and dried blood covers them. It occurs to him the only emotion within him at that time was uncontrollable rage. It had total control over his actions. He didn't have physical pain. Only rage. He was ashamed for what he did. It was out of character. Men like him were not supposed to act like that. He's a man of God. Rather, he had been a man of God. However, he was so angry to think that young man's life

63

had been cut short. That boy never knew joy, had never known love. His own parents rejected his love. Was there anything worse than losing a parent's love?

He remembers the accident. Perhaps he *was* a basket-case now. Maybe he did have emotional problems. It doesn't matter. Most he ever cared for were gone. He had made a new friend. His new friend had been taken from him too, ripped out of this world. He could have been that boy's new parent. He could have helped guide him through his difficult times. After all, that's what he was trained to do, counsel others in their time of need. It seemed what he had been trained to do, that which he thought was his calling, had now been all for naught. He was no longer a pastor. No longer a counselor. He was nothing. In his mind he was but a shell of a man, a ghost wandering the country. He now decided he would get away from people for sure. That was it. He didn't want to make friends with anyone. He wanted to be alone. He didn't want to even be with God anymore because God didn't want to be with him.

He works out and eats a breakfast bar. After striking his tent, he packs up and hikes along the Missouri River. A worn path, others had taken guides his way. At times, he runs into other folks fishing and camping. When given salutations, he obliges and returns them. However, he doesn't stick around to talk with anyone.

~ * ~

He spends the next week hiking the Missouri, fishing along the way, and detouring at times stopping in small towns along US-2 for supplies.

At a road-side convenience store in Wolf Point, Montana, he buys some supplies. Approaching the counter to pay, Jack happens upon the end of an argument between the clerk and a young man.

"Hey, fuck you, asshole," the young man says to the clerk.

The young man, who has a basket full of items, grabs a handful of candy bars at the counter, not paying for anything, running past Jack on his way out. Jack could have intervened, but he's done enough. It's not his place. He watches the young man hurry to his car, climb in, and zip away.

The clerk calls the police while Jack stands there waiting to pay for his supplies. After the clerk reports the crime over the phone, Jack pays his tab and hikes off.

~ * ~

For the next few weeks Jack hikes and camps his way along Fort Peck Lake, through the Charles M. Russell National Wildlife Refuge, and along the Upper Missouri River Breaks National Monument. Lush, sparse and full of wildlife, Jack lives the life trappers lived a few hundred years ago. He fishes for most of his meals, only encountering deer, rabbits, beavers and an assortment of other small creatures such as squirrels and birds. He doesn't happen upon any bears or wolves, thankfully.

He makes his way across Montana, Washington State, and ends up in Seattle, checking into a luxury downtown hotel late one night after a long day. He tosses his pack on the floor, strips down and draws a bath in a large in-room Jacuzzi bathtub. His first bath or shower in weeks, he just sits there, leaning up against the side, his arms outstretched on either side of the rim, with his head laid back on a pillow cushion that's attached to and a part of the Jacuzzi. He has never lapped in such luxury before, except once on his honeymoon in the Bahamas. He had lived the pious life. The Jacuzzi jets massage his lower back. He almost falls asleep.

After toweling off, he crawls onto the bed, never unpacking, or reading. Alone, hugging a pillow for the first time in a long time, he crashes in short order.

~ * ~

At dawn, Jack awakes and dresses in his workout and running gear. The hotel has a fully equipped gym so he engages in his first full workout in weeks.

Two women, perhaps a little younger than Jack, saunter in just as he wipes his face with his shirt tail, exposing his muscular frame. Cute, and in great shape for their age, the women's jaws drop, their eyes almost popping out despite his long hair and beard. He notices their stares, but looks away. *I got to get out of here.*

He slips out onto the street. There, he jogs through downtown Seattle. He has lost track of the days of the week. It must be a Saturday, or perhaps a Sunday, because the streets are empty, despite the early hour at around six o'clock. He doesn't care. Time is an alien concept to him now.

He zips along, stopping near the water's edge where he watches seagulls swooping along the waterfront. Against the stiff breeze, the gulls seem to float on air but go nowhere, lost in space/time. Overcoming the resistance, however, the gulls manage to make headway and disappear out to sea.

He circles back to the hotel, showers, and eats his first full-course breakfast he's had in weeks at the hotel's restaurant.

Back in his room, he digs in his pack and pulls out Sanders' cash. Not since leaving the funeral home has he spent any of it. It wasn't his to spend. He has only spent his own money.

He enters the hotel lobby and sits at one of those computers in the business room that hotels offer. He Googles and finds what he's looking for then prints the page he wants.

He walks up one street then turns onto another. He enters the Seattle LGBTQ runaway and homeless shelter, pulling up to the counter. "Hi, may I help you?" a young man says to him, smiling, but scanning his long unkempt hair and beard.

"Yes, please. I'd like to donate some money."

"Sure. I can help with that. We have a collection box over there by the window."

"Actually, it won't fit." He pulls the cash from his jeans. "I have about thirty-six thousand, mostly in hundreds."

The man's mouth drops open. "Oh, well. Wow. I need to get our director. Hold on. Don't go away." He scurries into a back room, returning with the director a moment later, an older man in his forties.

Jack tells them the story. Both men shed tears. Jack has to fill out some forms for such a large cash donation, but he puts Sanders' name on the forms. "The only thing I ask," Jack says, "and you must promise me, that you will make a placard honoring Christopher Sanders for this gift and put it up on your wall, right over there." He points to a spot next to another placard with a similar exclamation.

"Absolutely," the director says.
Jack shakes their hands then departs.

~ * ~

After two more days of living in luxury, washing his clothes, and stocking up on supplies, Jack packs up and departs, heading north.

Chapter Twelve

Your nightmares follow you like a shadow, forever.
Aleksandar Hemon, *The Lazarus Project*

A week later, after camping along the sound north of Seattle, he clears the border and hugs the ocean, meandering along trails and in and out of coves. He camps in obscure places, making minimal contact with others.

Well over a year has passed since he left Georgia, and Jack's hair has grown out. It hangs down on both sides of his face. He can now tuck it behind his ears and he has a full, bushy beard. He looks like one of those Duck Dynasty characters.

In a small town on the Canadian coast a couple weeks later, Jack finds a fish and chips restaurant. The hostess seats him at a table overlooking the ocean where he looks out the window at fishing boats in a small harbor. Fishermen scrub and hose them off after a day at sea. *Perhaps I can become a fisherman. That would be serene.*

"What can I get you, hon?" the waitress says, snapping him out of his daydream.

"House special, please. Fish and chips."

"Drink?"

"Milk, please. Thank you."

She scans his pack on the floor next to him. "Passing through?"

"Yes, ma'am."

She looks him over. "Thought it was Jesus himself sitting here."

"Pardon me?"

"You look like Jesus, with that hair and beard."

"Oh, I can assure you I'm not Jesus."

She continues to stare at him, making him uncomfortable. She's perhaps his mother's age, in her fifties, and has a salty-weathered look about her. She's been living and working here by the sea all her life. "Ma'am?" Jack says.

"Yes?"

"Fish and chips, please."

"Oh, yes. Yes, right away." She hurries to place his order with the cook.

What is it with all these people? Young girls whistling, others gawking, and this one standing there in a trance like I've descended from on high? Look like Jesus? Nonsense. No one knows what Jesus looked like. Jesus would look like a Hasidic Jew. He wouldn't look like Jack Douglas of Scots-Irish descent.

A few minutes later while watching the fisherman, the waitress delivers his Halibut and chips. He eats every last morsel. After he finishes, he thinks about what the waitress said. *Jesus?* He shakes his head. *Jesus and the fish and the feeding of the multitude. How many times have I given a sermon centering on that story?*

The waitress drops off his check, smiling at him again. *Is she flirting with me too? I've got to get out of town, get up to Alaska and out into the bush.*

It's late, and dark, but he walks north along the shore. He finds a cove next to the ocean surrounded by a forest to camp for the night. He pitches his tent, tosses his pack inside and crawls in. A cold autumn night, temperatures dipping into the mid-thirties, he strips off his clothes, including his underwear and zips up into his all-weather sleeping bag. He hugs his pillow again like he did that day his mother came to see him.

~ * ~

Jack stands on the side of the highway waving his hands, screaming, "Stop," near the overpass as Janette drives by with the children waving at him. He runs after the van as the tanker-truck crosses the center divider striking the van.

A fireball envelops the area, blowing right past Jack but not burning him. He sprints for the van through the flames and comes upon the scene. He opens the door to the van to discover the decapitated and burning corpse of his wife.

He glances at his children who are engulfed in flames.

He tries to get closer, but a hand upon his shoulder pulls him back away from the scene. A few feet from the van he slips through a black hole and is now standing in his room back at the man-camp in North Dakota.

He looks up and sees Sanders swinging from the belt on the pipe.

"Jack," Sanders says. "He's here for you too."

Jack struggles to go to him, but the hand on his shoulder holds him in place. He watches as the belt strangles the life from Sanders.

He glances at the skeletal hand on his shoulder then looks up at a faceless figure in a large black cloak. With its other hand, the figure wags its boney index finger at Jack.

~ * ~

He jolts up in his bag at dawn. Soaked in sweat, Jack unzips the bag and rolls it down to his waist. It's a frigid morning. He grabs a towel from his pack, wipes sweat from his face and torso.

Catching his breath, he looks at the urn hanging on his pack. "I'm so sorry, kid." Placing his palm on his chest, it feels as if an elephant lies across it, yet he sits upright. He puts his face in his hands, rubbing it, wiping tears away.

He opens his pack and pulls out his family photo, staring at it, tears dripping from his eyes.

After a minute, he unhooks it from a clasp inside his pack and squeezes it in his palm. He opens his hand, pulls back the largest blade of his jackknife, regarding it, the glint from the blade catching his eye. He presses the edge against his wrist near his vein. He raises the tip, pushes it down, breaking the skin. A small drop of blood pops out. He pushes it tighter against his wrist where a little more blood trickles out.

He grips the knife firmer, closes his eyes then hears something flutter, like a small horse, outside his tent. He opens his eyes, holding fast, a small amount of blood beading on his wrist.

He hears the animal flutter again then something brushes against the side of the tent. Then another animal brushes against the tent on the other side.

He lowers the knife and unzips the tent. Peering out through the opening, he sees a large stag standing nearby watching him. Stark naked, he eases out of the tent, stands, holding the knife in his hand. He looks back at a doe and her fawn next to his tent on either side. They move toward him. The doe sniffs his leg. The fawn sniffs the other and gently nudges him in the side. He reaches down to stroke the fawn's head. The doe bumps his hand, the one with the knife, but he holds firm. She bumps it again. He opens his hand, releasing the jackknife onto the ground. He strokes the doe too.

The fawn meanders over to its father stopping along the way to sniff the grass. The doe soon follows. Jack watches the stag lower its head to nudge the fawn along. The stag eyes him again before the three of them amble off into the woods.

He examines his wrist. A superficial cut, he walks into the cold ocean up to his knees. He looks out at the ocean churning before him, squats, and reaches down to splash water onto his face and over his shoulders. He washes the blood from his wrist.

He returns to his tent, towels off then sits on a log with the towel wrapped around him watching seagulls fly over. Glancing at the knife on the ground, he wraps the towel tighter around his shoulders. Considering the sky, he sighs and says, "Okay." Nodding, he continues, "All right, then."

A gull swoops down and stands on the end of the log looking at him.

"You're kidding, right?"

"Squawk," it says.

"I guess not."

"Squawk." It nods its head rapidly then flies off heading north. Jack ponders the direction it flew.

He gets up, reaches down to pick up his knife. Using water from his bottle he washes the blood off, wipes the blade against his thigh and stows the knife in his pack. He dresses, strikes his tent, packs up, and moves out, hugging the shoreline.

~ * ~

In Juneau, Jack checks into another luxury hotel for a few days to wash his clothes and resupply. Winter is coming.

He stops at a branch to his national bank where he withdraws cash for the next leg of his journey, wherever that may be.

He buys winter clothes, a parka, flannel shirts, insulated long johns, pants and heavy boots. He donates his summer clothes to a local church.

Back in his hotel room, he uses the phone to call the manager to the mailbox center in Puckett. "Hey, Thomas," he says.

"Jack?" a man says to him over the phone.

"Anything of importance?"

"Something from the IRS."

"You better overnight it. Glacier Hotel, room two-two-one. Juneau, Alaska."

"Alaska? Wow."

"Yes."

"How you holding up?" Thomas says.

"Fine, Thomas. Thanks. Don't know when I'll call you again."

"Okay, Jack."

Jack hangs up, stays a couple more days, and sends the IRS a money order for what he owns then checks out.

He heads out to Skagway then back into Canada to Haines Junction. Taking his time, enjoying nature, two weeks later he passes back into Alaska. He stops in Tok for a couple of days to buy supplies and wash clothes again.

In Fairbanks, he once again checks into a hotel, washes clothes, resupplies and withdraws more cash from a bank because the towns from here on out will be few and far between. Three days later, he mails postcards to Georgia and heads out.

Because of his long hair and beard, he looks like a prospector during the Klondike Gold Rush, or worse, which gives him an idea for his next route of travel.

While admiring the beautiful and rugged terrain, he struggles to wash away his horrors and focus on the trail along Highway 6 north of Fairbanks. The memories would probably haunt him the rest of his life he figures. *What can I do but keep moving?*

Although he hikes at a brisk pace, he's in no hurry. He travels about twenty-five to thirty miles a day, camping off the road out of sight, away from people, which is not difficult to do out here in the America's final frontier.

He looks down at his Fitbit wrist tracker he bought in Fairbanks, gauging the thirty miles he's hiked this day. He hits a button, learning that sunset is in fifteen minutes, so he pulls off the trail near the end of Highway 6 in Circle, Alaska on the Yukon River.

After setting up camp, he cooks on his Sterno stove, reviewing his Yukon River map. He traces the river all the way to the Bering Sea. He looks out at the river. *Blame this on Jack London.* He folds his map and reads in his guide book that the Yukon had been used as a thoroughfare for the Klondike Gold Rush. Several villages dot the river along the way. Some are thirty to forty miles apart, others sixty to ninety, the longest between Tanana and Ruby at one hundred and twenty miles.

He washes his dishes to ensure he gets the food residue off them lest a bear wander into camp and sniff around. Each night he packs his food then hoists it into a tree. He learned from his Appalachian experience.

~ * ~

A couple hours before sunrise the next morning, he doesn't jump up in a jolt this time, but he'd had another nightmare similar to the other. This time, however, he wipes the sweat away, crawls out of his tent, dresses and gets busy. *Get busy and keep moving. That's the only way I can fight this.* He sets up his small Sterno camping stove to heat some instant oatmeal.

While eating, Jack hears something stirring in the bushes behind him. He pivots on the log he sits upon and sees a large grey wolf appear, circling around behind his tent. It's a female and weighs about one hundred pounds, he guesses. She has a white fur underbelly, white face, and grey on top. Her bushy tail seems to wag. She stops beside his tent, watching him at about fifteen feet. He doesn't dare move. Jack had read how wolves normally avoided human contact, were predatory animals, usually hunting in packs. He scans the area for others. *Is she distracting me, so the others can pounce on and tear me apart, like those velociraptors in Jurassic Park?* He isn't her food source. *So, what does she want with me?* In packs they hunt deer and elk, working as a team. They also hunt rabbits and squirrels. He stares at her. She stares back at him. He admires her face. She has a typical wolf snout with a black nose, yet has reddish-orange eyes. "I don't have anything for you," he says.

She cocks her head, crosses in front of him, moving closer. She stops and continues to observe him at about ten feet. Her closeness doesn't alarm him, for some reason. He is calm and peaceful. It appears she is at ease with him too. So, he figures he should finish his oatmeal. *At least I'll die with a full belly.*

As he eats, she just stands there watching him. "I don't think you'd like this," he says, holding up his bowl of oatmeal.

She cocks her head again then sits down.

"Suit yourself." He finishes his oatmeal, licking his spoon. "Well, I have to wash this out and pack up." He stands, keeping his face toward her, reaching for his pack beside the tent. She turns her head, following his actions.

He washes his utensils, glances at her, just in case she charges him, but she lies down, her front legs outstretched like a dog. "What's this all about? You domesticated, like someone's pet?"

She looks right into his eyes, almost through him. He feels a sense of calm.

"Well, I have to move on. Thanks for the company." He packs his stove and strikes his tent. She never takes her eyes off him. While adjusting the straps on his pack, he hears a boat in the distance downstream. He looks up to see it heading upstream. He glances back at the wolf, but she is gone, as if she disappeared into thin air. "Huh," he says looking around. "Where did you go?" Just like that his friend is gone.

~ * ~

He follows the river as it bends this way and meanders that way. Jack notices wolf tracks on the path he follows, always leading in the same direction he heads. Several times he sees her ahead of him on the trail as if she's waiting for him to come along. Each time he approaches, she turns then trots off down the trail ahead of him. *Bizarre*. It's as if he is following her and she's his guide.

That night, he sets up camp on the riverbank. He fishes, catching a large Rainbow trout, about nine pounds. He flays and cooks it on a fire he's built.

While eating, he looks up to catch reddish-orange eyes coming toward him out of the darkness. Not afraid in the least, for some odd reason, he just sits there as that wolf stops about a dozen feet from him. "You're a curious one."

She studies him, cocks her head again, and sits.

He looks at the uneaten fish in the frying pan. "Trout?" He picks up a sizable piece, tossing it onto the grass at her feet.

She opens her large jaw, exposing massive teeth, and picks it up chewing. She licks her lips, looking over at him again.

"Half and half?" He picks up more of the fish, eating it. He watches her watching him. He licks his fingers.

She lies down, outstretches her legs. Jack picks up another morsel, tossing it toward her. She once again gobbles it down. He repeats the process until it's all gone. "No more."

He gets up and cleans his utensils while keeping an eye on her in case she attacks. However, she just lies there, studying his every move. He kicks at the fire, stomping out the embers. He undresses, tosses his pack and clothes into the tent. Standing there in his underwear, he looks back at her. "Well, thanks for the date. Goodnight." He crawls into his tent, zips it up.

He settles into his bag, staring at the ceiling of the tent. *If she was going to kill me, rip me apart with those huge teeth of hers, she would have by now. What in the world is this all about?*

~ * ~

Early the next morning, he awakes and crawls from his tent. A dusting of snow covers the ground. Pulling up his pants, he discovers animal tracks encircling his tent, as if something paced around it during the night. He kneels down to examine an imprint by swiping his fingers over it. The imprint is as large as his outstretched hand.

He stands, looking around. No wolf, nothing. *What is she doing?*

He works out, eats, packs up then moves on down river.

A crisp, sunny day, his breath solid white as he exhales, he makes his way into the small village of Beaver, Alaska and enters a general store. Seeing no one there to greet him, the only patron inside, he calls out, "Hello?"

An old Inuit man with long white hair appears from the backroom. "Hello."

"I need some supplies, sir."

"Yes," he says, squinting. "Please." He waves his hand around the store. "We have everything you need." He sits on a stool behind the counter, watching Jack.

"Thank you." Jack goes down an aisle but notices the man's eyes trailing him. *Does he think I'm going to rob him?* Jack finds Sterno, matches, some freeze-dried foods, and other supplies. He heads back up the other aisle, places his items on the counter, the man watching his every move, making him nervous. *It's like the woman at the fish and chips restaurant. Is it because he looks like Jesus? No, that's ridiculous.*

He spots a paperback book rack next to the counter and picks up one that catches his eye: *Tales and Traditions of the Eskimo*, by Danish geologist Johannes Rink. He sets it on the counter.

While ringing up Jack's purchases, the man smiles, looking at Jack as if reading words off his face. After each item is tallied, Jack stows them in his pack.

At last, Jack hands him cash.

He takes the cash, places it in his till, and pulls out Jack's change, saying, "I see in your eyes she has chosen you."

"Pardon me?" Jack says receiving the change.

"In your eyes. Just as the shaman said. You're path has been written."

Jack has no idea what he's talking about. "Yes. Well, thank you, sir."

"You are welcome. I thank you too."

Jack nods, shoulders his pack, and exits. *Nice friendly man. Odd. Although, he probably thought I'm odd all alone out here hiking at this time of the year.*

~ * ~

The river flows through the snow-covered riverbank. A few miles down the river, as Jack takes his eye off the path to admire the high riverbank, he hits a rut in the path just beneath the snow. He falls onto the ground, his pack taking a jolt.

The urn breaks off, bouncing into the river. Jack tears off his pack, jumps in after the urn. The river gently flows, so Jack doesn't have to struggle with any current. He grabs the urn and climbs onto the riverbank. Soaked, he sets the urn down next to his pack, stripping off his clothes.

In late December the sun rises at almost eleven in the morning and sets before three in the afternoon. He tries to hike until around six in the evening each day, but glances at his Fitbit learning it's two-thirty. The sun will set soon. Since he has to dry his wet clothes, he decides to camp here. He dresses in fresh clothes and hangs the wet ones on a tree branch. They freeze in short order. He pitches his tent, cuts some branches off a tree then starts a fire. He strings his clothesline between two trees near the fire.

He sits on a log to rest, eyeing the urn sitting in the snow next to his pack. "You made it, kid." He glances at his tracks in the snow leading to and from the spot where he had jumped into and crawled out of the river. At last he stands, picks up the urn, wiping the snow from its base. He struggles but manages to unscrew it. He sets the top down, walks back to the river's edge where he watches the water flow.

He kneels at the river's edge, tips the urn onto its side and gently shakes the ashes into the river. He watches as the ashes mix with the water, flowing downstream. He dips the urn in the water, washing it out.

He screws the top back on the urn then tosses it into his pack where it bounces off his Bible.

He fishes, catches another large Rainbow Trout and cooks it on the fire.

Those reddish-orange eyes approach from out of the darkness. She comes right up to him, closer yet, to within six feet where he sits on a small tarp on the ground near the fire. Because of her long legs and large shoulders, she towers over him. She could pounce and rip out his throat before he had the chance to react.

Except, she doesn't. She lies down and outstretches her paws in front of her, watching him.

He tosses her a morsel of fish. She gobbles it up in short order.

"Now this one was not as large as the other, so there's not much to go around."

She squints as if she understands him. *Crazy.*

He eats some more then tosses her some. Together, they eat it all. He cleans up. She crosses her front legs, resting her head upon them.

Her eyes follow him as he checks on his drying clothes. Hot to the touch, he folds and packs them.

He pulls from his pack a paperback he bought in Fairbanks, *The Alchemist*, by Paulo Coelho. Sitting down to read it by firelight, he looks over at the wolf, realizing he had gone about his business not looking at her. He had turned his back on her. "You're not going to eat me after all, like Little Red Riding Hood, huh?"

She raises her head.

"Where's your pack?"

She puts her head back down upon her outstretched legs, considering him.

He opens his book, continues to read where he left off. He comes upon a passage, reads it twice, first silently then out loud where an old king tells the main character, Santiago, "When you really want something to happen, the whole universe will conspire so that your wish comes true." He looks over at the wolf. "What's your wish?"

She raises her head again, as if she understands.

"I hope your wish comes true."

She blinks.

He continues to read.

After a Chapter, his eyes grow heavy, his head falling to his chest. "Yelp."

He raises his head to discover her towering over him, inches from his face. *Is she now going to pounce and tear me apart? Why now?*

"Yelp." She turns, heads toward his tent where she sits next to the opening.

What is she trying to say? He yawns, discovers the fire is only embers now. He closes his book, putting a marker in it. He gets up and snubs the embers out with his boots. He looks back at her still sitting next to the opening of his tent as if waiting for him. *Well, here goes nothing.*

He makes his way toward the tent, looks down at her, thinking, *I'm in some sort of dream world.*

At the opening he stops, tosses his book in, kicks his boots off, and strips down. Standing there in his underwear, he tosses his boots and clothes into the tent as well. He looks at her again, watching him. "Well, goodnight." He crawls into his tent, zips it up. Settling into his bag, he watches as her shadow circles around his tent several times. His eyes grow heavy again. He drifts off to sleep.

~ * ~

Around six in the morning, well before sunrise, Jack stirs. He pulls on his T-shirt, pants, boots, and climbs from the tent. He puts on his flannel shirt, his parka then notices the wolf tracks around his tent.

While eating oatmeal sitting on his tarp, he looks around at the dark woods behind him. *Why the circles around the tent? Why is she hanging out with me? She's a wolf in her element, unless she had been someone's pet. She must be used to humans, although I haven't seen any for days now, since the store back in Beaver.*

He packs up then heads down river.

A few paces down the path, she waits for him again, her reddish-orange eyes glowing in the moonlight. This time she does not move as he bounds closer. He passes her. "Good morning."

She wags her tail, turns, catches up and trots ahead of him.

I've found a new friend. Rather, she has found me, despite my best efforts.

Chapter Thirteen

What good is the warmth of summer, without the cold of winter to give it sweetness?

John Steinbeck

Jack has now been alone living off the river for more than a month, except for his wolf companion who shows up every day, sometimes several times a day. She sits with him each night by the fire. At every small village he discards trash and picks up cooking fuel and other supplies. He even discarded the urn. The locals chat with him, making small talk asking about his journey. *They must think I'm nuts, like one of those prospectors at the turn of the nineteenth to twentieth centuries, who came here, didn't know what they were doing and died in extreme conditions.* Although, each local he encounters treats him well, like he's a long-lost friend.

He eats fish, several times stalks and traps snowshoe hare. They weigh between three and four pounds, so he eats some and dries the leftovers. It can last him a few days. He also snares a few larger Alaskan hare that can weigh up to twelve pounds. They last several days. Yes, skinning a rabbit is a bloody affair, but Jack purchased a survival book in Fairbanks that includes a Chapter on how to do just that. The book also details how to build a rabbit trap. With a couple of sticks and the rope called a snare line, he can set up a trap in short order. No bait is necessary. When the rabbit comes along, he pulls on the snare line, trapping it. With sticks set up correctly to thread the line and give it tension, he snares rabbits, killing them quickly. After tracking a rabbit, setting up the trap, it can take a couple hours, longer at times, except it pays off when his provisions run low.

In Ruby, Alaska on the Yukon, he stops in a store and buys snowshoes and supplies. At the checkout he examines the snowshoes.

"Here," the clerk says, an old Inuit woman with wrinkled skin. She takes them from Jack and demonstrates how to use them. "You slip them on like this."

Jack watches. She hands the shoes to him. He tries them on. "Not easy," he says.

"They take some time to get used to." She squints at him as if the sun is in her eye.

He hands her cash. She takes the cash and gives him change. She reaches out to shake his hand. Taken aback, but assuming she's just being friendly, he shakes it and says, "Thank you, ma'am."

She smiles, half her teeth missing. "Your light *will* grow brighter."

He shakes that off, departs. *Nice, happy people. At least someone's happy.*

Back on the path, she waits for him. Jack catches up as she turns off the riverbank and heads up another path northbound. He stops and looks at her tracks in the snow. Glancing over at the Yukon River, he pulls out his map, unfolding it.

She trots back down the path, stopping about two feet in from of him. Turning around, facing up the path again, she scampers about ten paces away but stops to look back at him.

"Where ya going?"

"Yelp."

"You want me to follow you?"

"Yelp."

He scans his map, tracing his finger north. There is nothing, no civilization there. He sees Nome off to the northwest. *Well, it's what I wanted to do. Get away from the world. I could see more of the rugged interior and truly live the life of a Wildman. I certainly must look the part. Live the call of the wild. Thanks, Jack London.*

He folds, stows his map, and follows his girlfriend into the wilderness.

~ * ~

Days later, trudging along through the rugged interior, sometimes no path to follow, he sure is living the wild man's life hiking, camping and hunting. Although it has been cold for many weeks, and he trudges through snow, he hasn't lived through a real Alaskan winter. Sure, it has snowed, is cold and he has encountered a few storms, but no severe storms. He hasn't needed to use his snowshoes.

Now early January, he moves along at his usual clip. Around one in the afternoon, he detects scores of rabbit tracks. No river or stream to fish in, he stops to set his trap. After he perfected the art of building a trap, he saved and tied onto his pack the stakes he needed. He unties the stakes, sets the trap, and hides off the trail, holding the snare line with the noose at the other end several feet away.

He waits almost an hour before a snowshoe rabbit comes along. He holds the snare-line steady, but it sidesteps the trap. Jack tries to coax it toward the trap, but it scurries off.

Another one comes along an hour later. Jack holds steady, and the large Alaskan hare, about eight pounds, steps into the trap. Jack tugs on the noose and snares it. It struggles to get away but Jack holds on and rushes it with his knife. He grabs it by its ears and slices its neck, killing it.

He puts the hare aside and sets up camp.

Too early for dinner, he sits against a tree and opens the book he bought a while ago in Beaver, *Tales and Traditions of the Eskimo*. In it, Rink tells the story of the mythical amaroq, a gigantic grey wolf, which is also a word for wolf in Inuit, who stalks and kills foolish people hunting alone at night. *Lucky for me, I only hunt in the day. Although, if I have to die out here, what better way to go than in the jaws of nature?*

In the book, he learns, the mythical amaroq does not travel in a pack. Rather, it's a lone wolf. *My companion must not only be a lone wolf but perhaps a lonely one looking for companionship.* He smiles at that, looks up and watches her approach from the wood-line behind the tent. He realizes he smiled. He hasn't smiled for so long. He also realizes she's kept him company and taken his mind off his past.

"Where you been?"

She stops within a couple feet from him, looking into his eyes.

"I'll call you Amaroq."

"Yelp." Amaroq cocks her head and wags her tail.

Am I stark raving mad?

She examines the large hare on the log nearby and looks back at him.

"I need to cook it. For me."

She sits, as if waiting patiently.

I could reach out and touch her, but would she bite my hand off?

He gets up, makes a fire while she watches his every move. He skins the hare, cooks it on a rotisserie, turning it at intervals.

When it's ready, he sits against the tree again holding the cooked hare in a pan. He cuts off a piece and places it on the ground in front of her.

She picks it up, gnaws on it.

He cuts a piece for himself. He chews on it while watching Amaroq licking her lips. *Why not?* He cuts off another piece, places it in his palm, and extends his hand.

She lunges forward and takes it from him, gobbling it.

He eats more too. He gives her more from his palm; this time she licks his hand clean. When she licks her lips, he again notices her large, sharp teeth. Together, they finish the hare.

She examines him, cocking her head again.

"That's all I have. Next time you get to pick up the tab." He watches her lick her paws. *Have others ever been in a situation like this? No one will believe it. I don't believe it. Am I in some sort of mythical dream? Perhaps I died back there on the trail somewhere and didn't know it and am now a ghost destined to forever wander the Alaskan wilderness with Amaroq.*

She lies down, those reddish-orange eyes glowing from the fire.

He cleans up then sits, reading his book, Amaroq sleeping next to him.

~ * ~

A few days later, Jack treks along with about an hour of daylight left. Heavy dark clouds float toward him. A gentle wind picks up, blowing flurries about. He saw Amaroq earlier in the morning and noticed her tracks along the path but hasn't seen her since. *She must be hunting.*

Around six-thirty, well after sunset, Jack can't fight the wind and flurries anymore. Almost a blizzard, unable to see the path before him, he stops and struggles to pitch his tent. He manages to erect it, however, tosses in his pack, crawls in, and zips up.

The wind is bone-chilling and despite these modern, all-weather tents, it bleeds through, freezing him. The cold-weather sleeping bags are also high-tech, and it's recommended that one sleep in them with minimal clothing so as not to sweat during the night. Against the unforgiving howling wind, he strips down and slips into his bag.

He can't read because of the fierce conditions, the tent shaking in the wind, so he just lies there, and within a few minutes has warmed up. Because of his vigorous daily hikes, he always falls asleep at once. However, in bed at an earlier hour, it takes him longer than usual, so his mind races, thinking about his past, which he hasn't thought about much over this past month. Then it occurs to him that while out on the trail with Amaroq seeing her several times throughout the day and by his side next to the fire at night, he doesn't have time to think about much at all.

~ * ~

Sometime in the middle of the night Jack wakes up to the sound of his tent snapping in the wind. He unzips his bag to discover half of the tent has collapsed. He sits up and finds snow covering the collapsed portion. He shakes some off but cannot re-erect the tent because one of the supports snapped.

Within seconds of exposure, even inside the tent, he's chilled. He's sure his frozen nipples will fall off like icicles. He looks at his watch and the temperature reads twenty below zero. His legs and feet are cold, despite the bag. He grabs his parka and throws it over the bottom of the bag on top of his legs and feet. He zips up in the bag, keeping open a small hole to breathe through. The wind roars outside, and he hears snow pelting the tent. The tent snaps even louder in the gusting wind. He shivers, rubbing his arms and torso to try to keep warm. It isn't working. Shaking, his teeth clatter. *I guess I'll die here, freeze to death. I'll remain frozen until I thaw out in the spring and the animals eat me, perhaps a bear, or maybe Amaroq.* Resigned to his fate, he drifts off, welcoming his death. He's ready. It's time.

Chapter Fourteen

And ye shall dance with him too, the Reaper, but alas for him, not today!
Unknown

Jack opens his eyes. *Am I dead? This can't be the afterlife? No, it seems I'm still in this world because I'm warm and can feel the cold air filling my lungs when I breathe in through the opening in the bag. The sun has risen because of the red glow inside the tent. That means I've slept past sunrise.*

He feels this great weight upon him. *Has the snow buried me? It seems the weight of the snow is too heavy, however.* He unzips the bag to below his chin and discovers that most of the tent has collapsed from the wind or the weight of the snow. Only one corner over his left shoulder remains erect. The weight upon him rises and falls, as if it's breathing, except snow doesn't breathe. This snow breathes, however.

He tries to sit up, but the breathing snow is too heavy to budge. As he moves, the snow rises as well and climbs off of him. He unzips down to his waist and sits up to discover Amaroq sitting beside him, yawning. She slept on top of him. At some point in the night she had somehow crawled in. *Now I know I'm in some sort of mythical world, like in Rink's book, although this amaroq doesn't eat me.*

"Good morning."

Her massive head lunges for him. He closes his eyes expecting to be eaten now. No, she licks his face. He winces as she licks it several more times.

"Okay, okay. I love you too."

Amaroq crawls out through the front door of the tent. Jack sits and inspects the tent's opening. The zipper has been retracted, but is not broken. There are no tears in the tent. He zips it up and down. It works okay. *She must have used her nose and somehow pushed the zipper open. Huh.*

He crawls out of his bag and pulls on his clothes. A brisk morning, he emerges from the tent, squinting in the bright sun.

Amaroq stands facing away from him looking through the woods. Jack stands up, watching her scan the area. She turns to look back at him then trots off down the trail. *What just happened?*

He shakes the snow from his tent, tapes the broken pole with duct tape, folds and packs it away. For breakfast he cooks the last of his oatmeal.

He'll have a short hike this day because of the late start, sleeping past sunrise, so he starts out.

That storm had been the fiercest one he's encountered so far on this madman's adventure. The snow now deeper than he ever saw it before, he straps on his snowshoes and finds them awkward, falling more than once.

He follows Amaroq's tracks in the snow, since she knows where she's going. Around a bend in the trail, she stands, waiting for him to catch up then trots off down the trail ahead of him. He's given up on trying to rationalize this wolf's behavior. Whether this is a mythical world he occupies or indeed real, he gives it no more thought. Nothing makes sense to him anymore. Everything he had known or believed in makes no sense. The only thing that makes sense to him, or matters, is the NOW moment.

~ * ~

By early March and with the days growing longer, the snow begins to melt. Jack sets up camp on the Koyukuk River a little less than halfway between Ruby and Nome. He decides to stay a few days to rest and fish, that way he can stock up and have something other than hare to eat every day. Besides, he twisted his ankle the day before, and it still smarts.

By the third day he's caught several fish he can stretch-out for a few days. He washes his clothes and airs his pack. He rests on his bedroll, studying his guide. His eyes grow heavy. He hasn't napped during the day in such a long time. He slips off to sleep. ˙

~ * ~

Jack opens his eyes a crack upon hearing something rustling near him. He turns his head to see a male grizzly helping itself to his fish. At the beginning of springtime, the males come out of hibernation first, followed by the females and cubs searching for food. He lies still. *Play dead, right?* It has to be about seven hundred pounds Jack figures by eyeing its girth.

It must have sensed Jack's consciousness because it ambles toward him. *This is it. My wish of dying from the jaws of nature will now come true. With the size of those claws, jaws, and teeth, I only hope he slashes my carotid or bites my head off in a quick decapitation. What did I expect? I knew the dangers of this whacked-out expedition. I know I'm in the grizzly's domain. This is what they do. Kill their food, just like I have. I can't blame the grizzly, or anyone or anything but myself. Then again does it matter? I died that day when Janette and the kids died. I have nothing or no one to live for. Better than killing myself.*

He doesn't have the ability to jump up and scare this one off like he had with the black bear in Appalachia. This monster, when it stands on its hind feet, would tower over Jack at about seven feet at least. With his sprained ankle, he can't run or climb a tree either. He closes his eyes and finds peace.

Within inches of his face because he can smell the bear's fishy breath, he hears something growling, hissing and yelping, almost like a dog. He dares to open his eyes. The bear spins around away from him, fending off an attacker.

Jack raises his head to see Amaroq nipping at the bear. The bear charges her, but she keeps her distance. She counter-charges him, and he backs off. She runs around, nipping him from behind. He spins around, stands on his hind legs.

Yep, seven feet tall.

The bear roars, but Amaroq growls back at him. She goes for his hind leg, succeeding in getting in a good bite. The bear falls to all fours, turns, and slashes at her, hitting her leg.

"Yelp," she cries. Standing her ground, she attacks again. She gets in another lick, biting him in the side. He growls, turns and races off.

Jack jumps up and hobbles over to his pack. Amaroq lies down, licks her bleeding wound. He digs through his pack finding his first aid kit. He moves toward her carefully because he knows wounded animals can be defensive. He shows her his intentions. She seems to understand, which makes no sense to him.

Using small scissors, he cuts her fur away to reveal the wound. It's a gash, but not too deep. However, he has to stop the bleeding. Using an antiseptic wipe, he cleanses the wound, wiping the blood away. Using a gauze roll, he wraps it around her leg. While wrapping the gauze, he glances at her face. Panting from the fight, she watches him roll the gauze on. Her large, sharp teeth, inches from his face, again remind him of *Little Red Riding Hood*. *What big teeth you have.*

He tapes the wound. "Now let it scab over before you go and gnaw at the bandage."

She licks his face.

"Okay, okay."

He puts the kit back into his pack and looks back at her just sitting there watching him still panting. "We've got to move on, girl."

Jack strikes his tent, packs his dried fish and heads out.

He doesn't need to wear his parka anymore, just a flannel shirt and lighter jacket. He's in no hurry, but he figures it's best to get away from the river and other bears that are sure to show up to hunt for fish too. His guardian, Amaroq, stays close to his side along the trail. She doesn't run too far ahead of him now but hangs with him most of each day.

~ * ~

Soon, he'll be in Nome. He watches Amaroq trotting along ahead of him on the path. *Can she come with me? She's domesticated, right? I can't take her into villages, towns, or cities. Can I?*

After pitching his tent, he prepares to look for food. He gathers his hare trap. No sooner has he gotten it all together, does Amaroq saunter back into camp, carrying a fresh kill. She drops it at his feet and looks him over.

"Thanks. You know, I never thanked you for saving my life. Twice actually."

Panting, she sticks her injured leg out toward him. He retrieves his first aid kit, takes out the scissors, kneels in front of her and cuts the bandage off. It has almost completely healed. "Wow. You're a fast healer." He examines it. The gash is only a thin pink line. She licks at it. "It's been only three days, girl." She licks his face. "Yeah, yeah, I love you too."

"Yelp." She turns and meanders back out of camp in search of something else.

Jack skins, eats some of the hare, saving the rest for later, or for his girlfriend, he laughs. She has given him an internal sense of not only laughter but awe. *How can I leave her and go back to a city or town? Perhaps I can find property out here and build a shack and live off the land. I can do that. Be one with nature, one with the wild. That way I wouldn't be put in the situation of ever losing another again.*

~ * ~

Jack awakes one morning a few days later to find himself half-in and half-out of his tent, his bag on top of his legs. He sits up to find Amaroq lying next to him. He discovers he is completely nude and dirty, like he's been dragged through the mud. "What happened, girl?"

She sits up, making a motion with her head as if she's trying to say something. He reaches over, pets her head. She stands up and licks his face so hard it knocks him back over. She continues to lick his face.

"Okay. Okay." He sits up again to see that his gear is strewn about as if something had riffled through it. His pack is torn, and it's been dragged several feet away. His Bible and family photo lie nearby, the glass from the frame broken. He picks it up, knocks the rest of the glass out, the picture falling out of the frame. He places the photo in his pack.

He scrutinizes Amaroq. *There's no way she did this.* He looks near his feet and discovers she has dropped a fresh kill there. She wouldn't go through his pack because she's been delivering breakfast almost daily now. She has no reason to. He finds his Fitbit nearby in the dirt. It had been torn off. He examines it, discovering that three days have passed. He has lost three days. *Have I been somehow sick and passed out that long?* "What happened, girl?" He strokes her thick fur on the side of her face. She licks his face again as if cleaning him like a partner cat would. "Yeah, I need a bath, don't I?"

He washes in a nearby stream, gathers his gear, and heads out, Amaroq by his side.

~ * ~

Traveling west, Jack makes his way into the Kigluiak Mountains the last week in April.

He jumps in and swims around in a chilling but refreshing lake. He had run out of soap a while ago, so he just swims around. *There's nothing like being alone in the woods to bathe in the nude, no one around to be offended or shocked.* Although, forgetting his nudeness, he's sure he'd frighten the average person. He hasn't groomed in so long that his hair had matted, making him look like a Rastafarian. His sister and parents would never recognize him. They would have him committed if they did. He didn't carry a mirror, so he has no idea how he looks. Even though he washed his clothes when he had a lake or stream nearby, they are now frayed and don't come clean. *With these clothes I must look like a homeless person. Although technically, I am a homeless person.*

Amaroq shoots out of nowhere. "Yelp. Yelp." She sprints up to the water's edge, runs up and down the riverbank turning back and forth every few paces. Jack swims by, splashing water, teasing her.

"Yelp." She makes a lunge at him, like she wants to jump in, but pulls back.

"Come on," he says to her.

She enters the water, up to her sternum, but holds back. "Yelp. Yelp."

"Chicken," he says splashing at her again.

She snaps her powerful jaws at him, getting a mouthful of water.

"Okay. See ya." He holds his breath and submerges.

A spit second later, he sees her splash into the water near him. He surfaces. She swims over, latches onto his mopping hair, pulling him ashore. "Ow," he says, grabbing at his hair.

She drags him halfway up onto the bank and licks his face.

She must have thought I was drowning. "Okay, okay. Thank you. I get it. I get it."

He lies there watching her turn her attention to licking her wet coat.

He towels off and pulls on his underwear, but his hand tears through it. He pulls on his ragged jeans, also torn. *I must look pathetic.* His tent is torn too, and although he had duct-taped the pole, it won't hold any longer so he just lies out in the open with Amaroq by his side. The wilderness takes a toll on manmade equipment. *Nothing lasts forever.* He laughs. *Nothing.*

He considers Amaroq resting under a tree one day. He met her over three months ago. She has been with him ever since. By his side. *How can I leave her?*

~ * ~

Near Mount Osborn in the Kigluiak Mountains of Alaska's Seward Peninsula, Jack stops, looking south. Consulting his frayed, weathered map, he knows Nome is not far below him.

"Yelp."

He turns and sees Amaroq standing behind him on the hill, panting, looking at him.

He again scans the valley before him.

"Yelp."

He sets his pack on the ground, walks over to her and kneels, those reddish-orange eyes looking straight into his, those beautiful white teeth glistening in the sun. He scuffs her neck on both sides and presses his nose against hers. He puts his arms around her neck, his head resting against hers. He strokes her thick neck and whispers in her ear, "I don't know where I'm going. I don't know what I will do. I wish I could stay out here and live with you forever. I will never forget you, Amaroq. You *were* my guardian angel. I know that now."

She licks his face then stands, towering over him once more. She walks a few paces away and stops, looking back at him. A moment later she lowers her head then raises it, turns, and trots off from whence they came.

Chapter Fifteen

Every new beginning comes from some other beginning's end.
Seneca

Jack locates the Snake River, following it south to Nome.

A few days later, he breaks camp and walks the final stretch into to Nome. Nome is a small town on the Norton Sound of the Bering Sea. Jack read in his guidebook that Nome, population roughly thirty-six hundred, has a seaport used for freight, cruise ships and a boat harbor for commercial fishing operations. In 1898 gold was discovered on Anvil Creek and the rush was on, with the village swelling to about ten thousand. Today, salmon, halibut, Alaskan king crab fishing and tourism are paramount industries.

The Nome residents, some white, many Inuit or of other native Alaskan descent or mixed, stare at his ragged appearance as he passes, some pointing.

At River Street near the mouth of the river, he finds The Prospector Inn and Restaurant. It hugs the water where the fishing boats come and go from Norton Sound. Looking as good as any, with a rustic quality, he climbs the front steps of the two-story structure.

Inside, he sets his dirty, torn pack next to the door and shuffles over to the front desk. Mid-afternoon, the restaurant hasn't opened for dinner yet, he learns from a posted sign. Looking around, he sees no one. He locates a bell on the counter, dings it. Nothing, so he twangs it again.

An Inuit woman appears from an office behind the counter. She has long, shiny, grayish-black hair tied into a ponytail flowing down to her waist. Attractive for her age, she seems to be in her sixties. She approaches him slowly, examining the wretched man before her, he rationalizes. She doesn't say a word, only squints at him like the old woman back in Ruby, so Jack speaks up to break the ice, clearing his throat and saying, "Good afternoon, ma'am."

She raises an eyebrow, looking him over. He knows he must look pitiful, but she makes him uncomfortable by the way she looks at him, not like the church ladies or others who ogled at him, but in another way, similar to the clerk in Beaver.

"Just came down from the mountains and was looking for lodging for a couple days."

"I know," she says, finally speaking up and smiling.

She knows? Well, of course. Look at me. He pulls a wad of cash from his pocket and says, "Cash okay?"

She nods but continues to give him a curious stare.

He shifts, frowns and says, "Ah, you have a shower?"

"Yes. A communal one at the end of the hall upstairs."

"That's fine. How much a night?"

"Eighty-nine."

"Well," Jack says peeling off some bills. "I only have hundreds."

"Don't worry about paying now." She grabs a key off a board from behind her. "I can show you to your room."

"Don't you need me to fill out a registration or something?"

"No," she says shaking her head. "Not necessary."

Not necessary? "Well, then, I'm Jack Douglas."

She extends her hand. "Ulloriaq."

He shakes. It gives him a sense of warmth, as if a burst of energy shoots through his veins, like Amaroq had done when she licked his face. They disengage. "Upstairs," she says. "This way, Mr. Douglas."

He grabs his pack and follows her up the stairs. "Is there a barber nearby?"

"There's one on the other side of town, but he went fishing. Salmon. Won't be back for a few days."

"Oh."

"I have someone who can cut your hair."

At the top of the stairs, Jack finds about twenty rooms on the floor. Using an old key, she opens a door to a small single room. It has a double bed, a closet, and a small television setting atop a desk, not that he will use it. He places his pack on the floor next to the bed and glances out the window at the sound.

At the door, Jack waits while she retrieves a set of towels and a bar of soap in a wrapper from a hall closet and hands them to him. "I'll send up, Qaniit," she says. "To cut your hair." Again, she stares at him, squinting.

I must really look like a nut. Surprised she let me stay here. He doesn't know what Qaniit means. *Must be someone with an Inuit name.* "Thank you, ma'am. I'm sorry. Your name again?"

"Ulloriaq. Ul lor i ak." She heads off down the hallway.

Jack pulls the door closed, picks up and browses through a brochure from the desk. It details that the Prospector Inn had been built for the Gold Rush and had been remodeled twice, first in 1955 and again in 1999. It hosts twenty-two rooms and a restaurant serving fifty patrons. The front face looks like a building out of the old west. It has a front porch and an arched façade on the upper floor that obscures the crest of the slanted roof. The entire building was built on stilts and faces the ocean several yards away.

He grabs a towel, the soap, his toothbrush, and the last of his toothpaste and ambles down the hall. In the bathroom he strips, tossing his clothes on the floor. *I should ask that woman to burn them.*

He climbs into a clawfoot bathtub and ensures he stuffs the curtain inside. He notices a sign on the wall reminding users to do just that. He turns the shower on and soaps up for the first time in more than two months. *I hadn't minded, and Amaroq hadn't either.*

He soaps his hair as best he can, but it's a losing battle. It's so knotted and entangled he gives up.

He towels off and wraps it around his waist. He lifts his toothbrush along with the paste, studying himself in a mirror above the sink for the first time in months. *I look worse than Robinson Caruso. I hope I don't crack the mirror.* He stares into his eyes. Something about his eyes bother him, but he doesn't quite know what.

He squeezes the last of the paste on his brush, tossing the tube in the trashcan at his feet. He brushes and rinses.

He secures his dirty clothes, toothbrush, and exits the bathroom. In the hall, he struggles to latch the door. Someone behind him calls out, "Mr. Douglas?"

He jerks around to see who it is, but the mop of hair dangling in his eyes causes him to drop his filthy clothes. As he bends to pick them up, his towel falls off. Reaching for the towel, his foot flops onto the corner of it. Pulling on the towel, he topples over onto the floor. He looks up to see a woman, about his age, looking down at his nakedness.

"Are you okay, Mr. Douglas?" she says, looking away.

He grabs the towel, covering himself. She looks back at him. Looking up into her soft, blue eyes he says, "Yes. Yes, I think so. Thank you." Standing and blushing, he holds the towel bunched in front of his genitals, although his hips and legs show.

She glances at his lean, fit frame, but averts her eyes again, saying, "You needed your hair cut?"

"Yes. Yes, I did. Do. Thank you." He wraps the towel around his waist and she looks back at him.

She holds a folded tarp and small barber bag. She too looks at him like that woman downstairs did. *I know my appearance is monstrous, but what's with all these people staring at me like this?* All people make him feel uncomfortable now. Everyone. Although looking into her eyes, they remind him of his own a few moments ago when he glanced in the mirror. Her eyes seem as sad and vacant as his. A stunning, mixed-race woman, Inuit and Caucasian perhaps, she has long black hair similar to the older woman's, yet whiter skin. Not only uncomfortable by the way in which she looks at him, Jack is embarrassed she's been exposed to this episode of a naked mountain man before her.

"In your room?" she says above a whisper.

"Pardon me?"

"Your haircut? I'll cut your hair in your room."

"Oh, yes. Sorry." He picks up his rags and follows her into his room.

She spreads the tarp on the floor, centering the chair from the desk on it. He tosses his clothes on the floor. As he sits on the chair, dressed in the towel, she pulls from the bag scissors and an electric hair cutter. "How short?"

"Oh, well, take it all off, I guess. The beard too. Don't know when I'll cut it again."

She grasps a handful of hair, but hesitates. She appears to wobble a bit, as if she'd become ill.

"You okay?" he says.

She doesn't answer but regains her composure, and, using the scissors, starts gnawing at his knotty mess. His head jerks a bit as she saws some off. Strands fall to the floor, some landing on his chest.

He sits in silence as she works on lopping it off. He winces from the tugging on his roots. Her hands are rugged, like she works with them for a living. She turns the hair cutters on and says, "All the way you said?"

"Yes, please. Buzz it off."

She does as instructed then turns the cutters off after going over his head a few times. She brushes his head with her fingers, hesitating at first after the initial swipe.

Using the scissors, she snips at his long, ratty beard. It falls onto his chest, lap and the floor. With the cutters, she buzzes the rest of his beard off, leaving only stubble behind.

She starts to brush the loose hair from his chest, but hesitates after touching him, like she had with his head, pulling her hand away by a couple inches. Jack doesn't know what to make of this. At last, she gently brushes the rest of his beard from his chest. Her touch feels gentle and warm, and, as with that woman's touch, sort of shoots a burst of energy throughout his empty being. No one has touched him for so long, except Amaroq.

"Please," she says. "Stand?"

He follows orders and stands. She wipes the rest of the small strands from his stomach, bending over to brush the loose ones from the front of his towel. A little embarrassed because of the pressure against his genitals, he turns his head away from her.

She kneels and brushes the fallen hair back onto the tarp that had landed outside its perimeter, but stops a split second later. He looks down at her then steps off the tarp when she places the tips of her fingers against the back of his left thigh. *That was awkward and weird.*

In haste, she rolls up the tarp, trapping the fallen hair, and places it in the hallway. She's in a hurry now.

"How much do I owe you?" he says pulling the cash from his pants.

"Nothing."

"Nothing? Oh, I'd like to pay you something."

Fumbling to gather her barber tools, placing them in her bag, she doesn't answer.

"Ma'am?" He scrutinizes her silence. "Well, then, could you tell me where I can buy some fresh clothes?"

At the door, she turns and glances at his rags on the floor. "You're not going to put those back on?" She averts her eyes from him again.

"Well, just until I can get some new ones."

Looking at the door jam and not him, she says, "Put those and all the rest of your clothes in the hall. I'll get you some."

"Oh, you don't have to do that."

"*Yes*, I do have to do that. You're not putting those back on."

He examines his rags. *She's right. They're dirty, smelly, and torn. A homeless person would refuse to wear them.*

She takes a few steps down the hall. He calls to her, "Well, here." He peels off two, one-hundred-dollar bills from his cash roll. "Get whatever you can find. Need some, well, underwear." *How embarrassing that this gorgeous woman, a stranger, not my wife or mother, is going clothes shopping for me.* "Size thirty-two." He eyeballs his skinny waist and says, "Better make that thirty."

She comes back over to him but does not look in his eyes.

"If you need more, let me know."

"That's plenty," she says taking the bills and stuffing them in the front pocket of her tight-fitting blue jeans.

"I really appreciate this, ma'am."

She doesn't answer. He watches her disappear down the stairs.

Jack sorts through his clothes. *She's right, they all need to go.* His guidebook is torn and dirty, the pages falling out, so he tosses that in the trash can. He sorts and organizes the rest of his things, not much at all really. All material things he owns in this world lie before him. He needs a new tent and pack too. He'll get those soon before moving on.

Chapter Sixteen

A good deed is never lost.
Saint Basil

Qaniit returns a short while later with a pair of jeans, a dress shirt, a couple Prospector Inn and Restaurant T-shirts, socks, and a small package of underwear. "Just down River and left on Steadman," she says to Jack who stands in the doorway of his room still wrapped in his towel. She hands him the bag with the clothes. "You'll find a store there." She holds out her hand with some bills in it. "Your change."

"Please, keep it," he says. "For your troubles."

While he holds the bag of clothes with one hand, she reaches down and picks up his other hand, placing the change in his palm. "If you like," she says, "the restaurant is open at five. Best halibut and salmon in town. Grandmother is the best cook." She turns and goes downstairs.

He stands there watching her go. *Something about her. She seems warm, yet cold and sad. Distant.*

He dresses and locates the store on Steadman. He also buys new running shoes and shorts.

~ * ~

He heads down to the restaurant at six. A few couples and a small family, all probably tourists, sit eating their dinners. He waits at the counter next to the bar, dressed in his new jeans and a loose-fitting dress shirt. He now looks normal, feels like a million bucks.

Qaniit exits the kitchen, carrying an order still wearing her jeans, but she has changed from her Prospector Inn T-shirt into a button-down turquoise blouse. It contrasts well against her white skin and long, black hair she parts down the middle and ties behind the back of her neck. His eyes follow her as she delivers a meal to a couple sitting nearby, noting her soft Inuit high cheekbones and almost almond-shaped eyes.

Jack watches her work. It seems she does everything around here. She circles around, catching him off-guard in a trance, even though he looks right at her. "This way, Mr. Douglas." She pulls a menu off the counter.

Blushing, he follows her to a booth by the window overlooking the ocean. "Thank you," he says.

She nods, cracks a little smile for acknowledgement, using only her lips, and goes off. Jack scans the menu. An Inuit boy, middle teens perhaps, saunters over with an apron around his waist, his black hair tied in a ponytail. "Anything to drink, Mr. Douglas?"

He knows my name already? "Milk. Please."

The boy fetches the milk. "And to eat?"

"The halibut, please."

"Sure thing." He places the order.

A couple minutes later and with no one else to serve, the boy happens by. "Passing through, Mr. Douglas?" He leans against the booth.

"Yes."

"You're the talk of the town."

"Excuse me?"

He slips into the booth across from Jack and, looking around to make sure no one can hear, whispers, "The townsfolk. They're all talking about this man who came down from the mountains with the spirit of the amaroq."

Jack freezes. Doesn't know what to say. *Amaroq? How does he know about her?*

An old man, in his eighties at least, with long black hair and wrinkled weathered skin, enters the restaurant. Jack watches him whisper in Qaniit's ear. She motions toward Jack. The boy sees him approach, crawls out of the booth, and scurries away.

The old man wanders over to Jack, standing at the end of the booth, looking down at him. He has native Inuit beads and animal claws on a necklace. He wears pants, a button-down shirt; his fingers are long and bony, and his eyes dark. He doesn't say a word.

Jack looks him over. *What's this all about?*

At last the old man sits across from Jack, saying, "Give me your hands."

Jack doesn't know why he agrees, but he holds up his hands as if the man has power over him.

He takes Jack's hands in his, squeezes, and closes his eyes. Jack feels this energy run through him like he had with those women. He doesn't know what to make of this but plays along.

After a minute the man opens his eyes and says, "I have waited many moons." He reaches over and places his palm on Jack's head while holding both of Jack's hands in his other hand. "I have seen her too. Many moons ago. Her spirit lives in you now." He climbs out of the booth, looks down at Jack. "It is time."

Jack's eyes trail him to the door. He sits in total befuddlement, staring at the empty seat across from him. *Amaroq? Spirit? I have seen her too?*

"Your meal, Mr. Douglas," Qaniit says, pointing with her hand at his meal in front of him. He hadn't seen her approach or set the plate down.

"Oh. Oh, thank you."

She nods, presses her lips together again, and heads back to the kitchen.

The boy comes by to get Jack's dirty dishes after he finishes. "Can I ask you something?" Jack says.

"Sure, Mr. Douglas."

"What's her name? How do you say it?"

The boy smiles from ear-to-ear while holding the plate. "Qaniit. Pronounced, can e it."

"What's it mean?"

"Falling snow. She's my cousin. Owns the place. Well, half-owns it. Our uncle owns the other half. He's in Anchorage. The cook is our grandmother."

"Uolllll…"

"Ulloriaq. Ul or i ak."

Jack says, "Ul or i ak."

"Perfect," the kid says. He sticks out his hand to shake. "I'm, Akiak. Ak i ak. Means brave."

Jack shakes his hand. "That man earlier? Who was he?"

Akiak looks over his shoulder then back at Jack. "Shaman." He meanders into the kitchen.

Jack heads up to his room. He undresses, organizes his new clothes in the closet. Standing near the mirror hanging on the closet door, something on the back of his left thigh catches his attention.

He turns his leg to see. It's a long thin scar on the back of his leg running up and down at about seven, perhaps eight inches. It's healed, but he can see the thin scar tissue is pink. He runs his finger over it. *That's what she was looking at. I didn't think she was being inappropriate.* He runs his finger along the pink line again. *Huh, I don't remember injuring myself there.*

He climbs into bed and stares at the ceiling, unable to fall asleep. He has this strange feeling in his gut. He ate a fine and filling dinner, Ulloriaq cooked well, but his stomach feels empty. He grabs the extra pillow, hugs it and stares at his Bible and family photo on the nightstand.

~ * ~

Jack awakes, nude, covered in dirt and leaves in the woods. Groggy, he can't sit up, as if paralyzed, Amaroq standing over him. She looks past him, as if on guard.

~ * ~

Jack awakes. *Strange dream.* Shaking it off, he crawls out of bed and works out in his room. He dresses in his running shorts, shirt, and new running shoes.

A warm day in May, perhaps in the forties, he runs along at a good clip. In town, a few residents point at him, whispering to one another. An old weathered Inuit woman at an intersection raises her hand, as if commanding him to stop. He obliges. She places her hand on his sweaty chest. She holds it there for several seconds, Jack panting from his run. "It is true," she says. She turns, walks away.

Curious. He stands there for a moment, watching her walk up the sidewalk. He starts up again, circles back to the Prospector. Inside, a young couple waits at the counter to be seated for breakfast. Qaniit comes from the kitchen and glances at him. He looks away, hustling upstairs.

He showers, dresses in jeans and a Prospector Inn T-shirt then heads downstairs for breakfast. "Good morning, Mr. Douglas." Akiak escorts him to a booth.

"Good morning, Ak…"

He smiles. "Akiak. Say, Ak i ak."

"Ak i ak," Jack says.

"Perfect."

Jack sits, Akiak handing him the menu. "You were here when I left last night."

"I work both shifts on the weekends and in the summer. Breakfast is only three hours, and dinner is four hours. I run errands and things like that in-between."

Jack nods then hands the menu back to the kid without looking at it. "Oatmeal. With milk, please."

"Sure thing, Mr. Douglas." He smiles and zips off to the kitchen.

Happy kid.

After Jack finishes his breakfast, Akiak stops by to collect his bowl, spoon and glass.

"Thank you," Jack says.

The kid smiles, looks back over his shoulder, and slips into the seat across from him. "You fish, Mr. Douglas?"

Taken aback, Jack says, "Yes. Yes, I fish."

"I'm going after breakfast. Wanna come?"

The kid's being polite and friendly, but… "Well, no, I…ah, I, I don't think so." He shakes his head.

"Come on. You can help me catch some salmon, for the dinner crowd. Cruise ship comes in around four." He has this big smile on his face from ear-to-ear.

"I ah, well, I ah…"

The kid fist bumps Jack's hand on the table. "Could use your expert touch." The kid's smile goes on and on.

"Not exactly an expert." Jack scans his eager face. *I shouldn't do this. I can't do this. I can't. But...but...* "Well, I ah, I guess, just for today, perhaps."

"Great. Meet you out front at nine-thirty."

Qaniit comes by. Licitly split, Akiak says, jumping out of his seat, "Mr. Douglas's going fishing with me, Cuz." The kid smiles at her, runs off and out the front door.

She watches him go, looks down at Jack's bowl and glass. "On your tab, Mr. Douglas?"

"Yes, thank you."

He watches her carry off his bowl and empty glass. *If she exhibits anymore sadness, I'll die all over again, if I'm not dead already.*

~ * ~

Jack meets up with Akiak outside at nine-thirty. Akiak has all the gear for both of them, and he drives in a beat-up blue Tacoma along the Snake River Road heading the way Jack arrived in town. Upstream, they find a spot and pull over. Akiak takes charge and sets up the gear. He gives Jack a pair of waders, a fly-fishing rod and reel.

Jack watches the kid. He gets right in there and snags a King Salmon in short order. *He's the expert and has duped me to join him.*

Several minutes later, Jack reels one in. Not long after that, Akiak catches another one. He puts it in his fishnet bag and smiles at Jack like a kid in the candy store. They fish and catch several more.

Around noon, Akiak offers Jack a sandwich and bottled water he pulls from a sack. They sit on the truck bed, Jack admiring the beauty of the river. "You're good," Akiak says, squinting at him. "Been fishing long?"

"A few months."

"Where you from?"

Just what I don't want to do, talk about my past. "Georgia."

"Wow. Long way from home."

Jack glances at him while washing down a portion of his sandwich with water.

"I'd like to see Georgia." He chuckles. "I'd like to see anything. Been here all my life."

"You're young. What, sixteen?"

"Yeah. Good guess."

"You got time."

"When I finish school. But I'll probably live here and all that. Especially since grandmother and Qaniit need the help." He takes a sip from his water after a bite of his sandwich. "Grandfather helps Qaniit when he can. He runs a fishing operation and with halibut and king crab season, he's pretty busy with all that."

Jack looks out over the river, finishing his sandwich. "Where are her parents? Qaniit's?" *Why did I ask that?*

"They died in a plane crash when she was just a kid. Her father owned half the inn with his brother, Uncle Robert."

"Robert? Hardly an Inuit name."

"He's white. A banker or something in Anchorage. Not sure. A real shady person."

Jack squints at him. He looks out over the river.

"Her husband died in a bad storm aboard grandpa's boat while crab fishing two seasons ago."

"Qaniit's?"

He nods. "She's been crazy about working. I don't think she's taken a day off since."

Jack looks over at him. *Hence, her sad demeanor. I wonder if mine shows?*

"Strange thing, she doesn't talk about him. Took it very hard. I don't think she's gotten over it." He frowns.

Jack thinks about that while finishing his water. "I appreciate this."

"The sandwich? No problem."

Silence as Jack listens to the river talking to him.

"Mr. Douglas?"

"Call me, Jack, kid." *Why did I say that? I shouldn't have done that.* "What is it?"

"Thanks."

106

"For what?"

"For, well, you know. Coming fishing."

Jack senses that that's not what he wanted to say. "Sure, kid. Sure."

They fish for a couple more hours and have quite a catch to take back for the tourists.

~ * ~

Later that night, while in bed and unable to sleep, Jack first stares at the ceiling, then rolls over to look at the moonlight shining in through the window illumining his family photo next to his Bible. After quite some time staring at the photo, his eyes finally grow heavy and he drifts off to sleep.

~ * ~

Something with sharp teeth drags Jack by his ankle, although it doesn't appear the teeth have broken his skin or drawn any blood. He can't sit up or move. A pain shoots down the back of his left thigh. He sees treetops and grey sky above pass by, dropping snowflakes on his face.

The creature drags him into a crevice and kicks dirt and leaves onto him, burying him.

~ * ~

Jack awakes. A strange, almost recurring dream, he shakes it off and sits up in bed. He grabs a towel off the door hook and realizes he has now been here for two days. *I need to resupply, get a new pack and other items, perhaps a couple more days at most and be on my way.*

He dresses in his running gear and jogs through town, zipping along Front Street and up Steadman. A native man in his forties appears from nowhere, blocking his path. "Mr. Douglas?"

"Yes?" Jack says stopping to catch his breath. *Who is this and how does he know my name?*

"My grandfather has bequeathed this to you. You must wear it at all times for providence." He holds up a small silver chain with a claw dangling on it.

"I'm sorry. Who was your grandfather?"

"He was the great shaman you met the night you arrived."

Stunned, Jack looks at the object on the chain. *Was? Bequeathed?* "What kind of a claw is this?"

"The claw of the amaroq."

Again, someone has said her name.

"Please," the man says holding up the necklace indicating he wants to place it around Jack's neck.

Jack hesitates, but nods after a moment, being polite and accommodating.

The man unhooks the chain and places it around Jack's neck. He clasps it closed, the claw hanging there resting against Jack's breastbone.

"Your grandfather passed?"

"He has returned to the amaroq, yes."

The man turns and walks away, leaving Jack standing there trying to make sense of what happened. He fingers the amaroq claw, examining it. It gives him a strange, yet warm feeling when he touches it. *Nice, but peculiar people. I guess I should just indulge these folks with their traditions and superstitions.* He continues jogging.

~ * ~

Back from his run, he showers and goes downstairs for breakfast. There, three men sit in a booth engaged in a discussion. Akiak seats Jack at another booth not far from the men.

Qaniit comes over. "Breakfast, Mr. Douglas?"

"Yes. Please. The oatmeal and milk. Thank you." As he reaches across the table to grab the menu to pass to her, she reaches for it at the same time. Her hand falls upon his. They withdraw their hands as if they had been zapped by an electric shock. "So sorry," he says, picking it up, handing it to her.

He watches her return to the kitchen and notices Akiak whispering to the men in the booth. The older one looks over at Jack but Jack looks away.

A moment later, Jack notices the old man stand and approach him, Akiak following. "This is my grandfather," Akiak says.

The man offers his hand. "Malik," he says.

"Jack Douglas." He shakes his hand. "Pleased to meet you, sir."

"May I sit?"

Jack motions for him to sit. Malik throws Akiak a glance, raising an eyebrow for him to scram. He does. "I hear you're quite the fisherman?" Malik says.

"Oh, I don't know about that. Caught a few in the rivers and lakes."

"Yeah, quite the survivalist I hear."

"Word travels fast around here."

"Like the wind." He shifts. "Jack, I got a problem, and I was wondering if you could help out. Well, actually Akiak suggested it. Just for a little while until I can get a permanent replacement."

Jack listens, waiting for him to continue. Malik wears a native Inuit, turquoise, silver and black bolo tie with a flannel shirt. He has long, grayish-black hair, similar to Ulloriaq's.

"As Akiak told you, I have a fishing operation. I have three boats and am down three guys now. I may have to dock a boat. I just need one guy to keep the one boat operating."

"Oh, I don't know anything about commercial fishing, sir. Besides, I'm just passing through. Have to be on my way."

"Qaniit's agreed to give you free room and board. I'll pay you twenty an hour plus a fair percentage of the haul."

"No. No, I don't think so, sir. I really have to be on my way."

Malik sighs. "Oh, okay. I understand. Thank you anyway. Good luck to you, Jack." He gets up, shakes Jack's hand and returns to the men.

While Jack waits for his breakfast, Akiak collects dishes from the family that had just departed. He cracks a solemn smile and lowers his head as he passes Jack.

Qaniit delivers Jack's breakfast a couple minutes later and returns to her business, this time without her signature nod and that crack of a smile for acknowledgement. *Wow. It's as if I'm just a tolerated guest now, although that's what I want to be, just a guest passing through.*

He eats his breakfast in solitude. *I cannot stay here and get involved with these people and their troubles. I don't need anyone else's troubles. Look what happened in North Dakota. I just can't stay any longer. I don't want to make new friends. Bad enough the kid took me fishing.*

After he finishes his breakfast on the way to the stairs, he passes Malik and his men. Noticing they're reviewing ledgers, he hears Malik say, "It's gonna cost us thousands in lost revenue. I have to take one boat off-line. There's no way around this."

Jack stops just short of going upstairs, one foot on the bottom step. He looks down at his feet. *I shouldn't do this. I really shouldn't.* He sighs. At last, he turns around and goes back over to the men. "Okay. Just for a couple weeks."

Malik jumps up and shakes his hand. "Thank you, Jack. We're still short-handed, but at least we can team you up with Miles here."

Jack shakes Miles's hand and sits with the men. Miles is a mixed Inuit about forty years old. Jack shakes the hands of the other two men, one Inuit and one white.

Chapter Seventeen

Not knowing when the dawn will come I open every door.
Emily Dickinson

The next morning, Jack stands on the deck of a fifty-four-foot steel stern-trawler as it makes its way out into Norton Sound. "What does it mean? Nuliajuk?" Jack says to Miles who pilots the boat.

"Goddess of the sea," Miles says, steering the boat through the choppy morning sound.

Malik gave Jack fisherman pants, a jacket, boots, and deckhand gloves. *Reminds me of Ahab, or am I Ishmael? I wonder if Moby-Dick lurks beneath the waves.*

An hour later, Miles locates a suitable sandy-bottomed area at about five hundred feet depth. Jack and two other deckhands, one Ronny, a mixed-race Inuit, and Sky, an Inuit, both in their early twenties, get right to work. At intervals, Jack and the crew work on setting out the groundlines with its six-foot, hooked, octopus-baited lines called gangions. At each interval one end of the groundline is laid out, anchored and marked with a flag and buoy. They repeat the process with several lines.

Later, after all of the lines have been laid, perhaps up to ten miles of it, the haul begins. Miles operates the winch, called a girdie that whines and raises the catch. Ronny removes the fish, Sky works on recoiling the lines, and Jack ices the fish, storing them in the hold. After each set, the men re-bait the lines, reset them, and repeat the process for the second run.

This goes on for about forty-eight hours. The men only stop to eat, hit the head, and take a quick nap or two. After they fill up the hold, they return to the dock. They haul out the fish for a buyer who weighs and packs it in a refrigerated truck. Jack and the men clean the boat, preparing it for the next run.

"We'll go out again on Thursday, Jack," Miles says.

"Okay."

"Hey, listen. You're a quick study and did a fantastic job, like you've been doing it all your life."

"Glad to help out."

Miles pats him on his shoulder. Jack walks back to the Prospector.

Mid-morning, the breakfast rush over, Jack enters, heading to his room. He strips down, smells his T-shirt. *Wow, do I smell of fish.* He hears a tap at the door. "Yes," he says.

"Mr. Douglas," Qaniit says through the door.

Jack cracks the door and peeks out.

"Give me your clothes, please."

"Oh, you don't have to do them. I can wash them later."

"No," she says. "I have to do them now, or they'll smell up my inn."

Shrugging, he doesn't argue with her because it seems pointless. This woman not only owns this place, half-owns it, but *is* the boss. You don't argue with the boss. He hands her his fishy clothes through the crack in the door.

He grabs his soap, wraps his towel around his waist, and goes down the hallway. Qaniit placed his clothes in a laundry bag and set them on the floor by the stairs. He sees the bathroom door open. He stands outside the door as Qaniit tidies the shower curtain and floor mat after a previous guest. "Try not to get water on the floor," she says looking at him then quickly away. "I don't know why some can't read the sign."

"Yes, ma'am." He glances at her then looks away too.

He goes in after she comes out.

Just before closing the door she says, "Mr. Douglas?"

"Yes?" He turns to face her while holding the door open.

With her sad and withdrawn face looking down at the floor she says, "I want to thank you for helping out. With my grandfather."

"Sure," he says, nodding.

She presses her lips together and nods her signature acknowledgment while still looking away from him at the floor. She moves on down the hallway.

Jack watches after her as she picks up the laundry bag and descends the stairs. He comes out of his trance, closes the door, and climbs into the tub, making sure he tucks the curtain inside, lest he feel her wrath. He soaps up, scrubbing the fish smell from him. *She's an attractive woman, so somber, yet acts businesslike. Is that the way others see me? No emotion, dead inside? It's as if she too has had her heart or soul ripped out and discarded.* He towels off inside the tub. *I wonder where Amaroq is. Has she befriended someone else? I hope she's all right out there without me. Of course, she is. She's a wolf in her natural element. How ridiculous.*

Jack crashes on his bed after his shower.

~ * ~

Lying face down in the dirt, he can't move, can't get up, can't raise his arms or legs. Cracking his eyelids open, although he can't get them to operate all too well either, he sees his gear strewn about him, his tent collapsed, his things scattered.

He feels this great pain on the back of his left thigh. He then realizes something is eating him. No, something is licking the back of his left thigh. Its tongue is warm and it seems to be working on something. Whatever it is, or is doing, the pain dissipates.

~ * ~

He awakes in the late-afternoon. He remembers that time a few weeks ago when he awoke half-in and half-out of his tent covered in dirt with Amaroq sitting beside him. He can't piece it together.

He gets up, dresses, and strolls through town to clear his head. *I've been here about a week. I promised Malik two weeks on the boat, but I have to go after that. I've already become too attached to this new set of people, or rather they've become too attached to me, certainly that crazy kid.*

Walking along East 6th Avenue, three native kids, playing in the front yard of their home, between four and ten years old, run up and touch his arm, one rubbing it. The little girl smiles, takes his hand in her own. He doesn't know what to make of this, a perfect stranger to them. He plays along, pats the little girl on her head. The three of them giggle, wave at him, and skip off. Jack waves, smiles back at them.

He stands there remembering smiling at Amaroq when she played with him.

He snaps out of his thoughts and makes his way back to the Prospector. The restaurant has opened for dinner, and a few cruise ship passengers have arrived to eat. A small bar just inside the restaurant around the corner of the main counter runs along the wall with ten seats. Qaniit serves beer to two white men in their fifties. One has a pot-belly, the other a rosacea face, like he's been drinking all his life. Jack waits to be seated. These two chaps don't look like they came off the ship. Rather, they appear to be pretend sport-fisherman on an excursion to find their manhood. Akiak takes orders from guests, and his grandmother, Ulloriaq, meaning star, Akiak told him, works in the kitchen.

Akiak rushes by and Jack says, "Take your time."

"Thanks, Jack. Hey, listen. Grandfather said I can go along on the next haul. On weekends. I've been a few times. I asked to go on the Nuliajuk with you and Miles." He smiles and hustles off.

Good kid. He's so into helping his family. Jack seats himself in a booth.

Qaniit scurries by with a coffee carafe. She refills the cups for an old couple from the ship. She stops at Jack and says, "The usual, Mr. Douglas?"

"Yes, thank you. No rush."

Jack hears a ding from a bell in the kitchen. She sets the carafe down on its pad at the waitress station behind him, and, as she hurries off to the kitchen, the pot-bellied man at the bar says to her, "Another round, good-lookin'."

"One minute please, sir." She darts into the kitchen.

Jack realizes they are tipsy.

Akiak takes an order for a man in a booth then busses the table next to him. As he passes the men at the bar carrying the dishes, rosacea-man reaches out and grabs his arm, knocking the plates onto the floor, breaking them. "Damn, you need to be more careful, boy," rosacea-man says.

Akiak bends down to collect the broken pieces. Rosacea-man says to him, "Pour us some beers, will ya?"

"I'm sorry," Akiak says looking up at him. "I'm underage and not allowed."

"Well, goddamn. Run along and find someone who can."

Qaniit pops out of the kitchen carrying meals on two plates. "Are you okay?"

Akiak nods, picking up the broken plates. He stands and goes into the kitchen.

Rosacea-man belches and says, "He's okay. Another round, beautiful."

"I'll be right back, sir," she says, hustling off.

Jack hears pot-bellied man catcall her and say to rosacea-man, "She's got a fine set of tits and sweet ass, huh, Kenny?"

The old man at the table with his wife next to Jack looks at the men too. He frowns. Qaniit drops off their meal. The woman says to her, "Miss? Could we have some extra tartar sauce, please?"

"Yes, ma'am. I'll get it from the kitchen."

"Some more coffee, please?" a man with his wife at another table calls as she passes.

"Yes, sir. I'll be right back."

This time as she passes the bar, pot-bellied man grabs her arm. "Just pour us a beer, sweetie," he says.

"Yes sir, one minute please."

As she's about to go into the kitchen, pot-bellied man jumps up and says, "Goddamn lazy natives. I'll pour my own damn beer." He slips around behind the bar, carrying his glass.

"Please, sir," Qaniit says. "You need to come out from behind the bar. I'll get your beer."

He ignores her and grabs the beer spout, tipping it back to let the beer flow.

That's it. I can't take it anymore. I have to do something. I can't just sit here. Jack jumps up, shoots over to the scene. "Is there a problem here, gentlemen?"

"Who the hell're you?" pot-bellied man says, topping off his beer.

"You might want to call the police," Jack says to Qaniit.

Because pot-bellied man blocks her access, she has to walk in front of the bar to the other end where the landline sits just under the counter. She reaches in and pulls it up. Rosacea-man staggers off his stool, rushes her, grabbing the phone, saying, "You don't wanna go and do that, honey." He slaps her buttocks with his other hand. She slaps him across the face.

"You bitch," he shouts.

Before he can throw a punch at her, Jack grabs the man's arm as it comes forward and puts him in a choke hold, pulling him back. Akiak emerges from the kitchen. Rosacea-man struggles, so Jack lets him go. "I think it's time to call it a night," Jack says.

"I think you need to mind your own fuckin' business, mister," pot-bellied man says sipping his beer.

I tried doing that. "Please, you should go. Perhaps she won't press charges."

"Press charges?" Rosacea-man chuckles and sits on the stool.

"I'll call the police from the office," Akiak says. He turns to head in there, but pot-bellied man pushes him. Akiak falls and crashes into the wall. As Jack rushes to help him, pot-bellied man splashes his beer over Akiak.

Jack helps Akiak to his feet and turns to the man, saying in a stern voice, "You gentlemen need to step outside. Now."

"Fuck you." Pot-bellied man takes a swing at Jack, but Jack ducks, swings around and clocks him in the jaw. The man falls backward against glasses on the wall, breaking a few.

Rosacea-man jumps up to assist. He takes a swing at Jack, but once again Jack moves his head backward to avoid the blow and counter-punches him. Rosacea-man falls to the floor, knocking over a stool.

The old man sitting at the table next to Jack's booth rushes over. "You need some help?" he says to Jack. "I was a Green Beret, one of Jack Kennedy's first and still have a lick or two in me."

"Perhaps," Jack says. "Depends on these two gentlemen."

Pot-bellied man straightens up, rubs his face. Rosacea-man tries to stand, but pot-bellied man has to assist him.

Jack notices the men placed cash on the bar for their tab. He grabs the cash, peels off three twenties and hands them to Akiak. "This should cover the broken dishes and bottles," Jack says. "And another for your troubles." He hands Akiak one more twenty and presses the rest of the cash against rosacea-man's chest. "Good night, gentlemen. The door is that way."

They scowl at him and shuffle out the door.

"Got a hella'va hook," the Green Beret says to Jack.

"Thank you, sir. For your assistance too."

"Didn't do much, except intimidate them, huh?" He smiles at Jack and pats his shoulder. He returns to his wife at their table. The other patrons, standing to watch, all sit and resume their dinners.

Qaniit straightens up, wiping up the spilled beer.

"You okay?" Jack says to Akiak.

"Yeah, thanks. We showed 'em, huh, Jack?" he says smiling.

"Sure, kid. Sure, we did." He looks down at Qaniit wiping up the beer from the floor. Akiak goes into the kitchen and Jack returns to his booth.

Chapter Eighteen

Life is what happens while you're busy making other plans.
Allen Saunders

A couple days later, Akiak picks Jack up at the Prospector at four in the morning and drives to the dock. They prep the boat, and along with Miles, Ronny, and Sky, head out to sea.

The Nuliajuk chops its way through the waves. Jack, Akiak, and the men sit inside the cabin because rain pelts the boat. Ronny hands Jack a bottle of water. "Thanks," Jack says.

"So, Jack?" Sky says, "is it true?" He sips his coffee. "About the amaroq?"

Jack narrows his eyes at him. "Is what true?"

"That you saw the amaroq?"

"I don't know what you mean. I saw a wolf, that's all." He scans the men, including Akiak who studies him.

"Yes, but did it follow you?" Ronny says jumping into the conversation.

"No. More like I followed her."

"Her?" Sky says, his voice inflecting.

Jack sips water. *I don't want to talk about this.*

"I don't mean to pry," Sky continues, "but the amaroq, the female, only befriends and latches onto lost souls."

Jack looks at him then down at the floor.

"And her spirit becomes a part of the soul of the one she's chosen."

Jack can feel all eyes upon him.

"The male amaroq," Sky goes on, "well, he finds those deserving to die, usually the evil, and tears them apart. Eats them."

"Oh, that's all superstition," Ronny says, interjecting. "No one believes that anymore."

"That's because you're half-white, Cuz," Sky says, slapping his shoulder.

Miles cuts the engine to the boat. "Let's go. Fish to catch."

The men file out and prep the gear, baiting the gangions. Jack watches Akiak who looks back at him with that big smile from ear-to-ear.

They lay out all the lines and sometime later circle around and begin the haul against pelting rain. Miles operates the girdie, Ronny and Akiak remove the fish, and Sky re-coils the lines. Dressed in a long yellow-slicker fisherman's rain coat and pants, Jack ices and packs the fish. They all work on rebaiting the gangions, dropping them in again.

After sundown, they eat dinner in the cabin, Miles grilling up some halibut. Akiak crashes on the bench after dinner.

The storm passes, and the sea calms, so Jack joins Miles who smokes a long pipe on the deck. Jack sits on the gunwale, looking out over the moonlit sea.

"The kid's really taken to you," Miles says to Jack.

That's what I was afraid of.

"His father passed about three years ago. Had some rare cancer never heard of."

Jack glances over at Miles then back at the black sea below him.

"Then his mother ran off with some white guy. Lives in California somewhere."

Why are you telling me all this? He doesn't say anything but looks back at Miles smoking his pipe.

After a long silence, except for the lapping of the waves against the boat, Jack says, "I'm really impressed with your sense of community. Very hardworking people."

"Ancestors have lived off the land and sea for thousands of years." He puffs on his pipe.

Another long break in the conversation. "Sometimes that's not good enough," Miles says.

Jack looks at him to finish.

"Malik makes enough to pay the crew, keep things operating, but the inn is bleeding into his earnings."

"How so?"

"Qaniit's uncle. A real asshole. A banker in Anchorage. I'm not sure if he's even a real banker. More of a speculator or something. Qaniit inherited half of the inn from her father, but the uncle owns the other half. Gambled his money, took out too many loans, bankruptcy and all that. He really doesn't contribute to the operation."

Jack studies him. Miles shifts, relights his pipe. "Forced Qaniit to take out a second on the inn, and he isn't making his part of the payments. Malik's trying to cover, but bank's threatening foreclosure."

Jack looks out at a streak of moonlight reflecting off of, and dancing around on, the water.

"That inn is her whole life. Like she's married to it now."

Jack looks over at him again, thinking about that. He's right about that. She does everything there. She employs a woman who cleans the rooms each day, but Qaniit gets up at the crack of dawn and opens for breakfast. After cleanup, she runs errands to get supplies, makes minor repairs, keeps the books in order, then prepares for the dinner crowd. The operation runs seven days a week all year long because either boisterous fishermen come though during season, like those two the other day, or cruise ships and other crazy white tourists seeking adventure, some on Grizzly tours.

"Well," Miles says, "let's do another haul."

The crew works throughout the night. They stay out another day and fill up the hold. Jack retires to his room, avoiding Qaniit and turns in, yet leaves his dirty clothes in his laundry bag outside by the door.

Again, he lies there staring at his family photo and Bible until falling asleep some time later.

~ * ~

Jack hears something roaring. He lies face down in the dirt and feels a sharp pain on the back of his thigh. He tries to roll over, but can't. He sees a large brown creature tussling with something.

A few seconds later he hears an ear-splitting howl from what appears to be a wolf. The brown creature runs off into the woods.

~ * ~

Jack wakes up in the mid-morning sun. *That dream again. What happened to me? Did that happen?* He sits up, grabs a towel and wipes sweat off his brow.

He works out in his room and goes for a run through town.

He returns, showers, dresses in his jeans and a Prospector Inn T-shirt.

Downstairs, breakfast is over, the place is empty. Heading for the door, he hears someone in the kitchen say, "Oh shoot." He then hears water spraying.

"Hello," he calls out, opening the swinging kitchen door a crack. He peeks in and sees someone's legs sticking out from beneath the sink where water squirts out all over the place. He edges in to discover Qaniit on her back dressed in her jeans and T-shirt. Soaked, with piping tools beside her, she struggles with a pipe. Jack kneels down and says, "What is it?"

"This darn nipple," she says pointing to a pipe coming out from the back of the wall. "You need at least three hands to manipulate this. The water shut-off is just outside the back door."

"Oh, right," Jack says, sprinting to the door. He opens it and finds the main shut-off. He goes back in and kneels again. "What can I do?"

"Can you hold this wrench, so I can screw this elbow on?"

"Sure." He gets down onto his back and crawls under the sink next to her. A tight fit, he manages to squeeze in. His shirt and pants become soaked from the puddle of water under the sink.

"Can you hold that light on this?" she says.

He holds the light on the operation.

"See that little screw? That one there?"

"Yes."

"It has to go in there to tighten the rubber flange." She holds onto a wrench in one hand while steadying the flange in the other.

"Got it." He picks up the tiny screw and tries to screw it in, but it falls onto her chest. "Oops. Sorry." He reaches for it and struggles to pinch it between his fingers and thumb. His fingers brush against her wet breast. "Sorry, again," he says. He manages to pinch the screw and get it into its new home.

Using the wrench, she tightens one pipe onto the other. "Can you connect that line over there?" she says. "Here, give me the flashlight."

He passes it to her, their hands touching. He grabs the hose and stretches it across while she holds the light. He secures the hose onto the new nipple.

"I think that will do it," she says. "Hold on." She crawls out from under the sink, and he hears her open the back door and turn on the water. She comes back in and says, "Any leaks?"

"No. No leaks."

"Can you pass me the wrench and light?"

He does as instructed and shimmies back out. He goes to stand, but she grabs his hand, helping him up. "Thanks," he says.

"Thank you, Mr. Douglas."

"Sure." He darts to move past her and as she moves to pass him at the same time in the same direction, his wet chest and her wet breasts bump. "I'm so sorry," he says backing up.

She nods, and he shoots past her in the opposite direction, hurrying for the door.

"Leave your wet clothes by your door," she calls after him. "I'll put them in the dryer."

"Yes. Yes, thank you, Qaniit." He hustles up to his room.

In his room, he strips down, towels off, puts his wet clothes in a laundry bag and sets them in the hall.

He sits on the edge of his bed without a stich on and stares at the floor trying to catch his breath. A little light-headed, he rubs his face in his hands and glances over at the family photo resting upright against his Bible. *I have to get out of here. A few more days and I need to be on my way. I should get what I need and head back into the hills and find Amaroq. God, I miss her.* He looks down at the amaroq claw hanging on its chain around his neck, resting against his sternum. He picks it up and, holding it in his palm, squeezes it. He regains his composure. A sense of calm envelops him.

He dresses, zips downstairs and out onto the street where he walks through town for a couple hours.

Chapter Nineteen

We are just a drop in the ocean, but the ocean would be less because of that missing drop.

Saint Teresa

Jack's two-week commitment has now turned into three. Malik finally hired two new deckhands on the other boats, but is still short so Jack stayed, promising a little while longer until Malik rounds out a full crew on the Nuliajuk. While fishing, and with each run lasting between two and three days, Jack's days go by quickly, with no time to think about much, certainly his work takes his mind off his past. In between the runs, however, which last about two days, Jack tries to keep busy by exercising, running or walking through town, but when he hangs out at the Prospector, he sinks into depression again. He avoids everyone, even Qaniit, who works almost twenty-four seven.

Jack climbs out of bed, dresses, drapes his raincoat and rain pants over his arm, and heads for the harbor. While walking, Akiak pulls up in his truck. "I don't know why you won't let me drive you, Jack."

"Need the walk and fresh air."

Akiak crawls along in his truck, keeping pace.

Jack feels Akiak's eyes upon him. "What is it, kid? I said fresh air. That smelly exhaust isn't fresh air."

"It's just that, well, I dunno."

"You don't know? Spit it out so I can get my fresh air."

"Well. It's just that I'm so happy you came along when you did, Jack. I mean, because of you grandfather has been able to make a couple payments on Uncle Robert's half of the mortgage on the inn. Buys Qaniit some time."

Jack glances at him then back at the street in front of him. "Okay.

Something else?"

"It's just that, well, Qaniit is, you know. I mean, she's, well, she won't say anything, but I know she's a little happier too. That you came along and are helping out and all."

"Glad to help out. Now, please? My fresh air?"

Akiak smiles, in his usual way, from ear-to-ear. "Thanks, Jack." He zips off up the street.

Jack sighs. Carrying his raingear over his arm, he notices the amaroq claw bouncing up and down outside his shirt. He reaches down and tucks it under.

~ * ~

Setting out on the Nuliajuk, the ocean starts out calm and the skies clear, although after the first haul around noon, the clouds blacken and a light rain falls. It's not too severe, so they come around for a second haul later that afternoon.

Jack packs the fish in the hold. The rain picks up, pelting the crew. Three to five-foot waves crash against the boat, rocking it. The sky has darkened, and it looks almost like nighttime.

After the haul is stowed, Akiak helps Ronny and Sky re-bait the lines and drop them again while Jack stands talking with Miles near the cabin entrance. Miles says, "I'll be sorry to see you go, Jack. Whenever that is."

Jack glances over at him but doesn't say anything. He looks back at the boys working on baiting the groundline.

"You're a good worker and Malik's so grateful. Without you we couldn't have run the boats."

Jack nods. "Thanks, Miles. It's been a real learning experience and adventure." He starts for the ice hold.

"He's over the side," Sky hollers.

Jack twirls around and rushes over to the stern where he finds Ronny and Sky, but no Akiak.

"He's snagged on a hook," Sky yells, pointing to the black water below.

Jack rips off his raincoat, tosses it onto the deck and dives headfirst over the side. He kicks off his boots, grabs onto the descending groundline, pulling himself down hand-over-hand as it sinks rapidly on its own. The weight of his fisherman's heavy-duty rain pants impede his progress on the line, but he makes his way along it as the sinker pulls the line down into the deep.

Along the line below him at about twenty feet, Jack can just make out through the ocean darkness Akiak struggling to break free from the hook that snagged him. Jack slices open both of his hands on a few of the hooks and blood oozes out into the dark water, but he uses all the strength he can muster and races deeper, hand-over-hand.

Jack reaches Akiak, but Akiak has stopped struggling. Jack tears at the kid's pants where they snagged on the hook, ripping them apart, but he slices open his hands even more on this hook.

He frees Akiak, grabs him, and swims to the surface.

Using swimmer's rescue techniques, from behind and with his arm under Akiak's armpits, he swims over to the boat where he hoists Akiak up to the men. They place him on the deck. Jack climbs aboard. Ronny starts CPR.

Jack kneels next to him, turning his head to the side to clear the water. A sizable portion of seawater spills out. Ronny pumps Akiak's chest as Jack gives him mouth to mouth. "Breath," Jack says. "Breathe." *You're not going to die on me like Sanders.*

Jack blows into the kid's lungs again while Ronny continues pumping Akiak's chest. Jack blows yet another time. Akiak coughs and spits up water. He gasps, so Jack turns his head again to drain the water. Akiak turns onto his side, coughs again and takes several deep breaths, struggling for air. Jack pats him on his back expelling more water.

At last, Akiak catches his breath. The men help him sit up. "What happened?" Akiak says.

Miles hoists him with a bear-hug. "We almost lost you," he says, kissing his cheek. "Don't ever do that again."

Sky runs into the cabin returning with dishtowels. He bends down beside Jack, wraps Jack's bloody hands. He has badly torn them. "We've got to get him to a hospital, Miles," Sky says.

"Get in the cabin," Miles says to Akiak. "Stay there."

The men help Jack to his feet and into the cabin. Miles turns over the engine and opens up full throttle, heading for Nome. Sky turns up the volume on the radio and speaks into the handset, "Coast Guard Nome. This is the Nuliajuk. I repeat, this is the Nuliajuk. We need emergency medical services dockside. We are heading in now. We have an injury that requires medical attention. Over."

"This is U.S. Coast Guard, Nome Station. We read. Over."

"This is the Nuliajuk. We will arrive on-site in approximately..." he looks over at Miles who holds up three fingers. "Approximately thirty minutes. Over."

"Roger. Emergency services dispatched. U.S. Coast Guard Nome Station. Out."

In the cabin, Jack holds his hands higher than his heart so the blood won't run out. The towels become soaked soon enough, however. Sky grabs some more towels from a closet and rewraps Jack's hands with fresh ones. Ronny rinses the bloody towels in the small galley sink.

"I'm so sorry, Jack," Akiak says, his eyes watering.

"It's okay, kid."

Akiak sits next to Jack, places his arm around his shoulder, squeezing Jack and sniffling.

Jack looks over at him. "Next time you'll know to stand clear of the hooks."

Akiak nods, wiping tears away. Jack sits there, but he doesn't feel much pain. By the looks of the wounds, he will need stitches to close them. Ronny and Sky fuss over him while Akiak stays close the whole ride back to the harbor.

At the harbor, while pulling in, they see the flashing lights of an ambulance, many people standing around. It looks to Jack as if the entire village has turned out for the affair. Miles pilots the boat up to the dock where paramedics rush on board with a gurney. Malik, Ulloriaq, and Qaniit follow the paramedics onto the boat.

Jack stands. "I can walk."

"It's best you lie down and let us take over, Jack," says one of the paramedics.

He follows orders.

They strap Jack onto the gurney. "What happened?" Malik asks Miles.

Jack hears Miles tell them the beginning of the story, but the paramedics lift Jack off the boat, wheeling him away.

They load Jack into the paramedic truck. Just before they close the door, Qaniit jumps into the back of the truck. "I'll go with you, Dave." She sits on one side of Jack while one of the paramedics sits on the other. He taps an IV into Jack's arm and checks for vitals as the truck dives off to the hospital.

~ * ~

In Norton Sound Hospital, they wheel Jack into the emergency room. Qaniit waits outside. They set Jack up on an examination table as a doctor and two nurses come in. They peel off the towels from his hands.

The doctor examines him. Jack's hands have several gashes, however the wounds have closed and the bleeding has stopped. The doctor glances at the nurses. "Not as bad as they described on the way in."

Jack considers the wounds. *He's right. They don't look as bad as they first appeared on the boat.*

"I think a little skin glue, a few butterflies, and you're good to go," the doctor says.

The nurses wash the wounds, each taking a hand. The doctor applies skin glue. The nurses use butterfly bandages to hold the wounds together.

Several minutes later, with icepacks taped around his hands, Jack gets up, walks out into the waiting room where a crowd has gathered including Malik, Ulloriaq, Qaniit, Akiak, Miles, Sky, Ronny, and others he doesn't recognize. He stops short after seeing them. "You all didn't have to come down here."

Ulloriaq steps forward, hugs and kisses him on his cheek. The others surround him, those closest putting their hands on his shoulders, his arms and back. Ulloriaq whispers to him, "Thank you, Jack."

"Please. Please. I just did what I had to do."

Ulloriaq steps aside to allow Qaniit to move closer. She takes his arm in hers and leads him outside. The others follow. She helps him into Akiak's truck. She and Akiak climb in, he driving them back to the Prospector.

No one speaks during the trip. Akiak drops them off.

Qaniit guides him upstairs to his room where she helps him strip down to his underwear. She guides him onto the bed because his hands still have the large icepacks taped to them. She glances at the amaroq claw hanging on its necklace resting against his breastbone. "I'll be right back," she says to him.

He waits, looking at the icepacks.

A few minutes later, Qaniit returns, holding a dishpan with warm soapy water, a sponge, and a towel. She sets the dishpan on the desk then glances at his family photo resting against the Bible on the nightstand.

"You don't have to go to all this trouble," he says.

"You've done nothing but help us since you arrived, Mr. Douglas." She dips the sponge in the pan, squeezes it and turns to face him.

Yeah. Perhaps I'm nothing but trouble.

"If you hadn't been there on that boat, I would have lost another."

"I'm sorry about that," he says. "Your husband."

She nods and presses her lips together in her sad, signature acknowledgment. She starts giving him a sponge bath.

Taken aback at first, and a little uncomfortable, his eyes follow her moves. *I guess I shouldn't protest. She's in charge. Like I said, she's the boss.* She sponges his face, shoulders, arms, chest, and wipes him down with the towel. "Lean forward, please, Mr. Douglas."

Again, he follows orders. She sponges and towels off his back too. She rinses the sponge and sponges his legs and feet, getting in-between his toes, tickling him. She glances up, catches his eyes upon her, but goes back to work.

His heart beats faster and he feels a little lightheaded.

She runs the towel over his body to ensure she has dried him. She pulls the covers up to his waist, placing his ice-packed hands on top of the sheets in front of him.

He catches her soft, blue, but sad eyes again. *They remind me of the blue sky while hiking along the Yukon with Amaroq.* He feels that hollow ping in his gut again.

Picking up the dishpan to go, she says, "I'll check on you later, Mr. Douglas."

"Thank you."

At the door, she turns to him. "Thank you. For saving, Akiak. Goodnight, Mr. Douglas."

"Goodnight..."

She turns out the light, closing the door behind her.

"...Qaniit." He sits there in the dark staring at the door. He closes his eyes, squeezing them. He opens his eyes and peeks over at his family photo in the moonlight. He glances at his ice-packed, wrapped hands, then down at the amaroq claw. *I miss you too.*

He rolls onto his side, curls up with the extra pillow, and stares into the darkness.

Chapter Twenty

You cannot run from the wind, for it will always catch you.
Native American

He hears a gentle knock on the door. Jack turns over in the bed. "Yes?"

"It's me, Jack," Akiak says through the door." His voice rising, he continues, "You're awake. Can I come in?"

The sun has already risen. Jack glances at the clock on the wall. *Ten o'clock.* He has slept for almost eleven hours. He crawls out of bed, grabs a robe off the hanger by the door, putting it on. Opening the door, Akiak bursts through.

"Don't go away," Akiak says holding up his palms at Jack. "Stay right here. I'll be right back."

"I have to peeee," Jack says stringing out the word pee like a child.

"Oh, okay. Go pee, but come right back to your room." Just as fast as he came in, he shoots off down the stairs again.

What's with this kid? He steps from his room and recalls the event the night before. Looking down at his hands, he realizes the icepacks are gone. So, too, the butterfly bandages. In fact, there's no blood, no scabs, only thin pink flesh lines where the gashes had been. It doesn't appear his hands will scar too badly, if at all. *But how can this be? How could I have healed this fast?*

After the bathroom and back in his room sitting on the edge of his bed, Akiak enters carrying breakfast on a tray. He places the tray on the desk. "Got your usual," he says. "Oatmeal and milk." He smiles at Jack and pulls out the desk chair, motioning with his hand for him to sit.

"Thanks, kid." He sits at the desk.

Akiak opens a linen napkin, hands it to Jack as a waiter would.

"How're you feeling?"

"Good," Jack says. "Good." Jack catches him staring at him. "What?" he snaps.

"Well, I hope you don't mind."

"Mind what?"

"Well, it's just that you've been sleeping for three days and…"

"Three days?" Jack narrows his eyes.

Akiak sits in the other chair at the desk next to him. "Yes, well, you see the doctor, who's the nephew of the shaman you met, came by because we couldn't wake you up. You were alive and all, but in a deep sleep or something. The doctor said you were okay, all vitals okay, and it was not a coma he said, just a deep sleep to heal your body."

Jack flashes back to the event where he awoke to discover he had lost three days, where he was half-in and half-out of his tent with Amaroq standing by him. He looks at his hands again and over at Akiak. "What's going on, Akiak? I mean with all this?"

"I dunno. Grandmother says there are things no one can explain. It's like you just believe in some things, even though they don't make any sense."

Jack studies him, thinking about that.

"There's something else, Jack." He smiles.

Jack waits for him to continue, but Jack has to coax him saying, "Well, what is it? Spit it out, kid."

"Qaniit came in to take care of you."

"The hands?"

"More." He keeps smiling with a silly grin.

"And?" Jack says, his voice rising.

"She gave you sponge baths, well, because you sweated a lot. She also kept your lips moist with swabs. And she stayed with you, at your side, whenever she could."

"Okay, okay. Sooooo."

Akiak winks at him. "I think she likes you, Jack."

"Knock it off. Get out of here and let me eat breakfast in peace." He hears people talking downstairs. "Who's that?"

"Oh, Uncle Robert is here. Talking business with Qaniit and

grandfather." He closes the door, departing.

She likes you. Nonsense. The kid is just silly. He eats the oatmeal and washes it down with his milk. He looks at his hands again. *Makes no sense.* He glances at his clothes in the closet, not many really. *Everything I have in this world.* He stares at the floor and sighs. *Against what I've wanted to do, I've gotten way too close to these people. To this kid. Rather, they have gotten too close to me. I can't stay here. I don't belong. These are not my people. Actually, I don't have people. Any people. Anymore. I lost my people. I had wanted to start a business with Sanders, but, not this. Not here. Not like this.*

He stands and stares out the window. *Why did I pick this place? He looks down and touches the amaroq claw. Amaroq. That crazy wolf. Things you can't explain. The mythical amaroq? That's nonsensical.* Continuing to stare out the window, still touching the amaroq claw, he says, "What have you done to me?"

He showers and meanders downstairs. At the bottom of the stairs on his way to the door, he passes Malik, Qaniit, and a white man in his fifties sitting at a table talking. Qaniit's forehead rests in her hand, looking down at legal papers. She glances up, catches Jack's eye. "You okay, Mr. Douglas?"

He averts his eyes and says over his shoulder, hurrying for the door, "I'm fine. Thank you."

Outside, a cool gust of fresh air blows at his face. He takes a deep breath, and it feels as if his heart skips a beat. He feels his face flush. *Perhaps I'm up and about from the injury too soon? No, that doesn't make sense as my hands are almost healed, which doesn't make sense either, and I have been asleep for three days. Madness.* The amaroq claw flutters on the outside of his Prospector Inn T-shirt, so he stuffs it under the collar. His flushed face subsides, almost at the same time he had touched the amaroq claw.

He walks the streets for some time but he can't get away from the townspeople who come up to touch his arm, his hands. Even an old Inuit woman stops him, putting her palm on his cheek. He smiles and plays along. *I've got to get out of here.*

He doubles back to the Prospector to avoid any more people. He opens the door and finds the trio he had left earlier standing in the foyer. He tries to pass, but Malik says, "Jack, this is Robert Howell. Robert, Jack Douglas."

Jack glances at Malik, who looks pale, a little sickly. Jack looks back at Howell and they shake. "Mr. Howell."

"Mr. Douglas."

Edging around them to get away, he catches Qaniit looking at him. She looks away. He does too. He sprints up the stairs. Inside his room, he has to catch his breath. *Unusual for a die-hard runner. I never lose my breath like that.* He feels light-headed and has to lie down. His eyes grow heavy. He falls asleep.

~ * ~

With no clothes on, returning from a creek after bathing, he sees a grizzly tearing apart his camp. It head-butts him, knocking him to the ground. He tries to crawl away, but its claw snags on the back of his left thigh tearing it wide open. Lying there helpless and in excruciating pain, Amaroq sprints by him and tackles the bear. She's like a mad dog wrestling with it, both animals rolling around like logs sliding down a log shoot. She nips at it and howls an earsplitting tone Jack has never heard before. The bear scurries off.

She rushes over to him, licks his injury. The pain subsides, but he can't move. He passes out.

~ * ~

He awakes before sunrise. *Had that happened? Just like that? I don't remember it.* Jack turns the light on next to his bed, sits up, looking at his hands. There's no scarring. The wounds are indistinguishable with the rest of his flesh. He shakes his head and rubs his face in his hands. *I'm going mad.* He looks at the clock. Four-twenty in the morning.

He packs his clothes in haste in a small bag he bought. He couldn't find a large hiker's backpack anywhere in town, so he figures he'll find one in another town. He doesn't shower. He dresses and sneaks downstairs.

He pulls ten one-hundred-dollar bills from his pocket and places them in the ledger under the counter. He scribbles a note on a pad. It reads: "I'm sorry. I must be going. Thank you for everything. Jack."

He puts the note under a polar bear paperweight and tip-toes out the door. He walks over to the Nome Airport. At the counter, he says to the attendant, "I'll take the next flight out."

"Sure, Mr. Douglas."

I've got to get away to where no one knows my name.

"I have one to Anchorage in an hour. It's prepping on the tarmac now."

Jack looks out the window and sees an Alaskan Airlines jet being fueled.

"That's three hundred and fifty-eight round-trip."

"No. Just one-way please."

"You sure, Mr. Douglas?"

"Yes, please." Jack pays and checks in.

~ * ~

The plane taxies down the runway and departs as the sun rises. Jack looks out to see the harbor below, men prepping their boats. He turns away, covering his face with his hands as the plane banks out over Norton Sound and the Bering Sea toward Anchorage.

~ * ~

He checks into a hotel in downtown Anchorage. Jack goes right to his room and sits on the edge of the bed. *Where should I go? What should I do?* His mind races. He sees Janette and the kids again. *It has now been two years, or is it a thousand?* He thinks of Sanders. He thinks about Amaroq. He sees Akiak and the kid's big happy smile, fishing in the Snake River that day. He sees Qaniit. *She is such a beautiful, smart, and resilient woman. She deserves to be happy.* He sees her under the sink fixing the pipe. He sees her take his arm at the hospital. He watches her sponge bathe him in bed. He remembers how she looked at him yesterday. She seemed to have opened up just a little over the past couple weeks. *I hope she finds happiness and love again. She deserves that.* He looks up at the ceiling and says, "Please allow her to find happiness again. Okay?"

The ceiling doesn't answer him.

He looks down at the amaroq claw tucked into his T-shirt. He pulls it out and yanks it off his neck. He examines it for the longest time. He feels that pit in the bottom of his stomach again and a shortness of breath. He tosses the amaroq claw onto the bed and rubs his face in his hands. He gets up, stuffs cash in his pocket, and goes out onto the street.

He stands, looking up at downtown Anchorage before him. *Where to? Just walk to clear the head.*

He walks the streets for quite some time.

At sundown, he enters a small bar near the waterfront. Why? He doesn't know. *I've never done this in my entire life, walk into a bar alone.* He sits at the bar and scans the patrons, about twenty tough-looking sailor-type characters, men and women drinking beer. "What'll ya have?" says the barmaid. It appears as though she can go a round or two in the ring with him.

"Beer. Any kind. Doesn't matter."

She pours him one from the tap. He pulls his cash roll out and peels off a hundred from a bunch. She raises an eyebrow as he slides the Franklin to her. She cashes it out and puts his change down under a small weight on the bar.

He takes a sip and looks around. Three men, who look like fishermen, glance at him then away. He thinks about how these people hang out in a place like this much of their lives looking for something, whatever it is they're looking for. *If it fulfills them, who am I to judge?*

He sips his beer again. *Maybe this is how they cleanse their heads, wash away their pain.* He looks at his half-empty beer, or is it half-full? Doesn't matter. He finishes it and orders another.

He watches on the TV above him on the wall a local show on fishing. The expert fisherman demonstrates proper salmon fishing. He thinks of Akiak. *That crazy kid was the expert.*

He orders another beer.

Should I go back up north, into the wilderness? I have enough money left in the account to live off the land for many years. Alone. I don't need much. I only need a small piece of property near a river to fish perhaps. I could trap rabbits. Amaroq could come and live with me.

He orders and drinks yet another beer. Why? He's never done this either in his life. He got tipsy in college once with some guys, but never drunk. *What's wrong with me?*

He sits for quite some time and has several more beers watching another fishing show, this one on king crab fishing. *I hope Malik hires a replacement since the crab season is beginning in Norton Sound.* He has to squint to see the television now. He's lost count of the number of beers he's had.

He fumbles with his cash roll, peels off another Franklin, passing it to the barmaid. She returns his change and he leaves her a twenty-dollar tip. He exits and stands outside on the sidewalk, swaying, leaning against the wall.

He staggers down the street, stopping at the corner to look out at the water, the moonlight dancing around on it. It reminds him of that night aboard the Nuliajuk.

In an alley, he stops and vomits, almost toppling over. He wipes spittle from his lips and turns to go.

"Give us the money," someone says behind him.

He spins around to find the fishermen from the bar surrounding him. He doesn't know why he says it, but he does, slurring his words, "Gentlemen, you'll have to take it from me." He could easily take these guys, if he weren't drunk, but he is. However, he isn't about to just hand the cash over to them.

"Have it your way," the man says. The men attack him. He tries to keep them from getting the money, just to provoke them more, but he doesn't fight back. They punch, hit and throw him to the ground. Jack doesn't block their blows or resist as they kick and stomp him in the side, on the face, and in the head. They beat him badly and grab the cash. They drag him further into the alley, kicking and stomping on him more. The guy who took the cash kicks him in the face. Jack coughs up blood. The men saunter off down the alley.

He lies there in the stinking alley, bleeding from his nose and mouth, his eyes swelling shut. He manages to sit up to discover he's bled all over his Prospector Inn T-shirt. With both hands, he wipes at the blood on his shirt. Sobbing, he says, "I'm so sorry, Qaniit. I messed up your T-shirt." He crawls over and sits against a dumpster, looking at the blood all over his hands. He feels a chill. He wraps his arms around his chest, hugging himself. He reaches for his amaroq claw, but after patting his breastbone and digging in his shirt, he realizes he tore it off and left it on the bed.

He looks up, sees something at end of the alley looking back at him. It looks like a dog, but he can't see it too well squinting through his swollen eyes. It edges closer, stopping in front of him. "Amaroq?" *It's not possible. This is crazy.*

She licks his face, washing the blood away. He hugs her, stroking the thick fur on the side of her head. Sobbing, caressing her neck, he rests his head against the side of her face. "I'm so sorry, girl. I've let you down."

She licks him again and nudges his head. She turns, walks a few paces from him and stops, looking back, just like she had on the trails in the mountains.

"You want me to follow? Right?"

"Yelp."

He pulls himself up. She waits for him to catch up, turns, and heads up the alley. He follows, grasping at a sharp pain in his abdomen.

She turns onto a street. He does too. She turns a corner, heading up another street and he follows. A few minutes later he's back at his hotel. She trots into the hotel. He follows her. At the elevator, she goes in. He enters, standing next to her. He reaches down, strokes her head.

At his room, he opens the door and she goes in. Jack follows closing the door behind him. She stops, sits at the side of the bed. He sits on the edge, bends over and kisses her nose. He rolls over onto the bed, lies on his back, looking up at the ceiling. Amaroq hops up onto the bed and curls up next to him. He hugs her neck, squeezing it.

~ * ~

He awakes, still dressed in his bloody T-shirt and clothes, yet they have dried. He notices he is hugging the extra pillow. He opens his clenched fist to find the amaroq claw in his grasp. He rolls over and looks down at the floor but finds nothing there. He climbs out of bed, strolls to the bathroom, and stands over the toilet looking in the mirror while he urinates. He realizes his face isn't swollen or bloody. With his free hand, he rubs it over his face. *That beating happened, I'm sure of it, but how is it that my face has healed?* It's as if that beating had never happened. *How is this possible?*

Jack showers and packs his small bag. *I have to keep moving. Get out of here. Get out of Alaska. Go somewhere. Go anywhere, but keep moving.* Just before turning to leave, he spots the amaroq claw on the bed. He picks it up and stuffs it in his pocket.

In the hallway, he discovers the do-not-disturb sign hanging on his door handle. He doesn't remember putting that on.

At the front desk he checks out. "Three nights, Mr. Douglas," the concierge says. "That'll be four hundred fifty-three and twenty-nine cents."

"No. I was only here the one night. I checked in on the twelfth."

"Ah..." the concierge says dragging out the word, "today is the fifteenth, Mr. Douglas. You've been here three nights."

"Three nights?" He hesitates. *Three nights? Why always three days and three nights?* "Yes," he says at last. "Yes, of course." He pays his bill.

He stands on the street staring. Déjà vu. *Where to?* He starts walking and ends up near where he'd been beaten. He finds his way over to the Port of Anchorage and sits on a sea wall. *Maybe I could get a job on a cruise ship. I've been a deckhand on the Nuliajuk, so how different and difficult could that be? The Nuliajuk. I hope Malik found a replacement and has her still up and running without me.*

"Mr. Douglas?"

Jack turns to see a man he does not recognize approaching.

"What brings you down to Anchorage?"

"Do I know you?"

"No, not really. I worked on the Aga. Malik's other boat in Nome? I saw you come in on the Nuliajuk a few times."

"Oh," Jack says. *Seems I can't get away after all.*

"Malik had to let us go. The crew. He shut down the Aga. Might have to sell it. I'm looking for work on a ship here in Anchorage."

"Selling the Aga?"

"Yes. He's trying to put together enough to buy out Qaniit's uncle and pay off his share of the mortgage for the inn. The uncle is forcing a sale of the inn so he can pay off his debts. Malik can't bear to see Qaniit lose it after she's worked so hard. It's her life, ya know."

Jack nods, squints at him in the sun.

"But, that's not the half of it."

"Why's that?"

"Well, you know Malik is sick?"

"No. Didn't know that."

"Yeah. Battling some form of leukemia for a while now. He might have to close the whole operation because it's getting worse."

Jack looks out at the sea again.

"So, he laid you off too, huh?"

Jack looks back at him but doesn't answer.

"Well, anyway, you take care. I got an interview on a cruise ship." The man hustles off.

Jack sits there. He sighs and rubs his face in his hands. He keeps seeing Akiak smiling at him. He sees Qaniit's sad, lonely blue eyes looking at him then darting away. He feels that ping in his gut again. Yet this time, it turns to pain. His face grows heavy. He's lost energy.

For some reason he sticks his hand in his pocket and squeezes the amaroq claw. He feels a burst of energy, jumps up and hurries back to the hotel, checking in. He puts on his dress shirt and uses the business center to locate what he's looking for.

He finds the office in a small building downtown on 4th Avenue. The office he goes into has no receptionist or greeter, so he heads down a short hallway and finds the door open where he knocks.

"Yes?"

"Mr. Howell?"

Robert Howell glances up from his shabby desk with strewn-about papers.

Jack enters. "Jack Douglas? We met a few days ago."

"Yes. Yes, come in."

"I want to talk to you about the Prospector Inn. I hear you're selling it."

"Was."

Jack stands at the desk, Howell not offering him a seat. "Someone bought it?"

"Well, not quite, but I have a verbal agreement. Donald Prescott? Qaniit's late husband's brother? He's going to buy out my half. Has some crazy notion that it puts him closer to Qaniit and that she'll take to him now. He's been trying to snag her since Mark died."

Jack cocks his head. "I'm sorry?"

"Yes, well, Donald's a real character. He's the older brother, and they all met up there on a fishing trip. The way I understand it Donald tried to make it with her during and after his rocky relationship with his wife, but Qaniit rejected him for Mark. Mark was the more handsome and smarter of the two, and he actually played hard to get with her. Donald regularly was accused of beating his wife. He had a kid with her, but they divorced and he and Mark worked together on Malik's boat, but Malik had to fire Donald after he kept making advances on Qaniit. After Mark died, Donald even tried to make it with Qaniit at the funeral. Can you believe that? He chased her around the kitchen, but she slapped him across the face. Should've seen it." He chuckles. "He would've hit her if weren't for me running in to see the commotion and stopping him."

Jack steadies himself by holding onto the crossbar of a chair in front of the desk. He puts his other hand into his pocket and feels the amaroq claw resting there, squeezing it.

"I have a picture of all of us on a fishing trip." Howell holds up a picture he has on the table beside him with other photos.

Jack takes the picture from him and looks it over.

"That's Donald," Howell says pointing, "His wife, my wife there and the rest of us you know."

Donald, perhaps late twenties at the time, overweight and pre-balding, sits with his arm around a woman. He wears, what Jack has heard some call, a wife-beater tank top. He doesn't smile in the picture, rather smirks. Jack scans Howell and his wife, Qaniit and her husband, Mark, both smiling. He's never seen her smile. She has a beautiful smile. An attractive couple, her eyes look different, more life to them. He hands the picture back to Howell. "Is it final?" Jack says.

"Well, not final, but verbally. The papers are being drawn up as we speak and should be ready in a few days."

Without thinking, Jack blurts out, "I'll double the offer."

"Double?" Howell examines him.

"Cash."

"Cash? Well, that would be two hundred thousand for double."

"Two hundred it is."

Howell leans back in his chair. "What's your angle?"

"No angle. I'll have the papers drawn up so Qaniit's name is the only one on the deed. She owns the whole Prospector outright. I don't want her, or anyone else to know who gifted this. Anonymous payoff."

"You got your eye on her."

"No eye. I can have the money wired in a few days. Then I'm on my way. Leaving Alaska."

He leans forward. "Well, Donald's gonna bust a nut." He chuckles again. "He's a fuckin' hothead. But, money is green. Deal, Mr. Douglas."

Jack shakes his hand and hurries out.

He finds a real estate law firm and instructs the lawyer to draw up the papers so Qaniit will own the whole business. She'll only incur a mortgage for the balance, about one hundred thousand. The lawyer includes language on the documents, stating an anonymous donor paid off the uncle. It's all hers free and clear, no strings attached.

He locates a branch to his bank in Anchorage and finalizes the deal. Howell signs the papers two days later, and the bank wires the money to Howell's account.

Chapter Twenty-one

There are some things one can only achieve by a deliberate leap in the opposite direction.

Franz Kafka

Jack waits around for a week to ensure the deal is finalized, including Qaniit signing off and the deed recorded.

He waits a couple more days after that for documents to be sent from his box in Puckett and to tie up some loose ends with his bank. He has less than thirty thousand left. *I'll have to get a job now for sure. Perhaps go back down to the port and see if anyone's hiring. Maybe a steward on a cruise ship? I could work on another fishing boat somewhere along the Aleutians as a greenhorn on a boat for the upcoming king crab season.*

~ * ~

More than two weeks after arriving in Anchorage, he grabs his bag, tosses it over his shoulder, holding it by one strap, and checks out of the hotel again.

Outside the lobby, adjusting his bag, feeling good about what he's done, he sighs, looks around. That pit in the bottom of his stomach hits, making him feel woozy. He grasps his amaroq claw in his pocket, squeezing it. It gives him that sense of calm again. Peace. A sense of energy. *I'm ready for the next Chapter in my life. Whatever, wherever that is.*

Curbside, turning to head off down the street, a truck honks and snaps him out of his tranquility. That familiar-looking blue Tacoma pulls up next to him.

Akiak jumps from the truck. "Jack," he shouts. He had forgotten to put it into park because it starts to roll away. He jumps back in and puts it into park then hustles out again, running up to Jack, giving him a huge bear hug.

Jack, taken aback, at last raises his arms and pats the kid on the back.

"I knew it was you. I knew you did it. I just knew it."

"Okay," Jack says. "Okay. Don't squeeze me to death."

Akiak pulls back and says, "I knew you'd come back. I just knew it. I told Qaniit you really cared. I told her that. This was all part of your plan, huh?"

Defeated, Jack says, "How did you find out?" *No secrets are safe in Alaska.*

"I called Uncle Robert and said it had to be you. He said no, but I know when he's lying. I've caught him lying before and I know it in his voice. I told him to tell me where you were or I'd tell his wife he cheated on her. I caught him in one of the rooms screwing a tourist a few months ago when he came up to talk about the inn."

"How did you get down here? There are no roads from Nome."

"A cousin owns a ferry that runs between Nome and Prudhoe."

"You drove down from there? All by yourself? On a learner's permit?"

"Yes. He says he can take us back."

"You gotta move this truck," a valet calls out.

"Can you drive, Jack? I'm really tired and don't want to fall asleep and cause an accident or something."

I didn't need to hear that. I don't want to go back. I can't go back. But look at this kid. Look at that grin. And Qaniit? I don't want to see her again. However, I can't let the kid drive all the way back on his own and risk an accident.

Before he can say anything, including no, Akiak jumps into the passenger seat, leaving Jack standing there. Akiak looks at him, smiles, and says, "Let's go, Jack. Come on. Get in." He taps his hand against the door below the window.

Defeated again, Jack tosses his bag into the back of the truck, gets in and pulls off.

"Take a left there." Akiak points.

Jack turns, looks at the kid who smiles back at him.

After Jack navigates through Anchorage with his co-pilot directing him, Akiak says, "I don't think you know grandfather is sick."

Jack glances over at his face that's turned to sorrow, then back at the road. Akiak sniffles, wipes a tear away. "He's dying, Jack. He has leukemia or something. They don't tell me much because they don't want to worry me. I overheard the doctor. You know, the one who treated you, saying he only has a few months, if that." He wipes more tears away.

Jack takes one hand off the wheel and puts it on Akiak's shoulder, squeezing it.

~ * ~

In Cantwell, Jack pulls off for gas, waking Akiak from a nap. The station has a diner so they go in for lunch.

While eating, Akiak says, "I have a confession, Jack."

Jack raises an eyebrow. *Now what?*

"I kinda spied on you." He winces. "I mean, like a detective."

Jack puts his sandwich down, sips milk, waiting for him to continue.

"I hope you won't be mad at me."

"What is it, kid? Spit it out."

"Well, after you left, I just didn't want to believe the note you left. That you couldn't stay. That you were sorry and all. I mean, I knew you cared. I knew you were all that everyone says you are."

"What is it they all say I am?"

"The good one. The Morningstar."

Jack freezes, thinks about that reference. "What does that mean?"

"I'm not really sure. Something about your spirit and the amaroq."

"What about my spirit?" *I thought I had lost it.*

"I'm not really sure."

"You're not really sure about a lot of things."

"No." He looks at his half-eaten sandwich.

"What about the spying?"

"Well, I mean. You're not gonna be mad at me?"

"I'm not going to be mad at you."

"You promise?"

"I promise."

"Well, after you left, I just didn't wanna believe it. I couldn't believe it."

"Believe what?"

"That you didn't like us." His head droops.

Jack sighs. "Akiak, I like you. I like your family. I think they are very beautiful people. You are very hard-working people who care about each other. Care about the land. Care about the sea. Care about your people."

Silence. Jack waits for him to continue. Akiak only looks down at the table. "There's more. What is it?"

"Well," he pauses, "I knew there was something wrong, Jack. I'm sorry."

"Sorry about what?"

"I went on the Internet and saw it. Saw the story in your local paper."

Jack now looks down at his own half-eaten sandwich. *This is exactly what I didn't want to happen. Didn't want anyone to know about me. Didn't want anyone to feel pity for me. Didn't want anyone to care about me. Didn't want to let anyone in.*

"You're still listed as the pastor of your church. It says you're on sabbatical and they have a temporary pastor. I'm so sorry, Jack."

Jack looks him over. "It's okay, kid. Really. It's okay."

"Are you? Going back. To Georgia I mean?"

Jack shakes his head. "No. I'm not."

Akiak takes a bite of his sandwich. He washes it down with soda.

Jack finishes his sandwich. *What am I going to do now? I have to drive the kid back. How can I leave him? Look at that kid's face. It would crush him. It's like I've become his older brother or something. The brother he never had. His grandfather is dying. Qaniit could lose his fishing company unless she can find some help with that. Okay, I'll go back and help out a little while longer. However, at some point, I have to leave. I just have to.*

"I have more to confess." Akiak frowns.

Jack looks at him, raises both his eyebrows. "Yeeeess?"

"You promise you won't be mad at me?"

Jack sighs again, this time in a playful way. "I won't be mad at you." And before Akiak can jump in to ask him if he promises, Jack says, "I promise."

"Well, I sorta told everyone. You know. About what I found on the Internet."

This time Jack sighs for real, but says, "It's okay, kid. But," he wags his finger at him like a nun standing over a disobedient child, "don't go on about it. It happened. It's in the past. I don't want to live in the past."

"Sure. I promise." Akiak lowers his head, yet raises his eyes, looking up at him.

"There's more?"

He nods.

"What else?"

"Well, I sorta told everyone what you did. For Qaniit."

"Sorta?"

"Yeah."

"That was supposed to be a secret."

"I'm sorry."

He nods. "All right. Let's get out of here."

"I'm paying."

"You don't have to."

"I want to." Akiak snatches the bill and heads to the register. Jack shrugs, waits for him at the door. He leads Akiak out with his hand on the kid's shoulder.

Chapter Twenty-two

A man should learn to detect and watch that gleam of light
that flashes across his mind from within.
Ralph Waldo Emerson

Akiak asleep, his head resting against the door, Jack drives on through Fairbanks, seeing the turnoff to Highway 6 for Circle, Alaska. *How apropos that I've come full circle.*

On Highway 11, hours later, they cross the Yukon River, stopping at the Yukon River Camp on the other side. Jack fills the tank and the extra gas cans Akiak keeps in the bed for additional gas because there isn't much out here between towns. While filling the cans, he recalls his trek down the Yukon and his first encounter with Amaroq not far from here. *Again, I hope she's doing okay out there without me.*

He continues on, driving this empty stretch of highway that meanders all the way up to Prudhoe Bay. It's some of the most beautiful scenery in the world, even at night.

Jack's mind races. He looks over at the kid then back at the road. *How am I going to handle this? Businesslike. Help out the Nasak family. Get them through this tough time. Work on the crew of one of his crab boats. Get them through the season then be on my way.*

Several miles out of the village, Jack becomes drowsy. On the side of the road, not far ahead, an animal stands, the truck's headlights catching its reddish-orange eyes glowing back at him. "Can't be," Jack whispers, slowing the truck and stopping. "It just can't be." He stops a few yards from her. She looks at him, her eyes shining like lasers and hitting Jack in his eyes. She lowers her head acknowledging him, raises it again, turns, and trots off into the woods.

"What's going on?" Akiak says yawning and stretching.

"Did you see that?"

"What?"

"Right over there." Jack points to where she had stood.

"No. No, what was it?"

Still looking to where she had been, Jack says, "Nothing. Just an animal cut across the highway."

"You want me to drive?"

"Yeah. You had better take over for a while."

They exchange seats. Jack's eyes grow heavy and he drifts off as Akiak drives on.

~ * ~

Jack stands several feet away off to the side watching the attack play out in front of him like he had been transported back in time and was an unseen observer:

He sees himself walking up the path naked toward his tent to find a grizzly tearing apart his camp and going through his things, the grizzly charges and head-butts him knocking him down, he tries to crawl away but a claw from the bear's massive paw snags the back of his thigh ripping it open, Amaroq sprints out of the woods wrestling, rolling and growling on the ground with the bear until she jumps up howling an ear-splitting tone, the bear scurries off, she licks at his wound for several minutes causing the bleeding to stop and close up, she drags him by his ankle into a crevice and packs mud onto his wound using her paw, she covers him in dirt and leaves and stands over him on guard.

Over the course of the next three days that flash by in an accelerated way, like a fast-forwarded movie, he sees her lick his lips to give him moisture then using her paws uncover and drag him back to his tent where she pulls him in half-way, covering him up to his waist with his sleeping bag. She lies down next to him keeping watch.

~ * ~

He awakes as the sun rises, Akiak driving. Jack stretches and says,

"How long was I out?"

"A few hours." Akiak looks over at him.

"Everything okay?"

"Yeah, but you were having some kind of a dream."

"Why do you say that?"

"You kept saying thank you and I love you over and over again."

Jack rubs his face in his hands. *Crazy. As the kid said, people just believe in things that don't make any sense.*

In Prudhoe, they wait most of the next day for the cousin to load the ferry and cast off. It seems Akiak has many cousins all over the place.

Aboard the ferry, Jack stands at the railing, looking out at the Beaufort Sea. Rounding Barrow, Akiak hands Jack a bottle of water. They stand in silence, sipping their beverages, watching the ocean pass by.

Jack puts his hand in his pocket to feel the amaroq claw. He pulls it out. "Can you do me favor?"

Akiak examines the amaroq claw in Jack's hand.

"Can you find me a new chain for this? I broke it." He hands it to him.

Akiak takes it, nods, and stuffs it in his pocket.

~ * ~

Late evening, the ferry pulls into Nome. Akiak drives the truck off the ferry and back to the Prospector. Climbing the steps and going back in, Jack feels his heart palpitating like that day he ran up the stairs. *I tried to escape, but am right back where I don't want to be. This crazy kid. Like Amaroq, what has he done to me?*

Akiak flips on the hall light. "I'll get a key and get you set up." Behind the counter he locates an available room key and hands it to Jack.

The door to the master suite at the end of the private first-floor hallway opens. Qaniit comes out in her summer nightshirt that hangs down to her knees, her hair hanging down on each side of her face.

"Sorry if we woke you, Cuz," Akiak says.

She edges closer and sees Jack but looks back at Akiak. "You didn't go camping, did you?"

Jack senses an angry tone in her voice.

"No, but look who I found," Akiak says, changing the subject, his voice rising.

"Grandmother is worried sick. You need to get home and wake her to let her know you're in."

"Yes, ma'am." He throws Jack a smile and runs out in a hurry.

They watch him go then look at one another. "You didn't have to do that," she says.

"It's done. No need to talk about it ever again."

"I'm going to pay you back." She goes behind the counter and opens a lock box pulling out the one grand he left in the ledger.

"I won't accept it," he says.

"I don't like owing anyone money."

"I didn't lend you any money."

She comes out from behind the counter and holds up the cash.

"I'm not taking that either."

"Mr. Douglas…"

She sounds exasperated, which is why he quickly cuts her off, "Good night, Qaniit." He heads for the stairs.

"Jack?" she blurts out as if she hadn't meant to.

He freezes at the bottom of the stairs, one foot on the bottom step. He accepted her calling him Mr. Douglas all this time because that way, he realized, and she was right, it was more impersonal, businesslike. Unattached. Now, that barrier had fallen. He doesn't turn back to face her.

"I didn't know. Akiak told me everything. I'm so sorry."

It feels as if someone has taken the wind out of him again, punched him in the gut like those men back in Anchorage.

She moves toward him, standing a couple feet away facing his back. "Jack?" she says at a whisper.

He closes his eyes. He doesn't want to turn around. He doesn't want to face her.

"Are you okay?"

"Yes. Yes, I'm fine. Thank you. Goodnight." He runs up the stairs, leaving her standing there.

In his room, a different one but similar to the other, he tosses his bag onto the desk and sits at the edge of the bed, looking at the wall. His mind races. His heart races. His face flushes and he has this nervous feeling in his stomach. He reaches for his amaroq claw but remembers he had given it to Akiak to fix. He thinks about everything. He thinks about nothing. After a long time, he strips down and crawls onto the bed, lying there staring at the ceiling, hugging a pillow.

~ * ~

He awakes the next morning. *I need to keep to my routine. Workout. Run. Keep busy, keep moving. Don't hang out at the Prospector. Stick to business, helping Malik fish. That is all. Just like on the oil rig. Eat out or buy food to eat in my room. Perhaps try to avoid all people except for those on the boat. On the job.*

After his pushups and sit-ups, he goes for a run.

He passes Akiak, heading to the Prospector in his truck. "Jack, can you come visit Grandfather at his house? I can drive you there after breakfast."

"Sure, kid." Jack jogs on.

"Welcome back, Mr. Douglas," an elderly native man calls out as he passes.

Jack nods and keeps running, turning down another street.

"Hi, Mr. Douglas," a woman with a small child says as he runs past her, the child waving at him.

"Good morning," says another.

Jack, a polite man, nods to them all, but keeps his distance. He returns to the Prospector, sweaty from the summer morning. Just inside the foyer, he wipes sweat from his face, using his shirt-tail and notices Qaniit working in her ledger at the counter catching him doing that.

The lockbox sits open on the counter. She holds up the ten Franklins and says, "I'm putting this in a savings account."

Heading for the stairs and not looking back at her, he says, "It's yours to do whatever you wish."

"Jack," Ulloriaq calls out from behind him.

He freezes at the foot of the stairs and turns to see her hurrying from the kitchen wearing her cook's apron. She rushes him, throwing her arms around his sweaty torso, hugging him, burying her face in his chest. "I'm so sorry," she says.

He looks over at Qaniit who glances at them, then away. He hesitates, but at last raises his arms around Ulloriaq's shoulders. She doesn't seem to want to let up, despite getting his sweat on her apron, arms and face because she only comes up to his mid-chest. "Jack?" she whispers.

"Yes?" Because she spoke softly, he lowers his head so she can speak into his ear.

"Your light *will* grow brighter." She kisses his cheek, straightens her apron, and pulls away. Passing Qaniit on the way back into the kitchen, she says to her, "Yours too."

Qaniit, watching her grandmother pass, glances at Jack who looks over at her. She turns her attention back to the ledger just as fast. He turns away from her at the same speed, sprinting up the stairs.

After breakfast, Akiak drives him to the house where Malik, Ulloriaq and Akiak all live. A small, simple elevated one-story box home with a porch leading into the living room with two bedrooms, Malik sits in a recliner in the living room. He looks pale but rises to greet Jack, shaking his hand. "Please, sit," Malik says motioning for Jack to sit on a sofa adorned with a large crocheted, snow-capped mountain scene. "Thank you, Jack," Malik says, sitting. "For what you did."

Jack nods.

"What're your plans?"

Jack glances up at Akiak standing beside him. "Well, I guess I can help out a little while longer. Whatever you need me to do."

Malik leans forward. "I'd like you to take over the Aga."

"Take over?"

"Yes. I can put together a crew, mostly young men, but need someone to run it."

"I'm not qualified to skipper a boat."

"I don't trust those boys. I mean, they're all too green. Red king crabs are out there now, and we've got to bring them in. All the boats are making a killing. I got Conrad, who is the most experienced, worked with me last crab season, but he needs a strong hand. Jack, you're a natural. A natural-born leader. A quick learner, smart, and can jump right in with little training."

"Oh, I don't know, sir."

"I can help out," Akiak says. "Show you the ropes. Until school starts, of course." He looks at his grandfather.

Malik looks back at him, signaling with his eyes that he sort of approves of that idea. "Whaddaya say, Jack?"

"Well, I...I guess so. Get you through the crab season." He looks at Akiak who smiles at him but wipes it away and looks at the ceiling.

"Thanks, Jack. Again." Malik rises. "You can take the Aga out when you're ready. She's a big beauty. I could have sold her for quite a sum, but, well, this is our life. I provide jobs to the community and product to the buyers. I couldn't let them all down."

"I understand, sir." Jack puts out his hand to shake, but Malik hugs him. Jack slowly raises his arms and pats him on his shoulder blade.

"We'll get up you set up," Malik says, pulling apart. "Here's a book on crabbing." He picks up a book off his end table and hands it to Jack. "All you need to know. The manual for the Aga is in the wheelhouse under the wheel."

"Yes, sir."

Akiak drives Jack back to the Prospector. Looking at the crab fishing book in his lap, Jack glances up at Akiak giving him that silly grin. "What?" Jack snaps.

"You're gonna be great."

"Yeah? You keep getting me into all sorts of trouble."

"You're welcome." He smiles again and drops him off.

Jack sneaks in to avoid Qaniit. He zips up to his room. He lies in bed reading all he ever wanted to know about crab fishing.

Chapter Twenty-three

The purpose of life is a life of purpose.
Robert Bryne

Jack arrives at the Aga before the crew. He boards and unlocks the cabin then climbs the stairs to the wheelhouse. He lays the crab fishing book on the console and locates the manual under the wheel in a compartment. The Aga, he reads, means mother in Inuit. The Aga's a one-hundred and eight-foot steel-hull boat with a Caterpillar-built D398 turbo-charged after-cooled engine that produces eight hundred and fifty horsepower to drive three stainless steel propellers. It has two backup engines for auxiliary power.

He sizes up the console then strolls about the deck and, using the manual, inventories the equipment, the supplies, the first aid kits, the radio, the GPS, the emergency fire extinguishers, the life vests and raft. He goes below deck to look at the engines and the cabin that can house ten guys with its bunks, galley and head.

Akiak drives up in his truck followed by three boys in their own trucks. Jack waits for them on board.

"Jack," Akiak says, "This is Conrad, your deck boss, Dylan and Jonah deckhands. Oh, I can be a deckhand too."

"You're the greenhorn," Conrad says, giving him a noogie.

Jack shakes each of their hands. Upon hearing the name Jonah, he raised one eyebrow, thinking about the Bible story and hoped the kid wouldn't be swallowed by a fish on his watch. All kids in their early twenties, Jack is indeed the elder on board. He hopes he can live up to the task. Conrad and Dylan are Caucasian and Jonah, Inuit.

The bait truck drops off the bait, codfish. Jack signs for it. The boys stow it in the ice locker. "Gentlemen," Jack says, "let's take her out for a haul."

"Aye, aye, captain," Akiak says, saluting him.

"Knock it off," Jack says. "You're just along for the ride." The boys stow their gear and raincoats in the cabin.

"Cast off," Jack says to them. He starts the engines. Two boys grab a line each and cast away. Jack edges through the harbor and out into the sound.

A beautiful day, Jack pilots the Aga at a steady pace at about seven knots, although the Aga can go twelve. The waves lap against her hull and the cool ocean breeze blows a steady headwind. All four boys stand on deck, surveying the water. Jack takes her out fifty miles, consults his computer monitors, deciding this is the spot for a good honey-hole, or area where reports suggest crab dwell.

Jack cuts the engine, climbs down from the wheelhouse onto the deck. "Now listen up," he says. "Pay attention." He looks over at Akiak. "Watch out for the launcher and stay clear of the pots. I don't need any broken legs. I don't expect bad weather, so we don't have to worry about the waves on deck. But don't fall overboard. I can't save you this time." He looks at Akiak again.

The eight-hundred-pound crab pots, box-shaped steel traps, are seven by eight feet, constructed of wire meshing. The Aga accommodates about one hundred and fifty, tightly stacked and lashed-together pots on deck.

Conrad operates the crane, lifting a pot onto the launcher, the flat metal hydraulic lift on a hinge. Akiak opens the trap door of the pot. He bait-rigs a bag with codfish, hangs it inside the pot, and closes the trap door. Jonah engages the launcher that lifts up on its hinge sliding the pot into the water. Dylan tosses the length of the rope, called a shot, into the sea. Akiak throws the buoys, used to retrieve the pot, into the sea after it.

It takes all day to bait-rig and put all the pots in where they will soak or rest on the sea-bottom to catch the crabs for the next twenty-four to forty-eight hours, depending on what they haul in tomorrow.

"Come up here, boys," Jack says over the PA to the crew on deck late that afternoon as he drifts the Aga. They climb the stairs and gather around Jack in the wheelhouse.

"You boys did a fine job," Jack says. "Get some dinner and rest. We'll navigate back to the first string in the morning and see what we get. We'll head in after we fill all the tanks."

"Yeah, get your beauty rest, Jonah," Dylan says, laughing and punching his arm.

"Ha, ha," Jonah says. "Keep him out here forever, Jack. Twenty-four seven. That way it'll keep him away from my sis."

"I'm marrying that girl, bro."

"The day you're my brother-in-law is the day *I* stay out twenty-four seven."

"What about you, little bro?" Conrad says to Akiak. "I hear you got your eye on Massak." He elbows Akiak in the ribs.

"I dunno," Akiak says. "She's only fifteen."

"Only fifteen?" Jonah chuckles. "You better hurry up then before she gets away."

"I heard he only likes white girls," Dylan says.

Jack scans the boys. *Typical boys. No different anywhere in the world.*

"That's not true," Akiak says. "I'm diverse."

"Diverse?" Jonah says, laughing. "Now that's funny."

Jonah catches a little smile on Jack's lips. "Hey, I got Captain Jack to crack a smile," Jonah says. "Look."

"Knock it off," Jack says, his hand resting on the wheel. "I might hit a wave or something."

"Hit a wave." Conrad laughs. "He's funny too."

"Hey, captain," Jonah says, "I hear ya got your eye on a certain native princess."

"I've got my eye on the ocean."

"His eye on the ocean," Jonah says. They all laugh.

Jack catches Akiak eyeing him, laughing too.

"She's one fine pretty lady," Dylan says, elbowing Conrad and winking. "You better catch her now, Jack, before someone else does."

Jack ignores that and says, "You can have first watch, Conrad. Here's the schedule, boys." He hands them a computer print-out for the night-watch schedule in the wheelhouse.

~ * ~

After breakfast the next morning at five o'clock, the boys prep for the haul. Conrad services the power block winch, a special mechanized winch with an aluminum pulley and a hard rubber-coated sheave where the string will wind up and raise the pots. The crew stands around, watching him work on it.

Jack brings the Aga around to the first string of pots. Jonah, as the pot-retriever, tosses in the grappling hook attached to a rope to capture the first string. His hook makes contact with the string. He pulls it in. Dylan passes off the string to Conrad who wraps it around the hydraulic winch. He hoists the string and brings the pot to the surface. Jonah and Dylan guide it back onto the launcher. Dylan operates the launcher, tilting it up at an angle back toward the deck. Jonah opens the trap door spilling a sizable haul of crabs onto the sorting table. Dylan shouts up to Jack, "We've got serious crab here, Captain Jack."

The boys whoop and holler. *A first sizable pot haul.* Jack smiles at the boys, admiring their childish enthusiasm.

Jonah and Dylan sort the crabs, using U-shaped hand-held crab gauges to measure their size and to make sure they are males. They toss the crabs to keep into the saltwater holding tank then throw back the crabs that don't meet specifications, namely the females and the juveniles.

With each pot, the crew hauls in dozens of crab. Jack has the crew re-bait the pots and drop them back in.

~ * ~

The Aga stays out for the week and fills up all three tanks.

Around noon a week after departing, the Aga pulls into Nome. Jack docks. The crew unloads the catch for the buyer who hauls it off. They hose down the deck, clean the hold and help Jack conduct the inventory.

Ulloriaq drives up to the dock with Malik. He climbs out, shuffling over to the boat with the aid of a cane. "How'd the boys do?" Malik says, steadying himself on the light pole at the dock.

"Good," Jack says. "They're a great crew."

"I'm glad," Malik says. "Akiak, you go over and help Qaniit with dinner. I need to talk with Jack."

Jack doesn't like the sound of that. Neither does Akiak who frowns, yet obeys.

"We'll go out again next week, boys," Jack says.

"You got it, Jack," Conrad says. The crew hustles off.

Jack follows Malik down the dock to the truck. "Climb in, will ya, Jack?"

Jack climbs into the truck, sitting in the middle of the seat while Malik sits next to him. Ulloriaq drives them over to the office on the other side of the harbor.

Jack follows them into a small, one-story, one-room office where a sign on the door reads, "Nasak Fishing Company." Malik hobbles over to a desk and sits. He pulls out a key, handing it to Jack. "For the office, Jack."

Jack regards the key.

"I'm bringing on Rhonda Perch to help out here in the office. She used to work for me a while back. But I need someone to, well, sort of help manage all of this. Buyers, supplies, payroll, insurance. You know, all that business stuff."

"I didn't go to business school, sir."

"Yes, but you managed a, well, a church, right?" he says as if trying not to upset Jack.

Jack doesn't answer. He looks over at Ulloriaq. She presses her lips together.

Silence. Everyone waits for the other to say something, anything.

"Jack, I'm dying." He looks at his wife. "Ulloriaq and Qaniit know much of this, but they need help. You'll be compensated, of course."

I can't believe they're doing this to me. Putting this on me. This is not part of the plan. I promised them a while, but not forever, yet I can't tell them that here, now, under these circumstances.

"I trust you, Jack. You're like none I've ever known. What you did, I cannot believe anyone else on this whole earth would have done that." He looks at his wife again. "Ulloriaq doesn't know what I'm about to reveal, because I just found out."

"Sir, you don't have to say anything. About whatever you're going to say."

"I want to say it." He shifts in his seat. "Jack paid double for Robert's half of the Prospector to get him to agree to the sale."

"Double?" she says, gasping.

"Double," he says again. "Cash. Two hundred thousand."

Jack looks down at the key in his hand.

"Jack," she says coming over to him and squeezing his hand.

"Okay," Jack says. "Okay. Enough already. You people have been so kind to me. I'll stay a while to help out. To get things going. Get you through the crab season. I have one condition, however."

"Name it," Malik says.

"Actually, two things. We're going to hire some help for Qaniit. She can't do it all at the inn. The housekeeper is one thing, but she needs help in the restaurant, another waiter, perhaps a dishwasher too. Find a couple kids to help out after school or something."

"What's the other thing?"

"She needs to take a day or two off a week. For herself. Do anything to get away from the place for a few hours." He looks at Ulloriaq. "You too. We'll make it work."

"Well," Ulloriaq says, "you'll have to tell her that."

"You're her grandmother. She won't listen to me."

"She won't listen to me either."

"We'll see about that then," Jack says.

Ulloriaq twists her lips at him.

They drive Jack to the Prospector and drop him off.

Inside, Qaniit looks up from the counter while working in her ledger when he enters. "Leave your clothes by the door, Jack."

"No," he says. "You take care of business here and I'll wash them."

"But, Jack, I…"

"But Jack nothing." Before she can say anything further, he sprints up the stairs.

In his room, he strips down and tosses his clothes on the floor. He wraps a towel around his waist and heads for the shower. In the shower, he soaps up. He feels good about the haul he and the boys brought in. It would fetch tens of thousands of dollars to pay the boys a fine percentage, cover costs and keep everything running. It's good, honest work. Although he thought his former profession was as well, this work left him invigorated in a different way.

Downstairs, he heads for the door where Qaniit still works at the counter. "Do you want some dinner, Jack?"

"Oh, no. Thank you. I'll just find something on the town."

"You sure? It's no problem."

"I'm fine. Thank you." He hurries out the door.

Outside, Akiak pulls up in his truck with some items for the restaurant, vegetables and fruit. He climbs from his truck.

"Jack," he says in a subdued tone with a long face gathering his grocery bags from the truck's bed.

"You okay, kid?"

"School starts Monday."

"So. You're a kid. Finish school."

"I'd rather go out with you."

"Look. Here's what you do. You finish school, take some business classes, and take over the business."

"I thought you're taking over the business?"

Jack frowns. "It's your family business. I'm just an employee."

"It could be your family business," he says, smiling.

"What are you talking about?"

Still smiling, he says quickly, his voice rising, "You could marry Qaniit and it's all in the family."

"Would you stop with that nonsense? You have to be in love to get married."

He continues to smile at Jack in a cheesy way.

"Knock it off," Jack says. "Don't be ridiculous."

"I saw the way you looked at her."

"Hey, I was a man of God." He pulls away from the kid and walks into town. *That kid's gonna get me in more trouble.*

Jack doesn't find anything to eat that fancies him. His stomach empty, yet for some reason he doesn't feel like eating, he meanders back to the Prospector, sneaks in, and darts up to his room. He strips down, lies on the bed, looking at the ceiling. He can't sleep. He tosses, turns on the light, and tries to look through a new Alaskan guide book he bought in Anchorage before Akiak showed up. He can't concentrate, so he closes it and picks up off the nightstand his worn, creased and fading family photo. He looks at it for the longest time. It has been over two years but seems like yesterday. He runs his fingers over his children's faces, stopping on Janette's. After a couple of minutes, he puts the photo back onto the nightstand against his Bible, staring at it. He curls up with the extra pillow, hugging it again.

Chapter Twenty-four

What is a friend? A single soul dwelling in two bodies.
Aristotle

Akiak starts the new school year.

Summer has slipped away and autumn arrives. Jack skippers the Aga on several runs. Sky joins the crew. As the deck boss, Conrad supervises and teaches them all the jobs because Jack might need to switch up the two crab crews between the boats.

When piloting the boat and supervising the boys, Jack feels at ease, similar to how he felt with Amaroq. He misses her. He never thought he would crab fish the Bering Sea on a commercial fishing boat. Although working the drilling rig took his mind off his past for the several months he was there, it didn't compare to this. While supervising the boys, he admires their camaraderie, their banter about girls and life, their innocence, and their sense of wonder working out on the sea. In-between hauls, however, he hangs out at the office, pushing papers and keeping busy. He stays away from the Prospector except to sleep. He often eats alone in the office or his room. He even sneaks into the kitchen after hours.

After the crew set the pots one day, they hang with Jack in the wheelhouse who teaches them techniques on skippering. "Hey, Jack?" Dylan says, "I did it."

"Yeah?"

"I proposed to Jonah's sister."

"You dog," Conrad says, looking at Dylan but slapping Jonah on his back. Jonah glares at him.

"Congratulations," Jack says. He looks at Jonah and says, "Jonah, shake his hand."

"Oh, Jack," he says, whining.

"You congratulate your brother-in-law to be or I have to can you." Jack winks at Conrad who smiles back at him.

Jonah frowns. "I can't even think about this creep touching my sister."

"Are you kidding?" Jack puts his arm around Dylan, pinching his cheek. "Look at this cute face. Your sister will be a lucky woman to have such a stud." *I can't believe I said that. I've never acted this way before.* "Now, come on. Get over here."

Jonah edges closer. Jack whispers in Dylan's ear. Jonah snaps, "What?"

Dylan outstretches his hand. Jonah squirms but reaches up to shake it.

Dylan grabs his hand and pulls him in for a bear hug, kissing him on his cheek. "Yuk," Jonah says, scowling and breaking from the embrace.

Conrad laughs. "He just wanted to practice for his sister on you," he says.

Dylan and Conrad roar as Jonah wipes the cooties from his face. Jack has a large grin across his face too. "All right," Jack says. "Get out of here and clean up below."

The boys file out. Jack sits alone in the wheelhouse, looking out at the Bering Sea rolling before him, the Aga gently pitching from side to side. He sits back in the skipper's chair, monitoring the navigational equipment.

They stay out for a full haul, a little over a week and a half this time.

~ * ~

Akiak works dinners at the Prospector after school, and breakfast and dinner on the weekends.

One afternoon after school, Akiak drives up to the Prospector around four o'clock to help prep for dinner. Grandmother hasn't arrived yet because he doesn't see her truck. Grabbing a bag of vegetables from the bed of the truck, he zips up the porch steps and hears someone inside, shouting.

He enters and sees two retired tourists creeping down the stairs. The

man says to Akiak, "In the kitchen, I think. There's someone fighting."
They hear a loud crash of pots and pans and more yelling. The man looks
at his wife as Akiak rushes into the kitchen.

He sees Donald, Qaniit's deceased husband's brother fully dressed
but simulating intercourse by thrusting his pelvis and grinding it up against
Qaniit at the wall. "Why do you play so hard to get?" Donald says,
struggling with her. "You know you want it."

She hits him over and over and tries to push him back. Akiak hasn't
seen this man in a long time, but he has grown even more of a flabby belly,
is bald, except for a thin comb over, and wears jeans and a dirty T-shirt.
Donald grabs and holds Qaniit's arms above her head and leans in to kiss
her. She knees him in the groin. "You cunt," he shouts in agony, recoiling
and slapping her.

Akiak throws the bag of vegetables onto the floor and dashes over
to him, kicking pots and pans strewn about on the floor out of his way. "Get
your hands off her." He charges Donald as a linebacker would.

Donald crashes into the prep table and wrenches his back.
"Awwww," he screams. "You fuckin' punk."

Akiak darts over to guard Qaniit who has a bloody nose and mussed
hair. She brushes at her hair and wipes blood onto the back of her hand.

"You little fuckin' Injun." Donald attacks Akiak, throwing a punch,
hitting him in the gut.

Qaniit breaks away and runs over to the counter. Akiak gets in a
couple punches hitting Donald in the face and neck, but Donald throws
another punch striking Akiak in the eye. Akiak steps back, smarting.

Qaniit picks up a large butcher knife, points it at Donald while
holding it at her waist, and in firm voice says, "Get out, Donald."

The man and his wife open the kitchen door and step inside. "We
called the police," he says. "They're on the way."

Donald, sweating like a hog, straightens himself and surveys Qaniit
holding the knife and the couple standing at the door. "This ain't over." He
sticks his tongue out at her moving it up and down like a snake. Making a
fist, he tightens his face, looks over at Akiak and says, "You watch it,
Injun."

Still training the knife on him, Qaniit backs up to allow him to pass.

Donald swaggers past the couple who hold open the swinging door. The woman enters the kitchen while the man stands in the doorjamb, watching Donald depart.

"You okay, Cuz?" Akiak says, rubbing his eye.

Shaking, she says, "I'll be okay." She sets the knife down and grabs a plastic reusable food bag, gets ice from the freezer and applies it to Akiak's eye.

The woman grabs some paper towels off the holder, wets some, and offers them to Qaniit. "Here, honey. Your nose is bleeding." Qaniit pinches her nose and wipes the blood away with her other hand holding the towel.

~ * ~

Jack works late in the office with Rhonda Perch, a mixed Inuit. "So, the invoice," she says pointing, "you sign it here, and here. We file it in the tray on the filing cabinet for collection."

Malik told Jack that Perch, in her fifties, worked for him before. She stopped to raise kids and had been helping with the grandkids, but they were all adults now so she agreed to return and help out. "A lot to learn," Jack says.

"Running a business ain't easy, but you'll get the hang of it."

"Thanks, Rhonda."

"Well, I'll come in tomorrow, but in the afternoon, I'm babysitting for a cousin."

"Family comes first," Jack says.

Rhonda gathers her purse. Just before going through the door, she turns to Jack. "Jack?"

"Yes?"

"Thank you."

"For what?" He stands at the filing cabinet, holding the invoices looking back at her. "I'm the one who should be thanking you because I have no clue about any of this."

"You're a true friend to the Nasak family."

Jack watches her go. He sits behind the desk, rubs his eyes with the thumb and index finger of his left hand, and scans the papers on the desk.

A little while later, Jack yawns, stretches, closes the office and walks the mile back to the Prospector. At the porch stairs, he stops and sees the restaurant is dark. *Huh? It's not past six-thirty. Why is the restaurant closed?*

Inside, he looks around but sees no dinner crowd, no Akiak, no Qaniit, no one. He goes into the dark kitchen. *It's unusual, because it amounts to a substantial loss in revenue for the Prospector. Something is not right.*

He heads back into the lobby by the counter and glances around then looks down the hall to Qaniit's room. He sees a light under the door so he heads down the hall and taps lightly. "Qaniit? You there?"

A moment later, she's standing on the other side of the door. "Yes?" she says through the door.

"Why is the restaurant closed? Something wrong?"

"Oh, no. No. We had to close it for the night for a situation. We'll open for breakfast. I can make you something."

"What situation?"

"Nothing to worry about. I'll be up in a few minutes with something to eat."

"Thank you, but I can make my own dinner."

"No, Jack. I'll get it. That's an order. Stay out of my kitchen. You left the cheese out last time."

Oops. Busted.

"Put your clothes by the door."

He sighs. "You're impossible."

"Thank you."

"That's not a compliment."

"I didn't take it as one."

"Okay. Okay. I'm going up to my roooooom now," he says dragging out the word like a kid would to an authoritative parent. He heads upstairs.

In his room, he strips down and puts his clothes in a laundry bag. He wraps a towel around his waist, drops the laundry bag outside the door and makes his way to the shower.

He just gets back inside his room after his shower when he hears a tap at his door. "Coming." He opens the door, but Qaniit has placed a tray with his dinner on the floor and picked up the laundry bag heading for the stairs. "Qaniit?" he calls after her.

Dressed in her nightshirt below her knees, she stops at the top of the stairs but doesn't turn around. "I made you a sandwich," she says over her shoulder. She starts down the stairs.

Something's not right. She seems more solemn, if that is possible. I shouldn't run after her, I don't want to run after her. However, as a pastor, a counselor, he knew when people were not forthcoming. He knew when something was wrong. It's his nature to get people to open up so he can help them, guide them, and give them support. So, he grabs his robe from the hook on the door, hurrying after her.

At the bottom of the stairs, just before she is about to go into the laundry room, he catches up with her. "What's wrong?"

She stops but again doesn't turn around, her head down and away looking at the floor. "Nothing. Everything is fine, Jack."

"You're not good at lying." Dark, and from behind, he can't see her face. He would never put his hands on her and force her to turn around, so he shoots around in front of her. She looks away from him. He has to jockey his head to get a look at her face. "Would you stop?" he says in a teasing voice.

She does, but doesn't look up at him.

At last, he reaches in and turns the light to the laundry room on catching a glimpse of her swollen black eye. "What happened?" he says, his voice cracking.

"Just a little accident. Nothing to worry about."

"Qaniit, stop, please and look at me."

She slowly raises her head but still looks at the floor.

"This was not an accident, was it?"

Defeated, he senses, because she shakes her head slowly.

"Please. We're friends, right?" At last, he realizes this.

She nods at the same speed she shook her head.

"You're not going to tell me?"

She finally looks into his eyes. "Jack, I don't want to involve you." She looks away again.

"Well, I think your cousin and grandfather have already done a good job at that."

"You've got the company to worry about. I don't want to…"

"I'm not letting you pass until you tell me."

She looks at him again and says, her voice firm, "Last guy who stood in front of me got a knee between his legs."

Jack cocks his head to show her he's not playing.

"Okay. Promise me you won't go on about it. I can handle this."

"I can see that you did." He raises his eyebrows.

She tells him what happened.

"Where did he go?"

"He lives in Anchorage, somewhere. Already flew out before the police could get to him. They issued a warrant."

"Okay, but as long as I'm around, you let me know if he comes back."

"Jaaaack," she says.

"Qaniiiiit," he says imitating her.

She presses her lips together.

"How's the kid?"

"Matching eye, but his one is the left. He says he's going to show it off in school."

"Crazy kid." Jack reaches for and takes the bag of laundry from her.

"Jaaaack," she says like she had before.

"You're going to rest. I'm doing my own laundry, thank you very much."

She sighs. "Jack."

"Jack nothing." He raises an eyebrow.

Without thinking about or commanding himself to do it, he takes her hand, leading her down the hall to her room. Her hand is soft, warm, and makes his heart race. At her door, he lets her hand go. "Now get some rest. That's an order." As fast as their eyes lock onto one another, they look away.

"The laundry soap is in the cabinet above the washing machine and you wash in regular cycle and..."

    "I know how to do laundry, Qaniit. Goodnight."

    "Goodnight, Jack," she whispers after him.

    He heads back down the hall into the darkness.

Chapter Twenty-five

All say, "How hard it is that we have to die"- a strange complaint to come from the mouths of people who have had to live.

Mark Twain

On the Aga a week later, Jack skippers the boat back to Nome after another full haul. Making some serious money for the company, he's proud and pleased he's doing his part to help Malik while he battles his illness.

From the wheelhouse he sees Dylan standing looking over the gunwale. A little choppy on the return, a wave crashes up onto the deck, almost taking him with it on its journey back into the sea.

"Dylan," Jack yells over the PA. In an agitated tone, something the boys have never heard from him before, he says, "Get back into the cabin and stay there. That's an order."

Dylan looks up, saluting him.

"Take over," Jack says to Conrad in the co-skipper chair next to him. Jack bolts from his chair, hurrying down onto the deck. The other boys rush out of the cabin to see what's going on.

"Keep your head in the game at all times," Jack says, his voice stern. "You know those waves crash up onto the deck like that."

Sky says, standing there, "Come on, captain. Everyone knows how you're superman and saved Akiak. That you have the spirit of the amaroq."

"That's nonsense, and you know it," Jack hollers at him. "That was a once in a million chance. You see how choppy it is out here? They're no certainties in life. You know how you could be swept over and thrown back against the hull or worse, dragged under and chewed up by the propellers. Now, knock it off and pay attention."

"Yes, captain," Dylan whispers, his head lowered.

Jack is well aware of this myth the townsfolk spun, that he's some sort of spirit, god, superhero, or whatever crazy nonsense. He knows that's further from the truth. Yes, he worked out, and with his adrenaline exploding that day, had been lucky to save Akiak. However, he's just an ordinary man like anyone. Just an ordinary man.

He climbs the stairs, goes back into the wheelhouse and sits in the co-skipper's chair where he stares out at the sea in front of him. Conrad glances at him. "You want the helm, Jack?"

"What?"

"The helm. You want the helm?"

He snaps out of his thoughts and looks over at him. "No. No, you're doing fine." Jack's mind races. He keeps debating the same conflictions over and over again in his head. He thinks about how he's become a father-figure to these boys. How they need him. How Malik needs him to run the company. He wanted to come up here and start a new business. Change professions. Could he stay here to crab, salmon, and halibut fish year-round? Could he continue to manage Malik's business? Indefinitely? He debates all of this. He wants to stay, but he wants to leave. He's gotten too close to these people. Look what happened to his family. Look what happened to Sanders. Every time he got close to anyone they were taken from him. He had only wanted to open and run a business, alone, or with Sanders, not to get to know or get close to anyone. How crazy does that sound? He has to move on at some point, after crab season, he keeps telling himself. *Perhaps Ronny or Conrad or Sky can be promoted to captain and take over the Aga. Why can't Miles run the company?* Although this new job has taken his mind off his troubles, his past, he doesn't belong here. These are not his people. Then there's Qaniit. Despite the teasing he endures, he only likes her as a friend, right? She's very beautiful and smart, but he doesn't want to get any closer than he has already. She's not his people. Further, he senses, she doesn't want to get any closer to him because he feels her distance. He tried having a wife. She was taken from him. He tried having a family. They were taken from him too. He did everything right, per the Book. Still, it all had come crashing down. He doesn't want to take that chance again. Ever. *I can't.*

"You okay, Jack?" Conrad says.

He doesn't answer.

"Jack?"

"What?"

"Are you okay?"

"I'm fine. Why?"

He shakes his head, shrugs. "Can I take her in?"

"What?"

"The Aga. Can I take her in to dock?"

"Sure. You're ready."

"Thanks, Jack.

"For what?"

"Showing confidence in me."

"You're doing a great job." Jack looks out at the lonely sea again.

Back at dock, the crew unloads and cleans the ship. Jack inventories. He walks to the office, completes paperwork, staying late, and sneaks into the Prospector well after hours.

~ * ~

For the next several days he avoids everyone, including Qaniit, Ulloriaq and Akiak, even sneaking into the kitchen to make sandwiches late at night, making sure he puts everything back into the frig and cleans up after himself. He leaves his clothes outside his door for Qaniit to wash, lest she get after him. Twice now he spoke through the door when she came by, explaining to her that he was tired and going to bed. Truth was, however, he'd lie on his bed staring at the ceiling in the dark until he fell asleep each night. He tried reading a couple books he bought to help him get to sleep, but he couldn't concentrate. He's also having strange dreams where Amaroq stands over him yelping as if she's angry and scolding him. *Complete madness. Madness.*

~ * ~

Jack makes his way downstairs after his workout, a run and a shower one morning a couple days later. He ducks out the door without any breakfast. Akiak intercepts him on the porch. "Where've you been, Jack? Haven't seen you in a week."

"Got a business to run, kid. Aren't you supposed to be in school?"

"It's Sunday."

Sunday? He thinks about that.

"Hey, I forgot to give you this back," Akiak says. "I got it fixed a while ago." He hands Jack the amaroq claw on a new chain.

Jack studies it in his hand as if it's a long-lost heirloom.

"Here," Akiak says, picking it out of Jack's palm. He unlatches the clasp and puts it around Jack's neck where it rests outside his T-shirt against his sternum.

"Thanks, kid." He tries to get away.

"You okay, Jack?"

"What?" Jack snaps, going down the steps. "What are you talking about?"

"I don't know." Akiak shifts on his feet, looking down at him.

"You don't know? Then why did you ask me?"

"It's just that, well..."

"Akiak, you're the one acting strange."

"Are you sick or something?"

"Sick? I'm fine, kid. Get in there and get to work."

"Yes, captain."

"Knock off the captain nonsense."

"You're funny, Jack."

"Get to work."

Akiak goes inside.

Jack tries to get away but doesn't escape fast enough as Ulloriaq pulls up in Malik's truck.

"Good morning, Jack," she says through the open window, stopping near him.

"Good morning, Ulloriaq."

She climbs out. "You want the truck today?"

"No, thank you. I need to walk."

"Okay."

She closes the door. "It's not long now, Jack."

"I'm so sorry, Ulloriaq." Without thinking, he reaches out and takes her hand, squeezing it.

She looks into his eyes, like Amaroq used to. "Jack, whatever I can do to help, you just let me know."

"What do you mean? I should be asking you that." He lets her hand go.

"Just you being here is enough."

"Look, Ulloriaq, I truly thank you for your concern, but I'm fine. Everything's fine. Please. You have Malik to worry about, not me. Which reminds me, we've got to get you some help here at the restaurant. You should be home with him."

"You know who hasn't agreed to that yet."

"I thought you were going to talk to her," he says.

"I thought *you* were going to talk to her."

Jack looks over his shoulder back at the Prospector. "Well, we'll see."

"She's stubborn, but won't bite you, Jack."

"Yeah, I know. Stubborn. Not the biting." He tries to get away again.

"Oh, I forgot to tell you."

Jack turns back to her.

"The police arrested Donald Prescott. He's to appear in court in Nome. Not sure of the date."

"You think he's dangerous?"

She cocks her head and nods. "He's not stable. A hothead. Unpredictable."

"I want to know if he ever bothers anyone. Okay?"

She nods again. "Okay, Jack."

He walks off down the street, heading to the office.

~ * ~

One night a few days later, after spending most of the day in the office, Jack works on getting caught up with the paperwork, payroll, and

175

invoices, ordering, paying bills, and prepping for the next haul. Next to his desk, he takes a sandwich out of the small refrigerator he bought to keep meals in so he wouldn't have to mess up Qaniit's kitchen, and to avoid her.

Taking his first bite, the office phone rings. Quickly washing his food down with water, he answers on the third ring, "Nasak Fishing Company. This is Jack speaking."

"Jack? It's Qaniit," she says barely audible. "Grandfather passed. We're all going to the house now."

His heart skips a beat, not only because he hasn't heard her voice in days, but with this news. He doesn't want to go to the house. This is a time for family to be together. He is not family but an employee.

"Can you pick me up on the way?" she says.

Oh, great. Ulloriaq had given him the truck for a supply run for the boat this day. Although as a pastor he had helped those in this state of mourning, it's no longer his place. He doesn't belong, either as a family-member, or as a pastor. But, she needs a ride. "Okay," he whispers. He hangs up and drives to the Prospector.

Qaniit waits for him on the porch, her long, black hair blowing across her tender, snowy-white face. As he watches her walk over to the truck, he can't help but think how she has seen so much tragedy in her life. She climbs in, brushes her hair aside, tucking it behind her left ear and revealing to him such a sad face he feels *he* might die all over again. First her parents, then her husband, now her grandfather. Malik had raised her. Her protector is gone.

After she buckles in, he spontaneously reaches over, takes her hand in his, gently squeezing it. She looks over at him and he removes his hand, putting it on the wheel to drive.

They ride in silence. Jack glances over at her once, but she stares out through the windshield.

He pulls up, parks and shuts off the engine. She climbs out, starts for the house, but looks back at Jack sitting in the truck. She doubles back, comes over to the open driver window. "What's wrong?"

He looks at her. "Nothing. I'll take you back when you're done." He looks away from her.

"You're not coming in?"

"No. No, I, I don't think I should. It's a time for family." He looks back at her as her hair falls off her ear and covers half of her moonlit face.

She once again brushes at her hair tucking it behind her ear. "Jack, you've been a part of our family for a while now."

Family? He turns his head away from her again and reaches for the amaroq claw, squeezing it.

"What's wrong?"

"Nothing." Hiding it from her, he wipes at his eye to catch a tear.

Qaniit opens the truck's door, takes his hand. "Come on," she says.

"Are you sure?"

"I'm sure." She tugs on his hand, but he doesn't budge. "Would you come on?" she says, pulling.

Defeated, again, he gets out of the truck. As she leads him inside by his hand, his heart races.

The door opens to reveal many family members including aunts, uncles, cousins, and Ulloriaq and Akiak, who both spot the handholding as they come through the door. Qaniit and Jack release their hands. The family surrounds them. Ulloriaq hugs Jack. The aunts, uncles, and cousins all take turns hugging Qaniit and Jack.

Jack has flashbacks. Memories, sorrow, pain. A sniffling Akiak comes over and hugs him, dripping tears on his shoulder. Jack squeezes the kid and says, "I know, kid. I know."

They stay for a little while, until after the funeral director retrieves Malik's body. Jack drives Qaniit back to the Prospector, both riding in silence.

Inside, Jack heads for the stairs as Qaniit closes the front door. "Jack?" she calls to him.

He stops and half-turns to face her.

"Thank you," she says. "For coming in." She walks over to him, standing a foot away. "It means a lot to me."

His heart beats faster. He wants to run upstairs, crash down his door, and bury himself in the pillows and hide like he has done so many times these past weeks. "I'm so sorry, Qaniit. Whatever I can do to help." He looks down at the first step of the stairs.

She examines something on his face and reaches up. He flinches, but she wipes at a small tear welling under his eye. He closes his eyes, tight.

"I'm so sorry, Jack," she says.

He opens his eyes and discovers tears now dripping from her eyes onto her cheeks. He reaches up and wipes some tears from her cheek with the tips of his fingers. However, she sheds more and begins to quiver. He reaches out and pulls her close, hugging her tightly. She buries her face in his chest.

They embrace for quite some time. Sobbing, she soaks his Prospector T-shirt with her tears. After a minute, perhaps two, they pull back and look into one another's eyes. *Her soul is as void as mine.*

Out of nowhere, and at the same time, they kiss and hold it.

In an abrupt second, just as fast as they kissed, they pull apart. "I'm sorry," Jack says pulling away, looking down and away from her. "I...I don't know what I was thinking."

"No," she says backing away. "No. No, I'm sorry. I...I don't know what *I* was thinking."

She hurries to her room, Jack watching, feeling like a fool for letting that happen, taking advantage of her grief. *That is not me. Who I am. I've never acted like this in my entire life. What was I thinking? Was I thinking?*

He sprints up to his room and does what he had wanted to do all along, jump into bed, curl up, and hug his pillow. He glances over at his family photo propped up against his Bible. He lies there, staring.

Chapter Twenty-six

The heart wants what it wants – or else it does not care.
Emily Dickinson

"Yelp," Amaroq snaps, standing over him.
"What?"
"Yelp." She shakes her head from side to side as if she's trying to put to death a kill between her jaws.
"Enough. Enough already."
"Yelp." She nudges Jack's head and licks his face.

~ * ~

He awakes and glances at the clock to discover it is only two in the morning. *Even Amaroq messes with me while sleeping.* He lies there for several minutes unable to fall back to sleep. Jack tosses one way, then the other.

Thirty minutes later and thirsty, he puts his robe on then goes downstairs. He notices a light on in the office behind the counter, the door open just a crack. He heads into the kitchen and pours himself a glass of water, drinking it down. After rinsing the glass, Jack exits through the swinging door.

He stops again, eyeing the light coming from the crack under the office door. He edges over to the door and pushes it back just enough to peek through. Qaniit sits at the desk, going over papers. She looks up at him.

"Oh, I'm sorry," he says. "I didn't mean to disturb you."

"You okay? You want me to get you anything?"

"No. No, thank you. Just had to get a glass of water. Couldn't sleep.

You?"

She shakes her head, half her hair split over her breasts on each side and the rest down her back. She wears her summer nightshirt.

Her face, as sad as ever, the glow from the lamp on the desk illuminating her just so, yet she looks angelic sitting there. "I won't disturb you." He starts to close the door the way he found it.

"Jack?"

"Yes?" He pushes open the door to look in again.

"I want to go over these invoices with you tomorrow."

"Well, I'm wide awake. Let me see." He makes his way toward her.

She points to an invoice on the desk and says, "We use the same products from the same company here at the inn and on the boat. Get an extra discount."

Standing beside her, he leans closer to see, but catches a glimpse of her breasts down the front of her nightshirt. He looks away as fast as he can, trying to focus on the invoice. *Why did I do that?*

"So, don't you think the discount from the vendor should apply here?" she says.

He examines the invoice. "Yes. I think they discounted it here," he points, "but they forgot to include it here. They didn't total it correctly."

Inches from her face, obscured a bit by her hair that smells fresh like she washed it before going to bed, he stares at the side of her face. Resting her elbow on the desk and closing her fist, she taps the knuckle of her index finger against her lips. Jack watches her, his heart racing. *I have to get out of here.*

She glances up at him, pressing her full rounded lips together, catching his gaze. He looks back down at the invoice in a split-second. "I see that now," she says looking away from him just as fast and highlighting the section on the paper. She places the invoice in a paper-stacker and looks at another.

Jack moves around to the front of the desk to get some distance, pulling up a chair across from her. *Why did I look in here? Why did I come in to look at this paperwork now? Why don't I turn and run?*

"Can you add these up?" She passes him some invoices, a calculator, pencil and pad.

He fingers through about ten pages, tapping out numbers on the calculator and recording them on the pad. He glances up at her once and catches her watching him, her index finger on her lips. Again, their eyes dart away and back to the papers before them. "Here you go," he says, sliding the pad over to her.

"Thanks." She tucks her hair on the right side of her face behind her ear as she often does and presses her lips together in that same acknowledging way. She licks the tip of her index finger and fingers through more papers. Again, he stares at her but brings himself out of it before she catches him this time.

He scans the room, trying not to look at her. She glances up at him and says, "Almost done." She uses her pencil and puts check marks at the top of each corner on several invoices and places them in a different stack. "That's enough for now," she says. "Let's go to bed."

That sounded awkward. He believes she realized it too because just as fast as she said it, she blushed and jumped out of her chair.

"I'm just going to take the rest of these to bed to review." She picks up a half-dozen file folders with papers inside. While holding a water bottle and her keys in the other, she follows him to the door.

He holds the door for her to pass. At the same time, they both go for the light switch, one hand upon the other. "Sorry," she says, pulling hers off.

He turns the lights off and closes the office door behind him. She struggles with the keys in her hand. "Could you...?"

"Sure." He takes the keys from her, touching her again, his heart almost beating outside his body. He locks the door and hands them back to her, putting them into the same hand as the one holding the water bottle.

"Well, goodnight," he says.

"Goodnight." She fumbles with her keys and water bottle in the same hand. She drops the keys and a couple folders from her arm where she had held them against her breast, the papers scattering.

They bend over at the same time to pick up the folders. She secures a couple and he does too. He picks up the keys and stands, facing her. "Here you go," he says, handing her the folders and keys.

She straightens the folders and juggles the keys, almost dropping the water bottle this time.

"Here," he says, taking the water bottle and the keys back from her.

She follows him to her room. He swings open the door, standing with his back against it, holding the handle. She passes by facing him. "Thank you, Jack."

"Sure," he says reaching out to hand her the keys and the water bottle. Looking at her and not her hand, he drops the keys before she grasped them. He bends down and picks them up, coming within inches of her face, the front of his robe spreading to reveal his chest and tight-fitting boxer briefs.

Placing the keys in her hand and passing her the water bottle, this time she drops all the folders on the floor, the papers scattering again. "This is embarrassing," she says cracking a smile. "All thumbs."

That's the first time he's seen her smile like that. *It's a beautiful smile, even if it had been made for an embarrassing moment.* Looking at each other for only a split second, they embrace and kiss as fast as attracting sides of magnets. She drops the water bottle and keys.

As they kiss, he feels her soft breasts compress against his chest.

After a moment, he pulls away, turns his head to the side, and closes his eyes. She presses her face against his chest. They hold on like this for a minute, or two, Jack isn't sure. "I didn't want this to happen," he whispers in her ear.

"*I* didn't want this to happen."

He can feel her warm and moist lips against his chest. He rests his head on hers. "I have fought this, I think from the moment I met you."

"*I* have fought this from the moment I met you." She looks up at him, a tear welling in his eye.

They kiss again. She closes her eyes, breathes softly, and while only the thickness of one strand of hair separates their lips, he says, "I'm sorry for doing this to you."

"I'm sorry for doing this to *you*," she says, maintaining the distance between their lips.

"Do you really want to do this?"

"You keep taking the words out of my mouth," she says, cracking that smile again.

He, at last, smiles. "Only if you do."

"Only if *you* do," she says.

They kiss again and he closes the door, leaving the papers strewn about. She takes him by his hand, leads him to her bed, and pulls the robe off his shoulders where it falls to the floor at their feet. He lifts her nightshirt, revealing what he already knew, that her body is what most men dream about. He kisses her neck and she throws her head back, her hair dangling down to her buttocks.

He kisses her tight breasts, her aroused nipples and her neck. She kisses his biceps, chest and nipples. He sits down on the edge of the bed, kisses her stomach and puts his face against her thigh, kissing it.

She lightly pushes him by his shoulders down onto the bed and pulls his briefs off. She kisses him all over, working his chest, nipples, neck, stomach and thighs. It doesn't take much to arouse him. That happened at the door. She seems to be in charge, like she is with most things. She climbs atop, and they gently make love, her hair cascading down about his face as she lowers her head to kiss him.

He doesn't close his eyes as she looks into his. Her eyes seem different now. Fuller. She rolls over but keeps him inside her as he lies upon her. She digs her nails into his back.

He leans his head down and kisses her lips, her neck and her breasts, working on her erect nipples again. She writhes and, as he makes love to her, breathes deeply, turning him on more.

It's been so long that she must have released more than once. She's so warm. As for him, he tries to hold on as long as he can but can't any longer. Chest to breasts, he holds onto her, not letting her go, and releases.

He rolls to his side, but they stay together. After a few minutes of gentle kissing and caressing, he makes love to her again. He can feel her heart beating against his chest.

Several minutes later, her head resting on his upper arm, her lips pressed against the side of his chest and one leg between his, he strokes her hair, smelling it. She circles her finger around on his chest, playing with his amaroq claw.

Silence, except for their soft breathing for the longest time.

"Somehow you came through my door," she says. "*My* door."

"Sorry about that."

"Yeah. You should be. Look what you did to me."

"Look what I did to *you*? Now what do we do?" he says, continuing to stroke and smell her hair.

"I don't know."

After a long silence, he says, "I was a man of God. Now, I don't know what I am."

"You still are."

"How so? I walked away."

"You have a spirit. Inside you. If that isn't God, then nothing is." She looks up at him. He kisses her. Pulling back, she says, "And you *are* a God." She squeezes his bicep. "Look at you," she says, teasing him and running her fingers over his abs.

"Me? Look at you. Goddess." He pinches her nose.

"Okay, we sound like a couple of teenagers."

"You started this."

She puts her head on his chest and falls asleep. He lies there on his back, an arm around this beautiful woman's shoulder, thinking. *Akiak. That darn kid. Amaroq. That crazy wolf. What am I to do now? I can't leave. Not now, not ever. Right? Could I live out my days in this storybook world? Can it be so simple? Life's never simple.* He knows that. He thinks back to his losses. He looks up at the ceiling and whispers, "Are you going to let us have this?"

The ceiling doesn't answer him.

He drifts off to sleep with Qaniit beside him breathing softly in his arms.

Chapter Twenty-seven

Good deeds are repaid in kind.
Anonymous

The next morning Qaniit stirs, waking Jack. She looks over at him and says, "You still here?"

He kisses her, realizing he hadn't tossed and turned like he had for some time.

They lie there in silence, holding on for a while, her head upon his chest again. "Whatever happens," she hesitates, "let's never talk about the past."

He strokes her hair. After a moment he says, "Yes."

She runs the tips of her fingers over his abdomen. He becomes aroused. She runs her fingers down and along his thigh. She looks up at him and climbs atop. He kisses her breasts, enters her. They make love again. They take it slow and make it last as long as they can.

When it's over, neither disengages. She stays on top of him, resting her head on his shoulder, her breasts enveloping his chest. He lies there, breathing in her scent.

"After six," she says, glancing at the clock on the wall. "You're gonna make me late for the breakfast rush. Grandmother will be worried."

"Shouldn't it be canceled since, well, it's the day after?"

"Many of the guests have already paid for it. Included in the deal. Just can't cancel."

"Well, this is exactly the reason why we're going to hire you some help."

"We?"

"Yes, we."

"This is my place. For some strange reason my name is on the entire deed now making me the full owner. The boss."

"Ha. Well then, *the boss* is going to hire some help. With breakfast, with dinner, and other things."

"It's not that simple, Jack."

"We'll make it simple."

She sighs. "But…"

He kisses her again before she can counter him. Pulling back from her lips a fraction of an inch he says, "Your grandmother warned me you were stubborn."

"What're we gonna tell them?"

He thinks a moment. "Nothing."

Another minute or two goes by. She circles her fingers around his shoulder. He puts his lips atop her head and just breathes in through his nose, smelling her again. He could lie here with her all day.

"I'm worried, Jack."

"What is it?"

"I didn't want this to happen. To fall in love again. I certainly didn't want to fall in love with another fisherman."

He doesn't answer but thinks about that.

"I don't want you going out anymore. You hire someone and just run the company. From the shore."

"Well, we could do that. Let me see what I can do. I need a good captain to take over the Aga."

"Please. I couldn't go on, not again if you, well, I…"

He kisses her head. "I understand."

They lie there for a few minutes more.

Jack puts his robe on as Qaniit gets ready for breakfast. He slips out into the hall and heads toward the front desk.

Ulloriaq steps from the kitchen at that exact moment. "Oh, good morning, Ulloriaq."

"Gooooood mornnnnning, Jack?" she says, first narrowing her eyes at him then looking down the hallway and back at him again.

Using his thumb with a closed fist, he points over his shoulder and says, "Yes, well, I just spoke with Qaniit about hiring help." He goes right up to her, taking her by the hand. "Look. I'm covering for you today. You need to be at home. Tell Akiak to stay there with you. We'll come over after breakfast."

"You sure, Jack? I can cover for a couple hours."

"I just argued with your granddaughter, and I'm not arguing with you." He takes off her apron, escorts her to the door, and kisses her on her cheek. "I got this." He holds the door open for her.

Standing on the porch, she shrugs, turns and walks to the truck.

He showers, dresses and rushes downstairs. Qaniit works the kitchen while Jack takes orders, pours water, juice, drinks, and hustles around that dining room and kitchen like he had never hustled before. Even though eleven rooms at the Prospector are occupied, all the guests eat breakfast.

At nine o'clock when breakfast concludes, he sits at a table to get off his sore feet, sipping water. Qaniit comes from the kitchen. "What're you doing?"

"It's over. What do you think I'm doing?"

"It's not over. You have to wipe down the tables, restock the ketchup, salt, pepper and…"

"We're hiring someone to do all that."

"Maybe, but it has to be done now." She grabs his hand and tugs on him to stand.

"Okay. Okay." He stands. "What did I get into?"

"Yeah, what did you get into?"

He obeys orders. While she goes back into the kitchen to clean up, he checks each table and performs the follow-up chores she outlined. A few minutes later, he sees her exit the kitchen on the way to the office, looking over and smiling at him. *She's smiling now.*

~ * ~

Jack drives Qaniit to her grandparent's house. He takes her by the hand, leading her up the steps. Before Jack can open the door, Akiak swings it open from the inside. "I saw you walk up," he says with a long face.

"Hang in there, kid," Jack says patting his shoulder as he passes.

"Jack? I'm so happy the amaroq brought you to us."

Jack hesitates, but says, "Me too, Akiak. Me too."

Akiak hugs Qaniit and whispers to her, "I'm so happy for you, Cuz. You can be happy now."

The whole extended family has gathered once more. The funeral director arrives and Ulloriaq authorizes the service and makes all the arrangements.

~ * ~

A week later, three days after the funeral, Jack drives Qaniit and Ulloriaq to a law firm and meets Mr. Lamson in the office. An older white gentleman, he says, shaking Jack's hand, "Jack, I've heard so much about you. Everyone, please, sit."

They sit around a small conference table.

"So," Mr. Lamson says, "Let us review the will that Malik and Ulloriaq revised a couple weeks ago."

Jack glances at Ulloriaq who watches Lamson. Qaniit takes Jack's hand, squeezing it. As Mr. Lamson defines legal terms and reads general provisions of the will, Jack thinks back to the liquidation of his property more than two years ago. He had no one to leave his property to. Qaniit, along with Ulloriaq, will inherit the Nasak Fishing Company.

"That settles the house," Mr. Lamson says, turning a page of the will. "Oh, yes," he continues, bringing Jack out of his daydream. "As for Nasak Fishing Company, including all the property associated with it, the office and property attached, the boats, one half is bequeathed to Ulloriaq, Qaniit and Akiak Nasak equally, and the other half is bequeathed to Jack Douglas of Nome, Alaska, residence, the Prospector Inn."

Jack narrows his eyes and looks over at Ulloriaq and Qaniit then Lamson. "I'm sorry?"

"One half, Jack. You heard that right."

Ulloriaq, sitting on Jack's other side, says, "We wanted to do this, Jack. For all you have done for us."

"It should be in the family."

"It *is* in the family." She looks over at Qaniit.

"You two have me surrounded," he says. "This is a conspiracy."

"Don't look at me," Qaniit says. "She only told me yesterday."

Mr. Lamson cuts in, "I just have these papers for everyone to sign, and the company will be recorded as such."

Outside the office, just before they climb into Malik's truck, Jack says to Ulloriaq, "I suppose you know, then, that I'm in love with your granddaughter." He glances at Qaniit, not believing he said that.

"I knew that before you did," Ulloriaq says, climbing into the truck.

Qaniit looks at him, raises her eyebrows, shrugs, and climbs in behind her.

Jack gets in and drives, dropping Ulloriaq at her house before heading back to the Prospector with Qaniit. Malik and Ulloriaq had sealed his fate, if not Amaroq by leading him here. She had diverted him off the Yukon up into the woods and westward, eventually leading him into the mountains so that he could only head down into Nome to resupply. *How crazy did this all sound?*

Inside, Qaniit says to Jack, "Don't you think it's time you moved into my room? I mean, bring your things down?"

He knew this question and day would come. Still, he hadn't brought it up because he felt it was her room, not his, or theirs. Even though they had now made love several times, he wasn't sure he should move in, so to speak, although he had spent each night with her since. His belongings, not much really, were still in his room upstairs, living their own life. At her bedroom door he says, "Don't you think we should get married first?"

"That sounds ridiculous, Jack."

"What? Getting married?"

"We've spent each night together now. It's just your clothes that need to catch up with you. Hey, this is how you propose?" She goes into the bedroom.

Standing outside the bedroom door he says, "Well, no. I want to do it right, of course. Romantic and everything. Will you? Marry me?"

She shakes her head. "Not until you do it the right way. Romantic and everything, like you said."

"So, we're at a standstill?"

She goes back over to the door where he still stands, takes him by his hand, pulls him out of the way of the door which she closes, leads him into the room and over to the bed. "Either you bring your clothes down in the morning, or I will. I need to rent your room." She pushes him onto the bed. "Now undress."

"Yes, ma'am."

Chapter Twenty-eight

Evil doesn't rest.
Medieval Christian proverb

Jack hires new crewmembers, two brothers, white kids, one nineteen and one twenty, from Iowa seeking adventure. He updates the company's website and puts out help wanted ads on national job-hunting sites. Jack also convinces Qaniit to hire a waitress, a middle-aged woman looking for extra money to support her husband who has become ill and can't work. They hire a busboy doubling as a dishwasher, a kid from the local high school who wants money for a car to impress the girls.

For the time being, Jack still has to pilot the Aga because he needs to train a suitable skipper.

Jack drives Qaniit and Akiak to the courthouse. He holds her hand going up the steps. They check in with the court clerk and take a seat in the courtroom.

While waiting for a couple of cases to be heard before theirs, Qaniit taps Jack on the arm and points at Donald who struts into the courtroom, taking a seat on the other side. Donald looks over at the three of them, scowling. He looks away then back toward the judge.

"Next case," the judge says, gaveling.

The clerk reads from a paper, "Qaniit and Akiak Nasak versus Donald Prescott. Assault and battery."

"Please approach," Judge Saghani says. Saghani is an Inuit man in his sixties.

Qaniit and Akiak approach and stand behind a table. Donald swaggers over to the other table on the opposite side, glaring back at Jack.

"Qaniit, Akiak," Judge Saghani says, smiling at them.

"Your Honor," Qaniit and Akiak say.

Judge Saghani looks at Donald and says, "How do you plead, Mr. Prescott?"

Donald sneers at Qaniit and Akiak then looks back at the judge. "I think you're biased against me."

"You address this court with respect, Mr. Prescott. Now how do you plead?"

"I don't know."

"You either plead guilty, not guilty or no contest."

"Well, I mean it's their word against mine."

The judge sighs and scans papers the clerk hands him. "Look, Mr. Prescott. There were two independent witnesses who signed statements."

"Yeah, but where are they?"

"If you wish to plead not guilty, then we would have a trial and subpoena the witnesses." He scans through more papers. "Seeing how you have been through all this before with three domestic violence convictions, I'm sure you know how this goes. If you want to waste this court's time, that's your prerogative. I'm admonishing you, however, not to try my patience, Mr. Prescott."

Donald glares at Qaniit and Akiak, his face growing red. He looks back at the judge. "No contest."

"What's that, Mr. Prescott? I didn't hear respect for this courtroom in your plea."

"No contest, your honor."

"Now, that's better. Fifteen hundred dollar fine. I'm issuing a restraining order to stay away from both plaintiffs. You are not to go within one thousand feet of the Prospector or the plaintiffs. Do you understand, Mr. Prescott?"

"Yes."

"Pardon me?"

"Yes, your honor."

Judge Saghani bangs his gavel. Akiak follows Qaniit who picks up Jack on the way out. She takes his hand and they head for the back of the courtroom.

~ * ~

A couple days later, Jack returns to the Prospector from his morning run. He showers in his new private bathroom attached to Qaniit's room, or rather their room. He has now moved in, clothes and all. He's now living with a woman not his wife.

He drives to the office with Qaniit. She gets out of the passenger seat and Jack out of the driver's. They meet at the front of the truck, kiss and embrace. "I'll see you later," he says.

She embraces him again, not letting go and putting her head against his chest. He holds on, his lips on top of her head.

They stand there for the longest time holding on. "I love you, Jack."

"I love you too." He squeezes her.

She pulls back, kisses him again and climbs into the truck.

~ * ~

Across the street, in a rental sedan on the far side of the parking lot, Donald sits with a young man in his middle teens who looks a lot like him. Donald chugs beer from a can, downing the rest of it. He crushes the can, tosses it into the backseat and looks at the boy. "Pretty boy and his bitch are gonna get what's coming to them."

The boy pounds a closed fist against the palm of his other hand and says, "Let's beat the shit out him, daddy."

~ * ~

While working in the office, Rhonda enters. "Good morning, boss," she says.

"Rhonda, please. Just Jack."

"Just teasin' ya." She sets her purse on her desk, sits and fires up her computer. "I love the website. I got an application from a kid in Anchorage. He worked for Johnston Fishing Company there last season but saw your ad and the competitive rate you offered. I gotta say, Jack. You

193

got the business sense."

"Thanks. Couldn't do it without you. Who can I get to take over the Aga? None of these boys are mature or ready enough for that."

"That's a tough one. You don't think Conrad is ready? Perhaps Sky?"

"They need more confidence. More experience. If they can get more hauls, I might be able to pair them up with some more experienced crews and switch the boys around."

"They're good boys. Known them since the wee years."

"I know. I guess I'm just being overly cautious."

Rhonda works until noon and departs the office. Jack follows her thirty minutes later, departing for the Prospector to have lunch with Qaniit.

Outside, a beautiful blue-sky day, he locks the office door behind him.

"Hey, mister."

Jack turns to see Donald standing there with his son. "Mister Prescott. You're not supposed to be here."

"It's a free country. Besides, the order didn't say anything about this office or you."

Jack can't believe he's being confronted by another man like he had with O'Reilly. "I don't want any trouble, Mr. Prescott."

"We don't need to be so formal. Call me, Don. What is it? Jack, right?"

"What do you want, Mr. Prescott?"

"What do I want?" He chuckles. "I want you to get the fuck outta town, that's what I want."

"That's not going to happen."

Donald moves closer, stopping within a few feet of him. Jack can smell beer on his breath. "You stole the inn from me. And Qaniit was promised to me." He jabs his index finger into Jack's chest.

Jack sighs, backs up. "Look, Mr. Prescott, I paid for the inn. It belongs to Qaniit and how could you possibly believe she was promised to you? She's not property."

"My brother said if anything ever happened to him, I should look after her."

"I don't think he meant it that way."

"I don't care what you think." He steps even closer, his son next to him, pounding his fist against his open hand.

Jack can't believe these idiots are threatening him.

"Listen, pretty boy," Donald says. "My boy and I're fixin' to teach you a lesson." He steps within a few inches of Jack's face, Jack's back pressed against the railing to the office steps.

"Please, Mr. Prescott. I *don't* want any trouble."

"*He doesn't want any trouble*," he says, mocking Jack while looking at his son. "Oh, you brought this trouble on yourself. Stealing my inn and my woman." He takes a swing at Jack, but Jack dodges the punch and steps aside.

Donald falls forward into the railing but catches himself from falling over. "Get 'em, boy."

Donald's boy, a little overweight like his father, charges Jack like a steamroller. Jack sidesteps him too.

"Dammit, stand still and fight like a man," Donald says, coming at him again swinging.

Jack sidesteps him yet again. *It's sort of comical, as if two of the three stooges had arrived.* "Please stop, Mr. Prescott. I don't want to hurt you."

"The only one getting hurt is you. Now, get in there and get 'im, boy," he yells.

His son comes at Jack again, but Jack ducks, spins around, grabs the boy by the arm, and throws him onto the ground.

The kid goes down with a thud, his face hitting the gravel. He wipes blood from his face. "I'm bleeding, daddy," he sobs.

"Why, you son of a bitch." Donald rushes Jack again winding up for a punch, however Jack pops him in the face before he can follow through with the swing. Jack hears a loud crack. Donald falls backward onto the gravel, landing hard on his buttocks. He grabs his nose that spurts out blood. "You bastard. You broke my goddamn nose."

"I tried to warn you, Mr. Prescott. I'm sorry about that."

"You're sorry? You gonna be real sorry."

"I'm leaving now, Mr. Prescott. I suggest you should do the same.

Please do not come around again or I'll call the police."

Jack walks off, leaving Donald and his son on the ground smarting.

~ * ~

Jack takes Qaniit out to a local restaurant that night. Because she now has turned over the waitressing and other duties to hired hands, and Ulloriaq began working less and less because Jack insisted, Qaniit only has to supervise much of the time now.

"I'm curious," Jack says after they had finished their dessert. "I didn't want to bring this up, and it's the only time I will mention his name, but what does Donald do for a living?"

"I don't really know because he's had many jobs. Was a truck driver. Worked at a stone quarry or something for a time. Something to do with blasting the rocks. Why?"

"Well, I don't want to worry you, but I saw him. He's still in town."

"I figured. Akiak saw him driving through town, and I heard he harassed a waitress over at the Gold Rush Saloon. I know her and saw her at the market."

"Okay. Let me know if he comes near you or Akiak."

"You think he's up to something?"

"I don't know. You said he lives in Anchorage?"

"Did. He's lived in many places since Dolores left him."

"Okay. Enough of him." The waitress returns the check tray, Jack dropping a tip in. "Ready?"

"This was my first date in a long time, Jack."

"Same here." He reaches for her hand, squeezing it.

They head back to the Prospector.

Pulling up, he notices a truck parked on the opposite side of the street just beyond the Prospector. He glances at Qaniit, certain she didn't see it.

Approaching the steps to the Prospector, Jack glimpses a figure of someone lurking around in the shadows on the opposite corner of the inn. Qaniit and Jack go inside.

They traverse the hallway and come to their room, but Qaniit stops at the door when she discovers a ribbon tied into a bow on the door handle. "What's this?"

He shrugs.

She opens the door to discover the room decorated in balloons, ribbons, and rose-pedals on the floor and the bed, and glowing votive candles carefully placed all around.

She turns back to him as he closes the door. "What's going on?"

"You asked for it." He kneels on one knee, pulls out a small jewelry box and opens it to reveal a diamond ring inside. "Will you marry me?"

"Wow. What a rock." She takes the box from him, pulls out the ring, hands it to him and says, "Put it on, will ya?"

"You didn't answer the question."

"Of course, you fool."

He puts the ring on her finger and stands. She admires it and says, "You romantic." Throwing her arms around him, she kisses him. He picks her up and she wraps her legs around his torso. He carries her to the bed, leaning over, attempting to place her on it, but falls over on top of her. While deep kissing, they struggle to undress one another.

It takes some doing to undress, because they don't let up. He tries to unhook her bra but labors at it. She breaks out laughing, causing him to laugh.

Continuing to work on it, he says, "It's as if I'm back in high school. Not that I did this."

"Nobody taught you?" She pushes him off. He rolls to his side. She reaches around and unhooks it lickety-split then pulls his underwear off and climbs atop him. He enters her and she tosses her head back, her hair whipsawing down her back and onto his thighs.

As they make love, she writhes and collapses upon him, kissing him all over his face. Making love to her, he feels, is animalistic or primal in a way, like they are one with the wild, yet it feels spiritual. She rolls onto her side, and together they continue to make love.

It seems to go on forever, yet it seems too short. Jack loses all sense of time again, yet in a good way now.

Lying beside one another and entwined, they speak no words. No words are necessary. They fall asleep in one another's arms.

~ * ~

Sporting a bandage covering his broken nose, Donald cuts a chain-link fence to the entrance of a stone quarry with bolt cutters. Holding a small flashlight, he pushes open the gate just enough to squeeze through and makes his way across the gravel coming upon a small shack labeled: *Danger. Stay Out. Explosives.*

Using the cutters to lop off a padlock on the door of the shack, he creeps inside and breaks open a box labeled: *Dynamite.* He grabs three sticks, hesitates, but grabs two more for good measure. He stuffs the dynamite in his backpack and makes his way back out of the quarry.

Chapter Twenty-nine

A ship is safe in harbor, but that's not what ships are for.
William G.T. Shedd

Qaniit drives Jack to the Aga early one morning. They arrive before the rest of the crew. "We'll be back in a week, at most," he says, hugging her next to the driver's door. "Just need to perfect the crew, get Sky and Conrad ready to skipper. Fill up the tanks."

"Skype me ten times a day?"

"I will."

She won't let him go, squeezing him. She balls his T-shirt up in her fists. "I don't like this, Jack."

"It's going to be okay. I promise."

"That's what they always say. Like in the movies."

She's right about that.

She looks up at him, tugs on his shirt, pulling his head over where she can reach his lips.

"Hey, you're stretching out my shirt," he says, cracking a smile and breaking the kiss. She smiles too.

The crew arrives and passes them, whistling. "Let's go, lover boy," Conrad says.

"Yeah, yeah," Jack says. "Get on board and get her ready."

Jack watches Qaniit drive off. He's well aware that King Crab fishing is rated by the Bureau of Labor Statistics as one of the most dangerous occupations with a high fatality rate. The causes of such a high death rate include hypothermia, drowning and injuries from equipment. However, for him at least, he'll be in the wheelhouse as the captain most of the time.

"Listen up," Jack says to the boys. Jonah, Dylan, Conrad, Sky, Pete and Troy, the lily-white Iowa boys, gather around. "Safety. Safety. Safety. Think about what you're doing at all times. Use your heads." He scans their eager faces. "Okay, let's go." The crew casts the lines off, and Jack pilots the Aga out into Norton Sound.

~ * ~

He sits at a desk in a dark, cheap motel room wrapping fuses around the sticks of dynamite. After taping them off, Donald solders the fuses to a triggering timing device. He then solders the triggering timing devise to wires running out of a gutted, modified cellphone. His improvised explosive device, I.E.D, is ready. Now he just needs to figure out where to place it.

He swigs beer from a can and tosses it on the floor. He lifts another cellphone next to him and programs a number. He plugs both cells into chargers and goes over to the bed where he opens another can of beer, chugging half of it. He flips the television on and punches in the pay-for-view porn channel.

~ * ~

About fifty miles out, the crew lays the first string of pots. Deck Boss Conrad hoists the pots using the crane and places them onto the launcher-lift as guided by Dylan and Troy. After Pete tethers the bait bags with cod into each pot, Dylan operates the launcher-lift causing the pots to slide into the sea. Jonah tosses in the shots and the buoys. The pots sink where they will soak on the ocean floor at about five hundred feet.

It takes the crew most of the day to bait-rig and drop all the pots.

~ * ~

Jack drifts the Aga on watch in the wheelhouse that night as the boys relax in the cabin. He checks weather reports, making note of an approaching storm. Conrad, who doubles as the chef, cooks dinner below in the galley. "Dinner, Jack," Conrad says over the intercom. "Surf and turf."

"Crew eats first," Jack says.

"Aye, aye. We'll bring you up a plate."

"Thanks." In the captain's chair, he dials Skype on the computer.

"Hello," Qaniit says over the hookup.

"Hey, good looking," Jack says smiling.

"Everything okay?"

"Everything's perfect. These boys are really great kids. Hardworking."

"Do you really need to stay out a week?"

"Need to fill up the pots. You know that."

She sighs. "Please be careful."

"Are you kidding? The boys call me Captain Safety."

"Cute, Jack. No, I'm not kidding."

Conrad sticks his head in carrying a plate of salmon, steak, potatoes and green beans. "Hey, lover boy. The boys want seconds. I had to rescue this." He hands Jack the plate.

"Eat, Jack," Qaniit says.

"I can eat and look at you." He frowns at Conrad and signals with his head a get-lost-look.

"Geeze," Conrad says slipping out the door.

"Jack?"

"Yes?"

"I can't stand it that you're not going to bed with me tonight and not waking up beside me in the morning. You realize this is the first night we've not been together?"

"I'm that sexy, huh?"

"Well, that too. But that's not what I'm talking about. Stop teasing. I'm being serious."

"We'll be careful."

"You promise?"

"You don't have to ask me that again. I never break my promises."

"You promise?"

"Ha."

"I gotta clean up in the kitchen," she says. "I let Joey go early tonight. Something about a hot date."

"I'm jealous."

"Love you," she says.

"Love you back." He closes the connection to Skype and sits there eating, watching the ocean splash over the deck, the Aga rolling from side to side. He checks the approaching storm. Over the intercom he says, "Conrad? Sky? Come on up."

They arrive on deck a minute later. "What's up, captain?" Sky says.

"Look at the storm." He points at the computer screen. "What would you do?"

Sky looks at the screen. "Can we get around it this way?" He runs his finger over the screen, tracing the edge of the storm.

"It's about a fifty miles across," Jack says.

"Gotta go straight at it then," Conrad says. "Take the wind and ride the waves at a forty-five-degree angle."

Sky says, "Zig-zag to leave the boat in the trough long enough to turn to minimize the time you're in the trough then broad side to the swell to prevent broaching."

"Good," Jack says. "That's what we'll do then. We've got about an hour. Clean up below. Tell the boys to stay in the cabin. If they want to come up here, that's fine."

Sky and Conrad hustle below. Jack finishes his meal, studying the approaching storm.

~ * ~

An hour and a half later, Conrad, Sky, and Jonah hang with Jack in the wheelhouse while Troy, Pete and Dylan, stay in the cabin. Waves crash over the deck, and Conrad pilots the Aga through the storm. "Slower," Jack says.

The ship slices through the on-coming waves, rocking from side to side. Jonah grabs onto Sky next to him so he doesn't topple over. Jack braces himself with his feet against the wall in front of his co-skipper's seat while holding onto the railing.

The Skype on the computer rings. Jack hits the answer icon.

"Hello?" Qaniit says over Skype. The picture is broken and she fades in and out.

"Hey," Jack says. "What are you doing up?"

"Wha…you…do…?" she says, her voice breaking up.

"Training the boys."

Conrad takes a wave at a forty-five-degree angle, but the wave smashes up against the Aga, causing it to pitch quite a bit to the side. Jack loses his grip and falls off his chair. Sky and Jonah go flying by him, landing on the floor.

"Jack? Wha…ing on?" Qaniit says.

Jack pulls himself back up into his chair as Conrad steers the Aga into the next wave. Sky and Jonah pull themselves up behind Jack who sits in front of the Skype camera.

"Hi, Qaniit," Sky says, smiling, waving and throwing his arm around Jonah.

"Everything's fine," Jack says. "I'll talk to you later. Love you. Gotta go." He turns the Skype off and looks over at Conrad battling the wheel to keep the Aga steady. "You're going to get me in trouble."

"Sorry, Captain."

"You too," he says to Sky and Jonah. "Hold on."

"Aye, aye," Sky says.

They ride out the storm and by early morning it has passed. "Get some breakfast," Jack says to the boys. "See how the others made out. I'll take the helm."

They eat breakfast and clean up. Jack drifts the Aga and inspects the ship.

After breakfast, they raise three pots with a few dozen crabs, but the next three have less. "Must be because of the storm," Jack says to the boys on deck. "Let's re-bait and drop them again. Then get some rest."

~ * ~

The crew rests all day.

During the middle of the night, Jack checks the weather report on his computer, Conrad sitting beside him in the wheelhouse. "Another storm is brewing here," Jack says pointing at the computer.

"What do you think?" Conrad says.

"We'll pick up some pots in a couple hours and see what we get." He looks at the clock on the wall that reads one in the morning. "Give the boys two more hours. Go get some sleep. I got this."

Conrad nods and departs. Jack watches him go. The kid's ready to take over. He can turn the Aga over to him on the next haul and run the company from the shore. However, for this run, Jack has to make it worthwhile, monetarily. It costs tens of thousands of dollars to operate this vessel. To cover those costs, he has to return with at least most of the three tanks full. He sits there looking out at the black sea, missing this wonderful woman he has found. Although being a skipper on this boat gives him a sense of worth and wonder, he wants to be with her every night. He realizes that now. Besides, he knows that twisted character Donald still lurks about town. He doesn't want to be absent in case Donald harasses Qaniit or Akiak.

The Skype rings and he sees Qaniit. "You still up?"

"I can't sleep," she says.

"Me either."

"I saw that storm last night on the weather service."

"We made it through okay. Not that bad."

"Don't play with me, Jack."

Busted. "Okay."

"I see another one coming."

"It doesn't look as bad as the one last night."

"I said don't play with me."

"Yes, dear. Look, we're going to pull up some pots soon. Let me see what we get."

"This is your last run. You're gonna turn this over to Conrad."

"Yes, ma'am."

"Don't yes, ma'am me."

"Yes, ma'am."

She sighs. "You don't, I'm chaining you to the bed."

"That sounds kinky."

"You into that stuff, Jack?"

"I'm just into you."

"Oh, your father called and made the reservations. He spoke with Ulloriaq."

"Okay." Another call comes in over Skype. "Huh. Rhonda's calling. I'll call you back."

"Jack?" Rhonda says over the laptop at the office.

"What's wrong?"

"The Issumatar is coming in early. Miles's injured."

The Issumatar, meaning superior, is the other crab boat owned by the Nasak Fishing Company. This boat is one hundred, eleven feet long and piloted by the more experienced captain, Miles.

"How bad?" Jack says.

"Not sure. Back injury. He can't get up."

"Okay. Keep me posted. Get some sleep. We'll be back in as soon as we can."

"Will do." The Skype disconnects.

~ * ~

At three in the morning, the boys work on bringing up the pots, most full. With the waves picking up from the approaching storm splashing over the gunwales and rocking the boat, Jack steadies the Aga.

Each pot hoisted up contains a sizable catch. The boys whoop and holler with each haul, battling the pelting rain and strong winds. Because of this, Jack decides not to re-bait the pots. After the last pot is hauled in later that morning and lashed together on deck with the others, Jonah shouts up to Jack in the wheelhouse, "About half on tank number three, Jack."

"That will do for this haul," Jack says. "Batten it all down. We're going in." He logs details on the computer while the crew finishes cleaning up on the deck, securing the last of the equipment. Storm clouds turn the sky black, rain assaulting the Aga. Jack scans the weather radar on one of the computer screens in front of him.

In the wheelhouse with Conrad, Jack watches as Conrad opens the

Aga up to full throttle while continuing to battle the high waves that crash over the bow, the gunwales and the deck. Spray splashes against the windows of the cabin where Jack has confined the crew.

A few hours later the Aga pulls into port. Qaniit and Akiak wait at the dock. The boys moor the boat, Conrad cutting the engine. Qaniit and Akiak board, Qaniit running up to hug Jack. "I'm a wreck," she says.

~ * ~

On the far side of the parking lot, well out of view, Donald sits in his rental, watching them with binoculars. While holding the binoculars up to his eyes with one hand, he sips beer from a can with the other. He burps and spills some on his shirt. He lowers the binoculars, wipes the beer away with his hand, licking his fingers to get every drop. He raises the binoculars again, watching them. "You're not gonna have her for long, pretty boy. You'll be out of the way real soon. At the bottom of the fuckin' ocean." He guzzles his beer, burping again.

~ * ~

"You're in charge," Jack says to Conrad. "Make sure you inventory and sign for the catch, supervise the cleanup and secure the boat."

"I got it, Jack," Conrad says.

Jack puts his arm around his shoulder. "I may need you to take out the Issumatar for Miles."

"Thanks, Jack."

"You know it's all about safety."

"Yes."

"Good." After patting him on his back, Jack follows Qaniit off the boat. She drives them to the hospital.

Inside, a nurse directs them to Miles's room. "I'm sorry, Jack," Miles says.

"Don't worry about it," Jack says. "What's the prognosis?"

"They think I ruptured a disk. Might need surgery. Could be a few weeks before I'm back in action."

"Okay. I'm going to have Conrad take out the Issumatar until you're ready."

"What about the Aga? We're making a killing out there."

"Well, I might have to take her back out until I can find a replacement." He looks over at Qaniit who shakes her head at him and mouths the word "no."

"What about Ronny?" Jack says.

"I don't think he's ready," Miles says. "A little too uncertain and, well, not too level-headed. Not a leader. Too much of a follower."

"Sky?"

"He might be ready, but needs a steady hand the first haul or two."

"Well, you get better. Let me know if you need anything."

"Thanks, Jack."

~ * ~

After Conrad and the crew finish cleaning and securing the boat, Donald crawls out of the rental carrying a backpack. He makes his way over to the Aga, boards, and jimmies open a cabin window beside the door. He sets the backpack down, locates a bucket nearby, stands on it and leans in through the window. He half hangs in, half hangs out of the window but manages to reach over and unlock the door. Extracting himself, he bangs his head on the top of the window frame just before dropping to the deck. "Goddammit," he says. He surveys the dock to make sure no one heard him then picks up the pack and goes inside the cabin. He finds the hatch to the engine compartment, opens it, and climbs down the ladder. By an inch or two he squeezes between the engine and the hull.

Near the floor of the vessel on the other side of the engine, hidden from view, he stops and takes out his I.E.D. Using putty, he sticks the I.E.D. to the floor, hidden behind and just below part of the engine. He checks the cellphone indicting a full battery.

He shimmies back past the engine block and out through the hatch. He closes the hatch, locks the door to the cabin from the inside, pushing it closed.

Looking around to see if the dock is clear, he disembarks and sprints for his car, his flabby belly flopping up and down.

Chapter Thirty

It is always calm before the storm.
Anonymous

Jack awakes beside Qaniit the next morning. She stirs, rolls over on top of him and says, "No."

"Good morning to you too." He kisses her.

"You know what I'm talking about. Don't mess with me, Jack."

"Let me take the Aga out once more. Just to be sure Sky is ready."

She rests her head on his shoulder. "I'm not letting you go." He lifts his arms around her. She says, "Something has brought us together, and I have no intention of letting anything take you from me. No boat. No ocean. Nothing."

"Me from you? Never." *Yeah, I pray nothing takes you from me. Although, no matter what one does, will fate do what it does no matter? If I turn down this path, will the event that was to have happened if I had chosen the other path happen on this path instead? Did I choose wisely? Did it matter? Is it inevitable no matter the path I choose?*

~ * ~

A couple hours later, Jack and Qaniit wait for his parents at baggage claim. Upon seeing them approach, Jack goes up and hugs them. He steps aside and says, "Mother, Father, this is Qaniit, my fiancée."

Their eyes go wide at the same time and their mouths drop open. His mother glares at Jack, narrowing her eyes while his father stares at Qaniit as if she's an alien. "Mr. Douglas," she says leaning in, hugging him. "Mrs. Douglas," she says hugging her. She steps back and takes Jack's hand.

"Well," his mother says, glancing at the handholding. "This is quite the surprise, I must say."

"Here," Jack says releasing Qaniit's hand and picking up their luggage, one bag in each hand.

Outside, Jack loads the bags onto the bed of Malik's, rather, his truck now. "Mother, why don't you ride with Qaniit and Father can ride with me?"

They all climb aboard. Jack follows Qaniit and his mother in Akiak's truck. Not quite out of the parking lot, his father says, "You could have told us over the phone, Jack."

"I could have, yes."

"Do you love...?"

"Do I love her?" He glances over at his father. "That's what people do when they're in love. Get married. Look, Father, I can't even begin to explain what I've been through. You wouldn't believe any of it. So, I'm not even going to try."

"We haven't replaced you at the church. I've had retired pastors rotate based on the assumption you'll return to the ministry."

"I'm not going back."

"It's your home. Your people."

"It's my past. My future is here. This is my home now. These are my people now. Just like in Puckett, I've come to realize that so many people, despite me fighting it, depend on me. Here. Now. This is my new congregation."

"You saying you want to preach here?"

"No. I'm a fisherman. A businessman now."

"Are you sure? I mean, it's what you were destined to do. Preach. It's God's plan."

"I'm not sure if I believe that anymore. Was it God's plan to take Janette and the kids from me?"

"Well, you know better than most the answer to that."

"If that was His plan, then it's His plan that brought me here. To Qaniit. I saved a boy from drowning, Father. That had to be His plan too. If I hadn't been here, the boy would have died. I've helped save her business. Her grandfather's fishing business too. If that was His plan, then it's His plan that I stay here with Qaniit and run the company."

"Quite a leap from a ministry to a fisherman."

"Are you saying it is of less significance?"

"No, I'm not saying that. Of course not. Well, you were destined to lead a flock, Jack."

Jack glances over at him. "Was. Now I'm destined to run a fishing company."

Silence.

"She's very beautiful. I must say. Are you sure about this? I mean, you only just met her, right?"

"I can't explain it. From the time I met her, I felt it. You know how you just know. I fought it. Believe me. I fought it." Jack looks over at him again as he looks back at Jack. His father turns to look at Qaniit pulling up to the Prospector.

Jack and his father get out, Jack grabbing the luggage and following them in.

Inside, Akiak and Ulloriaq greet them. "Nice to meet you, sir," Akiak says, extending his hand to Jack's father. They shake. "Mrs. Douglas," he says shaking her hand.

Ulloriaq greets them too. "Akiak, take their bags up," she says. "We've prepared dinner," she says to Jack, Qaniit, and his parents.

"This way," Jack says, leading them to a table. The restaurant won't open for another hour for dinner, so they have the place to themselves.

They sit at the table, Jack passing out the menus.

Silence.

His parents scan the menus then set them aside. He catches his mother looking over at him, then at Qaniit.

"To get everything out of the way up front, Mother," Jack says, "we're getting married in the spring."

"Um," his mother says, "Yes, so Cannnn…"

"Qaniit," Jack says. "Pronounced, can e it."

"Yes, well," his mother says. "I must say. I am well, you know, it's…"

"We're in love, Mother, and I'm not going back. I belong here now. With Qaniit." He squeezes his fiancée's hand.

His mother doesn't respond but glances down at their handholding then over at her husband to say something, but he looks away.

"I've been on a long and incredible journey."

More silence.

Jack looks them over, then says, "Many things have happened to me," he looks at his mother, "and as I told Father, you wouldn't believe any of it. All I can tell you is something brought me here to this village, to these people and this exceptional woman."

His mother looks down at the table, straightening her napkin.

"This is my home now."

His mother tugs on her pearl necklace.

"I'm not asking for you to understand," Jack continues. "We're only asking that you accept our love and bless this."

His mother forces a polite smile.

Ulloriaq and Akiak serve a full course meal. Jack does most of the small-talking throughout the meal about Nome and fishing.

"We're all going to a wedding tomorrow," Jack says. "A boy from my crew."

"Are you sure, Jack?" his father says. "We don't know them."

"That's the thing about the people here. We're all family. Since I'm a part of the family, you're part of the family too."

His father looks at his wife who glances at Qaniit when she reaches for and squeezes Jack's hand.

After dinner, Jack escorts his parents to their room. "We have a full course breakfast. It's in the brochure in your room. If you need anything, just call zero on the house phone and it rings in our room downstairs."

His parents exchange glances, his mother raising an eyebrow. "Jack," she says, "are you sure about all of this? I mean, you experienced quite the trauma, I understand that. You run off into the wild, we don't see you for more than two years. You rush into this relationship in what, a few months? It's not, well, you know. Normal."

His father says, "We thought about trying to find you, and well," he looks at Jack's mother, nodding, "yes, help you."

"We've been over this. *I'm* not mental, if that is what you're thinking."

His mother says, "Well, we're not saying that." She looks at her husband as if she wants him to agree with her.

Jack sighs. "Look, this all just happened. I can't explain it. You're right. It was extreme trauma, despair, loneliness, anger. I sank into the depths of depression. Things happened to me that can't be explained. Fantastical things. You know I roamed around the wilderness, alone, for months. Hunting, fishing. I even had a pet wolf." *Actually, I think I was her pet.* "Anyway, for whatever reason, whether you say it is God's plan, or not, I found my way here, found these people who are extremely good, hard-working people with a strong sense of family. Despite not wanting to love again, even fighting it with all my might, running from it, along came this woman, who by the way has seen much tragedy herself." He pauses, scans their long faces, his mother pursing her lips. "I must say, she has fixed me, Mother. Father. Fixed me. She has brightened my blackened heart and empty soul. She is a good, beautiful soul, and I have found love again. I would hope you would give us your blessing."

His parents exchange glances.

"There's more to it," Jack says. "Right?"

"Jack," his mother says, looking over her shoulder than back at him, whispering, "I mean, she's a native."

Jack bites his lip. "Did I just hear that right?"

She sighs. "I didn't mean it like that."

"Then how?"

She looks at her husband, but says, "Well, you know what I mean."

Jack nods, disapproving, pursing his lips. "Yeah. Yeah, I know what you mean." He doesn't want to say it, but he does, "You really want me to preach? You're a Christian, Mother. I forgive you. Goodnight." Jack turns and goes downstairs to their room.

Qaniit has already prepared for bed. She sits against the headboard in her nightshirt, reviewing papers for the business. Jack prepares for bed, slipping in next to her. He cuddles up and puts his head on her lap. She places the papers onto the nightstand, running her fingers through his hair. "You okay?"

"Yeah." After a moment he says, "As God is my witness, I love you so."

"I love you too." She turns the nightstand light out and curls up with him.

Chapter Thirty-one

A mother's love is unconditional. Her approval is not.
Chinese Proverb

Akiak enters the local market. Inside, he gathers his usual supplies of fresh vegetables, mixes, and fixes for the dinner rush.

Pushing his basket up one aisle, he turns down another and almost runs into Donald. "Watch it, asshole," Donald says, pushing Akiak's cart into him.

Akiak pulls back, steering clear of him, but says, "You're supposed to stay away from me."

Imitating a whining child teasing another, Donald says, "You're supposed to stay away from me." He comes right up to within inches of Akiak's face and whispers, "Fuck you, Injun. You better watch yerself. This is a dangerous world. Shit happens." He pokes his finger into Akiak's chest. "I told you it wasn't over. You and your cunt cousin and her pretty-boy will get what's comin' to them." He strolls off with a six-pack of beer.

Akiak finishes his purchases, his adrenaline exploding. He drives over to the Prospector where he doesn't tell Qaniit or grandmother because he doesn't want to worry them.

~ * ~

Jack and Qaniit wait at the bottom of the stairs for Jack's parents. Jack bought himself a suit, the first one he's worn in more than two years, and he feels awkward in it. He also bought Qaniit a beautiful light-blue dress. He knows she's an angel, but wearing that dress against her snowy-white skin, her long black hair flowing over her shoulders and down her back, he can't take his eyes off her. Holding hands when his parents descend the stairs, Jack says, "All ready?"

His father nods; they follow him out and climb into the trucks.

At the church, Akiak sits next to Jack whispering in his ear, "I saw Donald again. At the market."

"Does he have a job? Anyone know what he's doing?"

"My sources tell me no. He's at the Snake River Motor Lodge. Just hangs out there and at the Gold Rush Saloon. Buys a lot of beer at the market."

"Your sources, huh?"

"I have a network of spies. Like M in James Bond."

"Okay, kid. Then I'm the *P.M.* and you report to me."

"You got it." He shakes Jack's hand and winks.

Dylan and his new bride, Malina are married.

At the reception in the church hall, Jack and Qaniit introduce Jack's parents to the guests, especially the relatives. Jack notices they're taken aback, like he was at first, from all the hugging as if they're long lost family.

Dylan and his new bride stop at Jack's table while making the rounds. Dylan beams. "We're going out Monday, Jack. Right?"

Jack says, while glancing at Qaniit, "Yes." Of course, she shakes her head and mouths the word "no" again. He looks back at Dylan and says, "Unless you want to go on your honeymoon first?"

"Gotta save up some cash for that."

"Okay. I'll see you at six. Best wishes, kid."

"You got it, captain." He goes to the next table with his bride.

Jack turns to Qaniit. She wraps her arm around his. "Just one more haul. Sky should be ready after this one. At least I'm in the wheelhouse and not on deck. Okay?"

"No."

Jack catches his mother listening. She says, "Is it really dangerous?"

Jack nods. "Yes, it is." He squeezes Qaniit's hand. "I've got a great crew and have trained them to be extra careful. So we'll be fine."

His mother glances at her husband then back at Jack. "I can't believe you're doing what you're doing, Jack," she says. "I mean, you were, well, you know."

Jack starts to say something but holds back. He figures it's pointless to say anything. He scans both of their faces. His mother looks at their entwined arms, Qaniit now resting her head on Jack's shoulder. His mother looks away, adjusts her napkin, folding it neatly next to her plate. She toys with the stem of her wine glass. His father glances at his wife then over at Jack and Qaniit. Jack looks away, scanning the wedding guests who dine and dance.

~ * ~

Donald sits in his sedan across the street watching as Qaniit, Akiak, Jack, and his parents exit the hall. They climb into their trucks and drive off. Donald takes a swig of beer, burps and tosses the empty can into the back seat. He wipes beer from his chin with the back of his hand and drives off in the opposite direction.

~ * ~

The next morning, Jack takes his parents to the airport. He unloads their luggage and walks them into the terminal. There, he says to them at the counter, "Thank you for coming. Thank you for your blessing."

"Well," his father says. "I do wish you well, son. I mean it." He looks at his wife who scans her ticket. "I can see how much she loves you. You know as well as I do that our love for one another is what God is all about. Just don't give up on God. He tests us, you know, in ways like Abraham, Job."

"Yes, I've thought about that, Father. Many times. With each subsequent tragedy. How many times do I have to take the test?"

His father doesn't answer. Jack hugs his mother and says, "Please come back for our wedding."

She kisses him on the cheek but doesn't say anything. "Father," he says, hugging him. He leaves them there at the check-in counter.

Chapter Thirty-two

Love cannot save you from your own fate.
James Douglas Morrison

That night, they dine out again and walk back through town after dinner, Qaniit holding onto his arm. Neither speaks, each enjoying the crisp autumn, moonlit night. He looks over at her and she looks up at him smiling. They make it back to the Prospector.

In their room, he peels off his jacket and throws it on the desk next to the bed. He undresses her, first taking off her jacket then her boots and her tight-fitting jeans. He sits on the edge of the bed and kisses her thigh, removes her socks, her blouse and kisses her stomach, takes off her bra, stopping to kiss her breasts, and removes her panties, kissing her there too.

She reciprocates, first kissing his lips then taking off his pants, his boots, his shirt, kissing him on his stomach. She removes his underwear, kissing him there, and pushes him down onto the bed. She kisses him all over, teasing him. At last, she climbs on top and they make love. She kisses his lips, his neck, nibbles on his ear and teases his nipples with the tip of her tongue.

After several minutes, he rolls over on top of her and gently reenters her, kissing her lips, her neck and her breasts. They hold on as long as they can.

He releases, yet holds onto her, not letting up, kissing and fondling her more.

Yet again they fall asleep in one another's arms.

~ * ~

The next morning, Jack stirs. Qaniit wakes and wraps her arm

217

across his chest. She presses her lips against his.

He tries to speak though her lips on his but can't.

She climbs atop and straddles him, pinning his arms to the bed above his head.

"Okay, okay," he says, grimacing. "I'm going to be late."

She won't let up. "If I can just find something to tie you up with." She looks around the room.

"God, you're so beautiful," he says reaching his head up to kiss her.

"Don't change the subject, Jack. I'm not playing."

He lays his head back onto the pillow and pulls her down toward him, holding her. They lie like this for several minutes.

He glances at the clock. "It's almost six."

"So."

He reaches for the phone on the nightstand punching in a number. After a couple rings, he says, "Sky? Jack. Get everything ready, do the checks and I'll be there as soon as I can." He hangs up.

"Okay, okay. I love you," he says.

"I'm not letting you go." She holds onto him.

"My last haul. I promise."

She squints at him.

"What kind of a look is that?"

He rolls her off and climbs on top of her. "It was actually quite a sexy look." He leans down and kisses her. "I'll be back in a few days." He heads for the shower. At the shower door, he turns to look back at her lying there, watching him. *God, I'm a fool for leaving you.*

~ * ~

Walking up the dock, still dark out because sunrise isn't until nine-thirty, Jack and Qaniit spot the crew on the Aga preparing for its voyage. Sky has taken charge. Dylan, Jonah and Pete inspect the pots, making sure they are all lashed while Troy packs the bait in the locker.

Jack hugs and kisses Qaniit. She places her head against his chest, not letting him go.

"Break it off, lovers," Sky hollers from the deck. "We're ready to cast off, captain."

"Yeah, funny," Jack says, breaking off the embrace.

Qaniit stands on the dock watching as the boys cast off. Sky at the wheel, he slowly pilots the Aga out to sea, Jack in the co-skipper's chair next to him.

~ * ~

Donald, sitting in his sedan watching from across the street on the far side of the parking lot, snorts, opens his window, and spits a hack out onto the ground. "Fuck with me. You're all gonna get what's coming to you." He punches a number into his cellphone, waits until the phone answers on the other end then enters a code. He hears a long beep on the other end of the line and clicks off his phone, tossing it onto the seat next to him. He chugs a beer and snorts again, this time swallowing.

~ * ~

The cellphone attached to the I.E.D. hidden below deck on the Aga lights up and the triggering timing device switches on, indicating a count-down of thirty-six hours.

~ * ~

Donald shifts into gear, hits the gas, but backs up into a fence. "Goddammit." He shifts into drive and zips off.

~ * ~

The waters are a little rough this morning, with waves splashing over the gunwales. Jack confines the crew to the cabin. "We'll take her out here," he says to Sky, pointing to a map on the computer screen in the wheelhouse, "Half-way between Nome and St. Lawrence. Where the Issumatar indicates there are some good honey-holes."

Sky, at the helm as the skipper-in-training, turns his attention back to the ocean in front of him, waves crashing over the deck as the Aga rolls from side to side.

"You're doing a fine job, kid. Keep her steady."

"Thanks, Jack. If you're okay with my skills after a couple of days, we could have Oscar from Scenic Nome Helicopters come out and airlift you back to your honey." He smiles and looks over at Jack.

"Ha, ha. Keep your eye on the ocean."

"I have to say. You know you have a glint in your eye."

"A glint? Where did you get that word?"

"I was educated, ya know. I have my associate's degree in mechanics from the community college."

"Good for you. You should now get a degree in engineering."

"Yeah." He looks out at the churning sea then back over at Jack. "So, what I mean is you're not so crabby now, pardon the pun."

"Crabby? I'll have more of glint in my eye when I'm certain you've mastered piloting this boat and can lead the crew so I can sit in an office all day and have lunch with someone much more beautiful than you."

He laughs. "See? You crack me up."

"Yeah. Yeah. Keep her steady. I'm going down to lecture the boys." Jack climbs out of his chair and heads below to the cabin.

In the cabin, the boys lounge. Pete and his brother, Troy, play Spades with Dylan and Jonah. "Follow suit, man," Jonah says to Dylan.

"I thought it was clubs," Dylan says.

"Diamonds," they shout at him.

"Aww, damn," Dylan says, throwing his cards onto the pile.

"He's still tired out from his wedding night," Pete says, smiling.

"Stop," Jonah says. "That's my sister you're talking about."

"And my wife," Dylan says, frowning.

"All right," Jack says. "All right. Listen up. We're not going back in until we fill up the tanks. The Issumatar is heading back in with a full haul. We have to match that."

"Yeah," Jonah says. "We can't let Captain Conrad one-up us."

"No, we can't," Jack says. "Pay attention to what you're doing. I need your head totally in the game. Watch the pots swinging around and make sure you're clear of the launcher. I don't need any broken legs." He scans their willing faces. "The weather report is windy, so it'll be choppy. Watch the waves over the gunwales. The water temp is falling and don't expect me to dive in for you. I'm not Poseidon."

"Poseidon?" says Dylan, laughing.

"Okay," Jack says. "Gear up in ten and let's drop the pots, boys."

"How's Sky doing, captain?"

"He *will* be the captain of the Aga on the next haul."

"Go easy on him," Jonah says. "He's really a sensitive guy."

"Yeah, right," Dylan says. "He's a hard-ass."

Jack goes back up to the wheelhouse and checks his computer. "Let's drop here," he says, pointing to a spot on the computer screen.

The boys on deck work on dropping the pots.

In the wheelhouse, Jack and Sky watch and monitor another storm approaching. "You see how it spreads this way," Jack says, pointing to the storm on the computer screen. "And the current is here, so if we swing around like this," Jack traces the route, "we can perhaps avoid the brunt of it."

Sky nods. Jack looks at him then sits back in the chair. "You make judgment calls, as you know," Jack says. "This is never worth the lives of your crew. If you can't out run it, or go around it, you'll have to head into it. Like we did the other day." They hear Jonah whistle from the deck. He signals okay. Sky increases the Aga's speed and swings around to another honey-hole.

The crew finishes laying all one hundred and fifty pots. After dinner, the boys play cards, watch movies, and catch some shut-eye.

~ * ~

The timer on the bomb counts down, showing twenty-four hours and two minutes.

Chapter Thirty-three

Woe, destruction, ruin, and decay;
The worst is death, and death will have his way.
William Shakespeare, *Richard II*

Throughout the next day the crew rests, plays cards and learns how to service equipment from Sky and Jack. They oil and service the crane, the launcher and the winch.

That night, Sky cooks a hearty supper of halibut and the boys share a cherry pie that Dylan's new bride baked from scratch.

Sky relieves Jack in the wheelhouse so he can get a plate. As he enters the cabin, he discovers the light's out.

"Surprise," the boys shout.

"All right," Jack says. "What's going on in here?"

"We saved you a piece of pie and got you an engraved paperweight," Jonah says. He holds up the paperweight and reads, "Captain Jack Douglas. Fisherman. In appreciation." He hands it to him.

The paperweight depicts a ship, a fish and a crab. "Thanks, boys."

"Your pie, Jack," Dylan says, handing it to him.

Jack sits and eats the pie with the boys who joke about fishing and girls.

After finishing his meal, Jack says, "Okay. Let's gear up and get it done."

"Aye, aye, captain," Jonah, the new deck boss says. "Let's go, ladies. Put your rubbers on and get out there."

Jack climbs the stairs to the wheelhouse. The Aga rolls in high waves. "First string there," Jack says to Sky, pointing below at the first buoy bobbing up and down in the rough waves. Sky slows the boat to an idle.

The Skype on the computer rings. Jack answers, "Hey, boss."

Qaniit's image in the Prospector comes on over Skype. "You done yet?"

"Almost," Jack says. "Back by the end of the week."

"Not funny."

"Look who I have here." Jack turns the computer to show Sky waving from the captain's chair. "Hey, Qaniit," Sky says. "Your man is driving me crazy. Couldn't you have tied him to a chair or something back there at the inn?"

"I already thought of that."

Jack turns the computer back to face him. "Enough of him."

"Hey," Sky says, frowning.

"We're about to pull up the first string. I'll call you in the morning."

"You better."

Jack glances at Sky who rolls his eyes and looks away.

"Jack, I can't sleep without you now."

"I know." They stare at one another for the longest time. The thought of what Sky told him, about Oscar flying out to pick him up, crosses his mind. "We'll be in as soon as we fill the tanks. I promise. Sky's ready for the next haul."

Silence. He watches as she wipes a tear from her eye and tucks her hair behind her ear as she always does. *God, don't let anything happen to this woman. Please?* "Gotta go," Jack says. "Love you."

She forces a smile, in a forlorn way. "I love you too."

Jack switches off Skype and watches the crew coming out of the cabin dressed in their gear. For the first time in a few weeks, he feels apprehension, a pit in the bottom of his gut. He reaches down and grasps the amaroq claw, thinking of Amaroq, then Qaniit. He misses both. He looks over at Sky again who now has a cheesy grin on his face. "What?" Jack snaps.

"Nothing." He looks down at the crew getting ready to haul in the first pot. "It's just that you too are so cuuuute."

"Knock it off and pay attention. This is where, as you know, it's critical you watch what these boys are doing every step of the way."

"Roger that."

They watch as the boys on deck hoist up the first pot with several dozen crabs. "No," Sky says, "I mean, it's a great thing. I've known her and the family all my life. You have saved her, Jack. I'm sure you know the sadness she was in since, well, you know."

Jack hears him but doesn't respond, looking down at the crew as they re-bait and drop the pot back in.

"We tease you and all," Sky says continuing. "You know you're the best thing that's happened to her."

Jack looks over at him.

"I mean that, Jack."

"All right. Keep her steady. I'm going down to make sure these boys are thinking safety. No one's getting injured or worse on my watch." He puts on his raincoat and exits the wheelhouse.

On deck, Jack pulls up to the boys. They raise another pot with a few dozen crabs and cheer. "Great work, boys. Re-bait and push them all back in. I think we've hit the honey-hole here. We're going back with a full haul."

"Aye, aye, captain," Jonah says.

Pete re-baits the pot and closes the trap. Dylan engages the launcher and slides the pot back in. As it sinks, Dylan throws the shot in and Troy tosses one buoy and Dylan the other. The storm kicks up, rain pelting them, waves pounding the Aga, splashing over the gunwales soaking the boys.

"Only one hundred forty-eight to go," Jack says. "Do all the same and use your noggins. Pay attention to detail."

Jack stands there for a moment, Sky steadying the boat, the boys preparing to raise the next pot. Jack breathes in the crisp, fresh ocean air. Although he wants to be with the woman he now loves, as much as he can day in and day out, he feels at peace and at ease on the boat with these boys. He understands Qaniit's fear. Although her husband had been a captain, too, he was swept overboard during gale-force winds when a waved crashed over the boat during a severe storm. He had been out on deck helping to fix a leak in the hydraulic hoses. The wave swept him over, and he was gone in an instant. They never recovered his body.

Jack glances up at Sky in the wheelhouse. "I better get back up there, boys."

"Yeah," Jonah says. "Make sure Sky is competent."

"You just make sure you're competent," Jack says, patting him on his back. He turns to head back up to the wheelhouse.

~ * ~

The timer on the bomb counts down five, four, three, two, one.

The explosion rips through the hull, the cabin and up into the wheelhouse. The entire boat shudders, knocking Jack and the boys over by the blast. A fireball billows high up into the air.

~ * ~

"Anchorage, British Airways two-niner-four," the captain in the cockpit of a British flight high above the explosion says. "We just saw a large fireball half-way between St. Lawrence and Nome. You might want to notify the authorities."

"British Airways two-niner-four. Anchorage. We copy. Will notify the coast guard. Out."

~ * ~

Jack rolls over on the deck, his ears ringing. He sits up, turns and sees the wheelhouse engulfed in flames. He pulls himself up and finds the boys scattered on the deck, regaining their senses.

Jack runs over to them, helping up Dylan, Jonah, and Pete but can't locate Troy. He peers over the gunwale into the churning sea below but can't spot him.

"Troy," Pete shouts. He too stands looking over the gunwale into the dark ocean below.

Jack turns, looks at the flaming wheelhouse as the boat lurches to the side. "Pete, Jonah, grab fire extinguishers and follow me. Dylan, get the life preservers and the raft ready."

Jack hustles over to the stairs of the wheelhouse where he grabs a fire extinguisher. Pete at first hesitates to abandon his effort in looking for

Troy but then follows Jonah. They grab fire extinguishers off the wall under the wheelhouse and meet Jack at the stairs. Jack sprints up the stairs, Pete and Jonah following.

With the heat from the fire radiating on his face, Jack pulls the pin and sprays the doorway to the wheelhouse but can't get it under control. The boys spray as well, however the fire is too intense.

The boat heaves to one side at about twenty degrees. Jack and Jonah manage to beat back the flames at the door to the wheelhouse and get just inside where they discover the instruments all burning. Sky's body lies on the floor, charred beyond recognition. The windows have been blown out.

They beat back more flames, extinguishing the fire on and around the instruments, but all the instruments have stopped working. Jack grabs the radio transmitter, but the hand-held microphone is too hot and has melted so he drops it. The radio smolders.

The computers destroyed, nothing in working order, the boat creaks and continues to roll over at about thirty degrees now. "Let's go," Jack yells at the boys.

At an angle going down the stairs, they hold on as another explosion rocks the engine room. A secondary gas tank exploded from the fire. They struggle to stand against the tilting boat but meet up with Dylan who has the raft and preservers on deck. The raft is a six-person heavy-duty polyurethane nylon ocean standard life raft able to withstand freezing cold temperatures equipped with a survival pack for twenty-four hours. Yellow and orange, it can be easily spotted by aircraft.

"We have to abandon ship," Jack says. "We need to get away from the boat, or she'll pull us under."

Struggling against the tilting boat, the pelting rain and waves crashing against the ship, they make it over to the gunwale. "It's going to be cold," Jack shouts. "Put your preservers on, and I'll pull the cord as soon we toss her in. Swim over to the raft as fast as you can and push it away from the boat."

Their faces white with terror, they put their preservers on. After a minute, they hoist the raft up onto the gunwale, steadying it against the angle of the boat. "Toss," Jack shouts. They toss it over as Jack holds on to the ripcord. The raft inflates as it flies over the side. "Jump," Jack yells.

The boys jump in, Jack following.

They crash down onto the water, but a wave throws them back up against the side of the boat. Jonah hits his head against the rising hull, knocking him out. Pete and Dylan swim for the raft as Jack swims over to Jonah, grabs him, swimming backward toward the raft.

Pete and Dylan reach the raft, swim with it, pulling it away from the sinking Aga. Jack struggles to follow them with Jonah in tow, the water already bone-chilling.

The boys manage to get a sizable distance between them and the boat. They climb into the raft.

Jack catches up. "Grab him," he says to them. They hoist the unconscious Jonah into the raft then help Jack in. He zips up the door to the raft.

Dylan and Pete catch their breath while Jack attends to Jonah. "He's breathing, thank God," Jack says. He feels Jonah's pulse. "Jonah," he says. He gently slaps Jonah's face. "Jonah. Wake up."

Jonah's eyes flicker.

"Jonah," Jack says again. "Can you hear me?"

Jonah's eyes flicker again. At last, he whispers, "Jack?"

"Jonah. You have to wake up."

"What happened?" His eyes open to only a slit.

"A wave caught us. Threw us back against the hull. Where's it hurt?"

"My head."

Jack examines Jonah's head and discovers a lump.

"What is it, Jack?"

"You hit your head." Jack removes his preserver as waves pound the raft. Pete and Dylan struggle to hold steady. Jack topples over onto Jonah.

Jack sits up, removes his jacket, flannel shirt, and tears off his T-shirt. His upper frame exposed, he puts the jacket back on, crumples up the T-shirt into a ball and dips it into the cold water inside the raft from their dripping clothes. He applies it to the lump growing on Jonah's head.

They hear a loud creaking. Pete unzips the door. They have a straight shot through the door to see the Aga capsize, the moonlight reflecting off the hull. Jack spots a large hole in the hull near the engine compartment. It appears the fire has been extinguished by the seawater pouring into the hull as only smoke billows from the hole now.

"What the hell happened, Jack?" says Pete.

"I don't know. I had the engine serviced a couple weeks ago and it was reported to be in perfect condition."

"I mean," Pete continues, "boats just don't explode like that."

"No." Jack shakes his head. They watch as the Aga slowly sinks into the sea, water now shooting up through the hole as the ship fills with water.

"Troy," Pete yells out through the door in the ceilinged raft. He looks out at the black ocean. "Troy? You out there?"

Jack glances over at him while holding the balled-up T-shirt against Jonah's lump. Troy is most likely gone, swept over the side and drowned by the crashing waves without a preserver. Even the most experienced swimmer in fifteen-foot waves can't survive this turbulence for long.

"I'm so cold, Jack," says Dylan, his teeth chattering.

"Look in the survival kit. There's a first aide blanket in there. Take your wet clothes off and the two of you huddle under that."

"Troy's out there, Jack," Pete says, his voice cracking and tears streaming down his face.

"I understand," Jack says. "There's a flashlight in the kit and a ring on the zipper. Gerry-rig the flashlight to the ring and keep it on so he can find us, but we've got to zip up the door or we'll freeze to death. Then strip and get under the blanket."

They hear a loud sucking sound and look out to see the Aga sink below the surface. Jack feels responsible as Malik's prized boat goes under. Yes, the boat is insured, but it has been in his family business for more than twenty years. *What happened?* Jack feels horrible and worries more about his survivors and his fiancée than himself.

Chapter Thirty-four

The sea is unforgiving.
Anonymous

Akiak speeds through the Nome streets just past midnight. He blows through stop signs, skids around corners and slams on the breaks outside the Nasak office, coming to a halt in the gravel parking lot, stones disgorging out in all directions. A coast guard pick-up truck, a Nome police car and a few other cars are parked there. He sprints up the steps and bursts through the door.

There, he finds Miles standing with the aid of a cane, Conrad, Ronny, Rhonda, Police Chief Cerrano, a deputy, and Jason Kent, the U.S. Coast Guard Commander. "I'm going with you," Akiak says to everyone gathered.

"Anchorage air traffic control reported an airliner flying from China to London spotted a large explosion at these coordinates here," Kent says, pointing to a computer screen Rhonda huddles in front of.

"That's the exact spot where the GPS tracker went cold," Rhonda says.

"Planes like that fly at what?" Miles says. "Thirty thousand feet?"

"Higher on transpacific flights," Kent says. "It had to be a very big explosion for them to see it at that altitude."

Akiak paces the room.

"We've dispatched a chopper," Kent says continuing, "but they won't be able to cover much of the search area because by the time they fly out, and calculating the fuel needed to return, they can't stay out in the search area for too long. Besides, another storm is picking up and coming in. I've got the cutter gearing up and they should be ready within minutes. All cargo ships coming in and out of the area have been notified and are searching too. See if you can organize other boats from town, Miles. The more out there the better."

"Okay," Miles says. "Conrad, get the boys together and fire up the Issumatar. Ronny, see if you can scrape together some boys and fire up the Nuliajuk." He looks everyone over and continues, "If the Aga went down, and they made it into the raft, it has a beacon and flares."

Everyone stands silent, contemplating that statement for a moment.

"What do you think happened, Miles?" Ronny says.

"I don't know. A boat just doesn't explode for no reason. Especially like that."

"Donald Prescott," Akiak says.

"What about him?" Chief Cerrano says.

"He threatened me a few days ago."

"I thought he had a restraining order?'

"He does. I ran into him at the market. He said all kinds of strange warnings about shit happens and we'll get what's coming to us."

The chief looks him over. "Where is he? Prescott?"

"Snake River Motel," Akiak says.

"I'll draft a search warrant on the pretense he violated the order. See what we can find."

Silence, everyone watches one another.

"What about the families?" Miles says. "Qaniit?"

"This is not going to go over well," Conrad says. "It might send her over the edge."

"We better tell grandmother first," Akiak says.

"We'll go together," Miles says. "Can we be ready to move out in, let's say, an hour, boys?"

Conrad and Ronny nod.

"Okay," Miles continues. "Everyone meet at the dock in one hour."

~ * ~

Jack turns on the beacon that blinks and sends out a signal. He affixes it to a ring on the outside of the raft.

"I'm so cold, Jack," Jonah whispers. Jack undressed him and all three boys huddle under the emergency thermal blanket. Their soaked clothes lie in a pile near their feet.

"I know," Jack says. "Here." He reaches under the blanket and massages Jonah's legs, his arms and rubs him down.

"Jack?"

"What is it?"

"I can't see."

Jack doesn't respond but continues to rub him to get his circulation going. Jack is cold, too, but disregards his discomfort.

The raft shakes and gyrates as fifteen-foot swells smash against it. The raft was designed so that it won't flip over, but it rolls from side to side like a bobble-head. The boys, quiet and shivering, slosh around inside it.

Jack says, "Keep the blanket over your heads because most heat escapes through there. Try to generate heat from your bodies to warm each other."

"What about you, Jack?" Dylan says.

"I'm fine. Just keep rubbing yourselves all over. Massage your muscles. Keep the circulation going to generate heat."

"He's gone, right, Jack?" Pete says sniffling.

Jack doesn't want to answer that but says, "I'm so sorry."

Jack works on Jonah whose eyes have closed. "Stay awake, kid." He gently slaps Jonah's face, first one side then the other.

Jonah's eyes flicker. "Jack?" he says, his voice barely audible.

"I'm here, kid."

"Dylan there?"

"He's right here."

"Dylan?"

"Right next to you, brother."

A wave strikes the raft, tossing them over onto their sides and back again. "What's up, man?"

"Dylan?"

"Yes?"

"You be good to my sister and take care of her. You hear me?"

"You're not going anywhere, brother."

"You gotta promise me."

"I promise."

"Okay," Jonah says, his eyes flickering again.

"Stay with me, Jonah," Jack says rubbing Jonah's arms and legs. Jack keeps working on Jonah as the raft tosses, turns, and shutters in the wind.

~ * ~

Akiak pulls up to the Prospector with Ulloriaq and Miles in his truck. Moonlight shining on them, they crawl out of the truck and go up the steps. There, they stop and look at one another before Akiak uses his key to open the front door.

Inside, Ulloriaq turns on the hall light. Qaniit opens her bedroom door and comes out, wrapping a robe around her. As they edge toward her, she places her hand on the wall and slides down to the floor. Squatting there against the wall, they rush her, Akiak getting there first to grab her arms, trying to pull her back up.

Qaniit, with the palm of her hand holding herself steady against the wall, says, "No. No. No."

"He's alive, Qaniit," Ulloriaq says taking her by the arm. "I know it."

Miles hobbles over as fast as he can.

Ulloriaq grabs Qaniit under her armpits and, with Akiak's assistance, lifts her into her arms. "I feel it. I know he's alive," Ulloriaq says.

Qaniit taps her open palms against her grandmother's shoulders. "I knew this. I knew it." Tears drip from her eyes.

Akiak says, his voice cracking, "We're gonna go out now and find him, Cuz. Trust me. We're gonna find them all. You gotta believe me. Ronny's getting all the boys together. The coast guard is out. Ships all over the Sound are out looking for them. I know he's alive. I just know it. You know what the shaman said."

With an angry voice, she says, "Why? He was in the wheelhouse.

Not on deck. I just spoke to him a few hours ago. He was in the wheelhouse."

"There was an explosion and we lost contact with the ship," Miles says.

She steadies herself and says to her grandmother, "I'm pregnant."

Silence.

Ulloriaq takes her granddaughter's cheeks in both hands and says, "He's alive. I'm telling you, Qaniit. You know how I know these things. You know what I know. We're gonna get him. I know that too."

"I'm going with you," she says, wiping the tears from her face with the back of her hands. "I gotta get dressed." She turns, rushes into her room, the others following.

Miles says, "You stay here, Qaniit. We'll bring him in."

"No," she snaps at him, turning around. "I'm going out there with you. You're not stopping me. You're not keeping me from him. No one or nothing is keeping me from him. You hear me?" she says, her voice rising.

"She can go with us on the Issumatar," Akiak says.

"I'm coming too," Ulloriaq says.

Nodding, Miles says, "Okay. Let's go."

~ * ~

An hour later Dylan says, "I think we're warming up, Jack. This thermal blanket works."

"Good. Keep rubbing and don't stop."

"Pete," Dylan says. "You gotta keep at it." He elbows him.

"My brother is dead," Pete says sobbing. "He's out there. All alone."

"I'm sorry," Dylan says. "I'm really sorry."

Jack puts his index and middle finger against Jonah's neck and feels no pulse. Kneeling next to him, he whispers into his ear, his voice cracking, "I'm sorry, kid. I'm so sorry." Jonah's eyelids are open a bit, so Jack closes them. He pulls Jonah's body to the side.

"What's wrong, Jack?" Dylan says.

"He's gone."

"Gone?"

Everyone's quiet for a moment.

"We're all gonna die, Jack," Dylan shouts, sitting up in a fit, sobbing. "We're all gonna die."

"Stop it."

Dylan shivers. Hysterically, he says, "We're gonna die out here and no one will find us."

Jack shakes him by his shoulders. "Get hold of yourself. We fight. Understand me? Never give up."

Dylan struggles with Jack who bear hugs him to stop him from thrashing. "You never give up. Don't ever give up. You fight and you fight. You hear me?"

Jack holds onto the sniveling Dylan. "Dylan?" He pulls back, holds him by the shoulders and looks into his eyes. "Okay?"

Dylan nods and whimpers as the raft continues to thrash around in the thirty-knot winds and ten to fifteen-foot waves. "Okay now," Jack says. "I need you to be brave. We're inside a state-of-the-art life raft. We have the beacon up. We will even get warmer in here as this is what it's designed to do. Keep us warm and safe from the elements."

Jack lets him go. "Pete?" he says.

"Yes?"

"You okay?"

"Yes."

Silence for a minute.

"My brother is gone, Jack. Gone."

Jack struggles against the topsy-turvy raft but pulls up next to him and takes his hand, squeezing it.

"I knew this was a dangerous profession," Pete says. "How does a boat just blow up like that?"

Jack thinks it over. He remembers Qaniit said Donald had worked at a quarry blasting rocks. *Could that be possible? O'Reilly murdered the young Sanders. Could it be possible that this man, Donald, was just as evil and would murder a crab crew? A crew of young boys? Three boys are dead. What kind of a monster does this?* Jack says, "We're going to get through this. Someone will find us. There are lots of ships out here. Cargo ships, crabbers." He sees Qaniit lying next to him, holding on tight. He misses her so much. He sees Amaroq walking next to him on a mountain trail. Still dressed in his pants and only his raincoat, he reaches down and grasps the amaroq claw. It gives him warmth and energy.

Dylan sniffles, Pete shivers from the cold.

~ * ~

A dozen boats, including the Issumatar, leave the harbor and sail out into Norton Sound.

A Coast Guard cutter, with a chopper tied down on its heliport, leads the way.

~ * ~

Jack kicks his boots off and peels off his wet socks. He rubs his feet. He keeps his rain jacket on because it doesn't absorb water.

"Keep rubbing your legs, boys," Jack says. "We're warming up pretty good as our heat is trapped inside the thermal raft. We're going to make it because there are ships all over out here and as soon as the boat went down, the GPS signal was lost so Rhonda in the morning tracking the boat will figure this out too." He waits for them to say something. Anything. "Okay?"

"Okay, Jack," Pete says. "I am getting warmer."

"Dylan?"

"Yes?"

"You okay?"

"Yes."

"Good."

The rain continues to pelt the raft and the gale-force winds thrash it about. They lie there in silence listening to the rain and waves crashing into them.

Huddling and shivering a few minutes later, a big wave crashes against them. Jack rolls over onto Dylan. He pulls himself up again but something smashes into the side of the raft, the living and the dead thrown together up against the other side. The raft tears open as this monster slashes through it. Water pours in and inundates the raft in no time at all.

Jonah's body floats off into the darkness. Pete disappears beneath the churning waves. Jack, thrown up against Dylan, grabs onto him and holds on as they float away from the raft. Their life preservers scatter and the raft deflates, air swooshing out of it faster than air being let out of a valve in a tire.

Jack holds onto Dylan in the water, with no raft, no life preservers, nothing.

Chapter Thirty-five

Never give up, for that is just the place and time that the tide will turn.
Harriet Beecher Stowe

Aboard the Issumatar in the wheelhouse, Qaniit sits in the co-skipper's chair, Conrad in the skipper's, Ulloriaq on a fold-up chair behind them. Qaniit stares straight ahead at the black sea and dark sky, her face frozen in determination. Conrad opens the Issumatar up to three-quarters full throttle.

"Issumatar, Coast Guard Nome Station. Over."

"Issumatar. Over."

"We picked up a beacon signal. We'll send that to you. Cutter heading that way now."

"Issumatar. Copy."

"Coast Guard Nome out."

Qaniit looks down onto the deck where about ten men have gathered. Conrad grabs the PA mike. "Listen up, men," he says over the PA. "Chuck, you're in charge down there. Every man wears a preserver at all times." He hangs the mike on the wall next to him and glances over at Qaniit. "The beacon means they deployed the life raft. They're alive, Qaniit. We're gonna find him."

She looks at him but doesn't answer. She turns back to face the unforgiving ocean.

~ * ~

"Chief," Judge Saghani says opening his door in the dark early morning seeing Chief Cerrano standing there on his porch.

"I have an emergency, your honor." He hands the judge the search warrant. "We have probable cause to believe Donald Prescott may be involved in an explosion aboard the Aga. The crew is missing."

The judge sighs, takes possession of the warrant and says, "Come in."

The Chief enters as Saghani holds the door for him to pass.

Inside, Saghani turns on the hall light and walks into the living room where he lifts his reading glasses off a table by a chair. He reads the warrant and looks up at the chief, raising an eyebrow. He grabs a pen from a cup of pens and pencils next to a crossword puzzle, scribbles his signature on the warrant and hands it back to the Chief.

"Thanks, Bob. We've got everyone out looking for them. I'll keep you posted and when this is over, you and Melissa come over for dinner."

"Sure, Bruno." Saghani shows the Chief out.

~ * ~

"Don't let go of my hand," Jack says, swimming and holding Dylan with one hand while dragging half of the deflated raft with the other. Jack still has his pants and rain jacket on. They make it over to the shipping container floating nearby. The shipping container fell off a ship on its way to or from China or another Pacific Rim country and the west coast, Jack figures. This is a regular problem as the big cargo ships weathered all the storms, but hundreds, sometimes a few thousand containers a year fall off ships, some sinking, and some floating for days or weeks until they slowly sink to the bottom. Some wash ashore all over the world.

"Stay with me, Dylan." Jack tosses the torn raft up onto the container. "I need your help."

"I'm so cold, Jack."

Almost thirty percent of the container floats above the surface of the water. Despite waves crashing over it, they have a chance to get up there and hold on. Jack pushes Dylan up. "Grab on."

Dylan reaches up, pulls, and Jack pushes him up and onto the container. "Give me a hand," Jack says.

Dylan, with no clothes on, except his underwear, reaches over, pulling Jack up. Jack grabs on and manages to climb up onto the container. "That side up there," Jack says pointing. "It's higher. Come on."

Jack grabs the torn-in-two raft, dragging it to the higher floating side. "Get under." He pulls the raft over onto Dylan. Jack removes his rain jacket and crawls under the half-raft with him. "This will warm us." Dylan's body shakes. Jack hugs him, rubbing his body to keep him warm as waves slosh over the top.

The other half of the deflated raft floats away. The beacon, attached to the ring on this half, flashes and beeps in the darkness.

~ * ~

Chief Cerrano and his deputies arrive at the motel. He holds onto the warrant that stipulates they are allowed to search the room and Donald's person based on a threat and reasonable suspicion. It does not give them authority to arrest him, however.

Inside, a deputy bangs on a room door. "Police. Open up."

Donald opens the door dressed in dirty tidy-whites.

"We have a warrant to search your room, Donald," Cerrano says. "You need to step outside." The chief hands him the warrant.

"You have no proof," Donald says, scowling.

"Proof of what?"

Donald doesn't answer.

"The warrant authorizes us to search you too," Cerrano says.

Donald scans the warrant.

"Step aside," Cerrano says again. He and two deputies, one carrying a forensics case, push past Donald, leaving him standing there with two deputies in the hallway.

"Stand there," the first deputy in the hallway says to Donald.

Donald tightens his face and moves aside.

"Tim," the first deputy says to the second deputy. The first deputy holds up his case for the second deputy to hold while keeping an eye on Donald. The first deputy opens the case and puts on rubber gloves. "Hold your hands out, palms up."

Donald crumbles the warrant and throws it on the floor but holds his hands cockeyed.

The first deputy frowns, takes out wipes from a kit, grabs one of Donald's hands and twists it, palms up. He swipes one hand then the other on both sides and puts the pad in an evidence bag. He takes out another pad, swipes Donald's arms as Donald hacks and swallows.

The first deputy secures that pad in another evidence bag and closes it, putting it back into his case.

Inside the room, the deputies find and place into evidence bags left over wires from the bomb, wire cutters, parts of the cellphone used to trigger the timer, pliers, a screw driver and they wipe the desk, nightstand and other areas.

"Next flight to Juneau is in one hour," the chief says to one of his deputies. "Get that and the swabs from Tim on that flight to the lab."

One of the deputies takes possession of the evidence bags, stopping in the hallway to get the others. Donald narrows his eyes at the bags in the deputy's hands as the deputy hurries off down the hallway.

~ * ~

"Issumatar, this is Coast Guard Station Nome."

In the wheelhouse, Conrad grabs the radio mike as Qaniit watches him. "Go for Issumatar."

"There's a Japanese freighter, the Niji, ten miles south, southeast of the beacon. They're steaming that way now. Over."

"Issumatar, copy. Out." He hangs the mike up, glances over at Qaniit then behind him at Ulloriaq. He spots the boys on deck, a few scanning the ocean with night-vision goggles.

~ * ~

Under the raft, Jack holds Dylan close to help transfer heat from one to the other. He continues to rub him to keep the circulation going. "Dylan?"

He doesn't answer.

"Come on. I need you to hang in there." He shakes Dylan. "Stay awake."

Dylan's eyes flicker.

Jack continues to rub Dylan down. A large wave smashes into the container, rocking it and spilling water over the top. Jack has to hold onto the ridged edges on the top of the container with one hand and the raft with the other so it won't wash over the side.

Exposed to the night sky, he sees the clouds breaking. By looking at the position of the moon, it must be about three or four A.M. That means sunrise is about six hours away.

"Dylan? You with me?"

"Yes, but I'm numb, Jack."

"You have to help me, kid. Rub your arms."

"Okay."

Each works on rubbing.

"Jack?" Dylan says.

"What's up, kid?"

"I only made love to my wife a couple times since the wedding. I mean, we waited until we were married because, well, she wouldn't ya know. I respected her."

Jack doesn't respond. He holds him tight, rubbing his back. The raft isn't keeping them warm because just as they generate heat by being under it and using their bodies, a wave comes along, slipping over the top of the container, dislodging the raft, letting the heat escape. Jack repositions the raft each time, begins all over again. If they aren't rescued soon, they will die of hypothermia. Jack remembers reading about Titanic passengers in the water. The water in the North Atlantic had been about fifty degrees, ten or more degrees colder than this water at this time. Titanic passengers were in the water, and scientists estimated that some could have survived forty-five or fifty minutes but not longer. With a human's body temperature at about ninety-eight degrees, fifty-degree water brought it down quickly. He and Dylan are not in the water, nor is it as cold, so perhaps they can survive for a few hours if they keep working on their circulation. They can't survive for too long, however.

"You hang in there, kid. Rhonda will be in the office soon, and she monitors the GPS tracking on the boats. She'll see the tracker off and get a search underway. I am sure of that."

Jack holds onto the shivering Dylan. "You have to fight. Come on, Dylan. Come on. For your bride. You hear me?"

Weeping, Dylan says, "I'll try, Jack. I'll try."

Chapter Thirty-six

When the world says, "Give up," hope whispers, "Try it one more time."
Unknown

Donald dresses, packs his bag, jumps into his rental and speeds for the airport.

He skids to a stop in the main parking lot, not bothering to turn in the rental car. He gets out, grabs his bag and scurries for the terminal.

Approaching the terminal entrance, he stops cold, spotting a police car parked there. He slinks over to the door, peers inside. He sees two deputies standing next to the check-in as if they're on surveillance in addition to the normal airport security.

Looking around, sweat beading on his forehead, he turns around and hurries back to his rental. He sits in the rental for a moment until he turns the engine over and peels out of the lot.

He drives back to the motel but stops short when he sees a police car parked there. Two deputies exit the motel and stand by their car. One deputy speaks into the microphone attached to his shoulder while the other scans the area. They climb into their patrol car then drive off.

Donald waits a minute, his eyes darting around. At last, he puts the rental into gear, backing up. He spins around then speeds off.

He zips over to the ferry dock where the ferry preps for a run. He stops short again after seeing the police car from the motel parked there. The deputies stand near the ferry talking with a man. "Fuck." He slams his fists onto the steering wheel. "Fuck. Fuck. Fuck."

He peels out yet again, winding his way over to the Snake River Road heading north.

~ * ~

The Japanese freighter Niji slices through the waves. Searchlights scan the water. The men on deck point at the orange and yellow object in the water off the port bow with the blinking beacon.

The Niji pulls up and idles. A man lowers a rope ladder over the side, climbs down holding onto a rope and a long boat-hook pole. At the bottom near the water, he leans over, tries to hook the raft, jabbing the pole forward a couple times. He tries several more times before snagging it. He ties the rope onto a ring on the raft. The men above hoist it up.

The man climbs back up. The men inspect this half of the Aga's raft with the beacon flashing on its ring. One man looks at another with a long face who shakes his head.

~ * ~

"Issumatar. Coast Guard Nome. Over."

Conrad grabs the mike. "Go for Issumatar."

"It's Kent. I'm afraid I don't have a good report. Over."

"Hold," Conrad says looking over at Qaniit.

She climbs out of the chair, stands next to him. In a flat, determined voice, she says, "Go ahead, Conrad."

Ulloriaq jumps up from her seat, stands next to Qaniit, holding Qaniit's arm. Conrad sighs and says, "Nome, go for report. Over."

"The Niji reports they found half the raft. Seems it was torn into two pieces. This half had the beacon. No sign of survivors. Over."

Ulloriaq grabs Qaniit from behind by her shoulders, steadying her. "He's alive. I know it. I feel it, Qaniit." Ulloriaq looks at Conrad. "We're not giving up, Conrad. You hear me?" she says, her voice rising.

"Of course not." He watches as Qaniit, with a tight face and showing no emotion, climbs back into the co-skipper's chair. She looks out through the front window, her eyes scanning the merciless ocean before her.

~ * ~

Jack drifts in and out of consciousness. He struggles to stay awake. He hadn't slept much the night before last because he stayed in the wheelhouse with Sky. He feels for Dylan's pulse. It's shallow and weak. He tucks the raft down around Dylan on one side then climbs on top of him to keep him warm, just like Amaroq kept him warm so many nights ago in that storm in his tent. He tucks the raft down around Dylan on the other side too.

Jack's eyes grow heavy. He can't fight much longer. He wants to keep rubbing Dylan but has to rub his own body to keep warm now. "Dylan," he says. "Come on. Don't stop. Wake up."

"I can't, Jack," he whispers.

"You have to hang on. Come on."

Jack fights against his heavy eyelids. Hypothermia is setting in, shutting down his senses. He also fights the waves splashing up onto and spilling over the top of the container that is sinking with only about ten percent now showing, the far edge level with the water.

His eyes flicker and close, darkness enveloping him.

Something pulls the raft off his head. He squints up to see Amaroq standing there. *Am I dead? Is it over? Can I now wander for eternity with her in the wild?* "I've missed you, girl."

"Yelp."

He looks around, sees the sinking container.

"Yelp." She licks his face. Her warm tongue sends a burst of energy throughout his body, giving him strength. She nudges his head.

He reaches down, grasps the amaroq claw, squeezing it. "I'm so sorry for letting you down, girl."

"Yelp." She again licks his face. Using her nose, she nudges him again. She lies down next to him. He pulls the raft up and over her, huddling.

His eyes grow heavy. He drifts off into the abyss with Amaroq warming him.

~ * ~

Donald pulls off Snake River Road several miles north of Nome. He drives down a dirt path, stopping near the river in a secluded area. Sweating, his hands shaking, he pulls his cellphone from his pocket and punches in a number. Not getting a signal, he says, "Goddammit." He tosses the cell onto the passenger seat, wipes the sweat from his forehead and crawls out of the car.

He hacks and spits into the river while unzipping his fly. He takes a leak then hears something rustling around in the bushes behind him.

He zips his fly back up. "Hello?" he says. "Who's there?" He scans the bushes, sees what appears to be a large animal creeping around, but he can't make out what it is. He hobbles back to the sedan, climbs in and shuts the door.

Sweating and out of breath, he drives back toward the main road. He kills his headlights when he spots a police car with its lights flashing approaching in the distance, heading his way. He backs up into the bushes out of sight as the police car speeds by.

He sits there in his sedan concealed in the bushes as the police car hurries back down the road with its lights flashing a few minutes later. After it passes, he turns around, drives back down to the riverbank where he turns the car off and waits. "Goddammit," he says banging his fists onto the wheel.

~ * ~

"Issumatar. This is coast guard cutter Tupilek."

Conrad, in the wheelhouse answers, "Go for Issumatar."

"We've arrived on scene. Debris stretch visible. Pot buoys from the Aga lined up. We'll trace the current. Tupilek out."

Conrad glances at Qaniit who doesn't show any emotion, her blank face staring out through the window.

~ * ~

Jack opens his eyes, discovers the raft half off him. He looks around for Amaroq, but she's not there. He looks down at his hand gripping the amaroq claw.

The sea has calmed. Swells of about five to seven feet splash up onto the container. Still holding onto Dylan, he looks up at the sun rising over the horizon. He puts his fingers against Dylan's neck, feels a faint pulse. "Dylan," he says. "Come on, kid. Wake up." He shakes him.

Dylan's eyes flicker.

"Come on, kid. That's it. You can do it."

Jack's feet slosh around in water. He rolls away from Dylan to discover the other half of the container submerged. It will sink in short order. There will be no place else to go but down into the sea. He looks over the edge, spots one of the Aga's pot buoys floating nearby. There's a pot on the sea floor, probably full of trapped crabs. Those crabs would never get out. They would, most likely, begin to attack and destroy one another until they all died. *I guess I might be joining them down there soon.*

Now very cold, his own circulation slowing, Jack looks up at the sky and whispers, "Though He slay me, I will trust in him." He looks at the encroaching ocean at his feet. "I will not give up." He grasps the amaroq claw and looks at the sky again, shouting, "You hear me?"

The sky doesn't answer him.

Dylan's breathing is now shallow. Jack embraces him. Slipping a little because of the angle of the sinking container, Jack pulls himself up, grabs Dylan by his shoulders. "Wake up and fight, Dylan." He shakes him. "Wake up." He massages Dylan's face, torso, arms, and his legs. "Wake up and fight."

Dylan's eyes flicker again.

"Come on, Dylan," he shouts. "I'm not giving up on you either." He keeps at it.

Dylan opens his eyes a crack. "Jack?"

"That's it, boy. Yes. You can live." He rubs him hard all over. "Come on. Come on."

"Jack," he whispers, barely audible. "I'm so cold."

"No. You're not. You are warm. You hear me? Keep telling

yourself that you are warm."

Jack loses his footing and slips backward down the tilting container. He manages to hold on, pulling himself back up. "I need you to crawl up there and hold on to the edge, Dylan." He grabs Dylan around the waist, pulling him up to the edge. Lifting Dylan's arms, he drapes them over the top edge of the container. "I need you to hold on. Here." He places one of his arms over Dylan's and reaches for the raft, tucking it around them. "Now hold on."

Jack assesses the situation. There isn't much surface of the container left. The angle at which it dips into the sea will pull the rest under soon. He examines the ocean, sees another buoy coming into view.

The container burps, air bubbling out near where they hold on. The container sinks a little more, only about three yards of it above the surface now. Jack moves his hand off Dylan to readjust the raft, but slides down the container right into the ocean and under the surface.

Chapter Thirty-seven

When you reach the end of your rope, tie a knot and hang on.
Franklin Delano Roosevelt

Donald snorts, waking up in the sedan by the river. The sun up, he opens the door, gets out and looks around. He grabs his bag out of the trunk, rummages through it pulling out a shirt. "Goddammit," he says. He looks into the bushes but doesn't see anything. He finds a spot, squats and defecates there. He uses his shirt to clean up.

He leaves the shirt, goes back over to his car, pulling out a cigarette. He lights up and stands by his sedan smoking.

He watches the river flowing steady then hears something rustling around in the bushes again. Scanning the bushes, he sees some sort of a large animal lurking around there. He flicks his smoke into the river, crawls back in his rental, closes and locks the door. He grabs a half-empty beer and chugs the rest, tossing the empty can over his shoulder into the backseat.

~ * ~

In the wheelhouse, Conrad and Qaniit scan the sea.

"Issumatar. Coast guard three-niner air rescue. Over."

Conrad says, "Go for Issumatar."

"Is that you, Conrad?"

"Rene? Hey, bro."

"Hey. We're about two miles off your port bow. We're heading south, southeast to follow the current. Cover the debris field drifting that way. Tupilek behind us."

"Roger."

~ * ~

Jack surfaces, grabs onto the container. He can't feel his feet and his body continues to shut down. He can't kick his legs very well either.

The container burps again. Air bubbles upward in a rush. Dylan's arms slip off. He slides into and under the water.

Jack dives under, swims down and grabs hold of Dylan's arm. He swims toward the surface, pulling Dylan with him.

He surfaces with Dylan just as the container disappears below the surface of the water, the final air spurting upward.

Jack spots the pot buoy a few yards away and swims for it, pulling Dylan along. He catches up with the buoy and drapes Dylan's arms over it. He performs the Heimlich maneuver to help expel water from Dylan's lungs.

Dylan coughs, spits up water. Jack holds an arm atop one of Dylan's arms upon the buoy steadying him so he won't slip off. Jack struggles to keep his eyes open as his breathing becomes shallower. It won't be long now. No options left, he resigns himself to the fact that he has done all he can to fight his fate. *Did I choose the wrong path?* His eyes flickering, he sees Amaroq standing on the water a few yards away, Qaniit petting her. With almost no breath left he whispers, "I'm so sorry, Qaniit. Don't ever give up. You must carry on. Without me. You must."

~ * ~

Akiak stands near the gunwale on the Issumatar with several men scanning the sea. "What's that?" one of the men says, pointing at something about one hundred yards off the starboard stern.

Akiak lifts his binoculars, spots the pot buoy and what appears to be two heads bobbing up and down with it. He notices the orange and yellow half of the raft floating nearby. He throws the binoculars down onto the deck. "Conrad. Men overboard." He points in the direction of the buoy, tears off his life vest, kicks off his boots and removes his jacket, throwing it at his feet. He grabs a life-ring, backs up on the deck, then runs, jumping over the side.

Struggling to hold the life-ring, he swims as fast as he can.

In the wheelhouse Conrad, Qaniit, and Ulloriaq jump to their feet, looking into the water at Akiak swimming away from them. Conrad turns the Issumatar hard to the starboard side, but because of the size the boat and the angle of the turn, he'll have to make a wide arch. While spinning the wheel, Conrad shouts into the radio, "Rene. Issumatar. Mayday. Man overboard. I think men overboard. Mayday."

~ * ~

Jack struggles to hold Dylan and himself afloat on the buoy as they keep slipping off. He must be kicking his legs because he holds their heads above the surface, but he can't feel them. He can't feel much of anything for that matter, doesn't even feel cold.

"Jack?"

Did I hear someone shouting, or am I hallucinating again? He tries to hold onto the slippery buoy with one hand and Dylan with the other arm, holding him against his chest now.

A wave hits him and he goes under but holds onto Dylan.

Something grabs him, pulls him up. He gasps, struggles to breathe, spitting out water.

For some reason, he finds his arms draped over a life-ring. His vision blurry, he can see Dylan's arms hanging over the ring too and another set of hands holding them all in place. *Is that Akiak? How can this be?*

A moment later, he feels this great rush of air blowing on him from above, the water churning all around. He can't keep his eyes open any longer. *It's time to let go.*

Chapter Thirty-eight

There are nights when the wolves are silent and only the moon howls.
George Carlin

Two frogmen jump from the chopper, a basket lowers after them. Akiak steadies, holding onto Jack and Dylan as the rush of wind from the chopper above churns the sea.

The Issumatar arches around, approaching.

Each frogman has a life-ring apiece. *"They're* from the Aga," Akiak shouts over the thumping sound the chopper makes hovering above them. "Take them first."

One frogman grabs the basket, putting Dylan in while the other holds onto Jack and Akiak.

The chopper lifts Dylan up.

~ * ~

In the wheelhouse, Conrad brings the Issumatar in closer but stops outside the rescue area to keep clear. He, Qaniit, and Ulloriaq watch as the chopper lowers the basket a second time. Conrad peers through his binoculars. "It's Jack." He hands the binoculars to Qaniit who watches as the frogmen place Jack into the basket.

"Conrad," Rene aboard the chopper says over the radio. "We've got three men."

Conrad says into the mike, "One is Akiak who jumped in."

"Roger that. You want to pick him and the two frogmen up and we'll get the survivors in to Norton Sound Hospital? The one on board has extreme hypothermia but is alive. We can stabilize on board with what we've got, but we've got to get in fast."

"I have to be on that chopper," Qaniit says to Conrad.

"Hey listen, Rene. I have Qaniit here. She needs to go with you."

"Okay. I understand."

~ * ~

In the water the frogmen put their fingers to their ears, nod, and give the chopper thumbs up, waving it off. The chopper repositions over the deck of Issumatar, lowering the basket again.

Conrad, Qaniit and Ulloriaq race down the stairs. Conrad helps Qaniit into the basket, strapping her in. The chopper lifts her up, heading for Nome.

On board the chopper a medic dries Dylan, inserts an IV then covers him with blankets.

The co-pilot helps Qaniit out of the basket. Over the pounding of the chopper blades, the co-pilot shouts to her, "Let us work, Qaniit."

She sits back as the men strip Jack's pants and underwear off. After they dry him, the medic taps a vein, inserts an IV. He attaches an automatic blood-pressure gauge to Jack's arm then wraps him in a thermal blanket.

The medic waves Qaniit over. All covered except for his face, she jockeys near, lies down and places her head on his chest. She closes her eyes.

~ * ~

He feels warm, the sun upon his face. The snow-capped mountains glisten before him, yet there is a haze all about. Jack looks over at Amaroq standing beside him. He kneels, strokes the sides of her furry head. "You crazy girl. I love you so." He kisses her nose.

"Yelp." She licks his face.

"Okay. Okay." He stands and she trots ahead of him.

She stops, turns. "Yelp."

"I'm coming. I'm coming." He follows her up the path into the mountains.

~ * ~

At twilight, the sun disappearing on the horizon, Donald turns the key, but the engine won't start. "Goddammit," he shouts. He turns the key again but it doesn't make a sound, won't even click.

He climbs out, opens the hood to look at the engine. He wiggles some wires then looks at the starter. "What the fuck?" It's burned, as if it had melted. "Fuck." He looks down river. "Goddammit!" He snorts, spits onto the ground, slamming the hood closed.

He grabs his bag from the trunk, pulls up his falling pants, and starts walking down the path next to the riverbank.

A few minutes later as Donald prods along, his shoes getting sucked into the mucky riverbank, he hears something on the path behind him as if it's following. He turns to look but sees nothing.

Continuing along, a short time later, he hears twigs cracking behind him as if something *is indeed* following. He stops, turns to look but again, nothing. "Who's there? Come out so I can see you."

He continues on for a little way further until he again hears something following, rustling around behind him. Turning to see he says, "Goddammit. Who the fuck is there? Show yerself. I've had enough of this bullshit."

Nothing.

He turns back to the path in front of him and sees a wolf standing there, its reddish-orange eyes scrutinizing him. "Get outta here," he says to it flailing his arms.

She doesn't budge but stares, cocking her head, examining him more.

"I said get outta here, damn, stupid wolf. Shoo." He reaches down, picks up a stone and tosses it at her.

She ducks her head; the stone sails past, landing in the water.

She still won't move, continuing to stare, as if toying with him.

"Have it yer way." He reaches down, picks up a stick and shakes it at her.

She cocks her head the other way.

He hears something behind him again. "Goddammit. Now what?"

This time he turns and sees an oversized grey wolf, larger than the other wolf, almost twice as big, with red, piercing eyes. Baring its teeth, dripping saliva, it stands there, sizing him up.

He drops his bag, the stick, and turns to run up the embankment but only gets a few steps before stumbling and falling face-first into the mud. He rolls over as the giant grey wolf with red eyes creeps closer. He kicks with his legs to push himself up the embankment away from the gigantic grey wolf. "Shoo. Shoo." Donald grabs at mud and rocks, throws some at the wolf, but falls short.

The large grey wolf stops and analyzes him, its teeth as large as a human hand. Donald keeps kicking to get away. He tries to get up, but the large grey wolf leaps and tears him apart, pulling off his arms then going for and ripping out his throat.

Amaroq stands there watching her counterpart tear Donald to pieces, his blood-curdling screams echoing throughout the valley.

~ * ~

Jack's eyes flicker, the bright lights of a hospital room above him. He looks down at his hand, finds someone holding it. Qaniit sits beside the bed, her head resting on his chest just below his chin. He breathes in through his nose, smelling her hair. *Am I alive? Is this real?*

She stirs, looks at him with those soft-blue eyes.

"Hi," he says. "How are you doing?"

She looks up at him. "How am *I* doing? Don't *ever* do that again."

"Never." He kisses her. "Ever." He looks around the room. "Dylan?"

She nods. "He's awake. They're discharging him today."

"I feel so awful about those boys."

"I know." She squeezes his hand.

"Do they know what happened?"

"A good idea. I don't ever want to speak that man's name again after I tell you." She hesitates. "They think it was Donald who planted a bomb. Chief Cerrano found his head along Snake River. Nothing else was found. Bruno said it appeared as if whatever had killed him, left only his head so they could find it and identify him."

Could it have been? While holding her with one hand, he squeezes the amaroq claw with his other.

Akiak peeks into the room. Jack waves him in. Ulloriaq and others follow including Conrad and Miles. "How long was I out?" he says to Qaniit.

"Three days," she says.

"Three days?" *Why was it always three days?*

~ * ~

A large camping backpack strapped to his back, Jack hikes up a path into the mountains. He turns and says, "Come on."

"I'm coming," Qaniit says, following him, her pregnancy beginning to show. "I'm not a mountain man like you."

He reaches out, grabs her hand, helping her up the path. "Just a little farther."

~ * ~

Later that afternoon, they pitch their tent in the Kigluiak Mountains then sit, holding onto one another next to a small fire.

Jack looks up, sees her come around from behind the tent. "Here she comes," he says.

"This is not possible," Qaniit whispers in Jack's ear. "No one except a shaman, a holy man, has ever seen her."

Amaroq stops, looks at Jack, then over at Qaniit. She edges closer and stands, towering over them.

"Hey, girl," he says to her. "I've missed you."

Amaroq nudges his head. He puts his hands on each side of her face, scuffs her fur and kisses her nose. She licks his face then moves around behind Qaniit coming up on her other side. Amaroq nudges her head too. Qaniit looks at Jack who nods at her. Qaniit reaches up and strokes the side of Amaroq's face.

Amaroq lowers her head and sniffs Qaniit's belly, nudging it slightly. She lies down next to Qaniit, outstretches her paws, and places her head on Qaniit's lap. Qaniit looks over at Jack. He kisses her.

While holding one of Jack's hands, Qaniit reaches down and pets Amaroq with her other

About the Author

James Charles has written six books. He is a former Administrator with the Los Angeles Unified School District and an Army Veteran. He lives in Hawaii with his wife, Linda.

Acknowledgement

Thank you to my sister Nancy Martin for catching some bloopers.

Also by the Author
at
Rogue Phoenix Press

My War with Hemingway

Zach, a young veteran, contemplates suicide after a horrific tour in Afghanistan when Ernest Hemingway appears and stops him.

He enrolls in college where he falls in love with Jessica, a young woman from a wealthy family. Her love stabilizes him, and Hemingway's appearances become less frequent, until she doesn't return to school after break. He confronts her father who tells him he is not to see her again.

Alone, haunted by the wars, and with his friend Hemingway pestering him, he descends into alcoholism.

Teaming up with one of Zach's army buddies, and in defiance of her parents, Jessica searches for him. But will they find him in time to save his life? And is her love enough to help him find redemption?

An Excerpt

Chapter One

I'm All Broken. They've Broken Me. E.H.

"Zach!" Micah yells from behind me. "Get back!"

I glance back at him and hold up a clenched fist. He stops, yet I edge closer to the young Afghan boy, no more than ten, eleven years old.

He is screaming, crying and flailing his arms. A vest of explosives covers his Perahan Tunban, Afghan robe. "It's okay," I say shouldering my rifle and putting my hands up to show him I mean no harm. "It's okay."

"Powell!" Sergeant Evans yells at me from near where Micah and the rest of my squad now huddle for cover behind a pushcart full of Afghan vegetables. "What the hell's wrong with you? Get your ass back here."

The boy, hysterical, falls to his knees with his hands raised to the sky as if he's appealing to Allah. Out of the corner of my eye I notice ten Taliban fighters scurrying up the dirty village street heading right for me, yet they don't seem to be real. They are like ghosts to me, or perhaps I'm a ghost to them and they can't see me. It doesn't matter. Nothing really matters, except this child in front of me who's caught between heaven and hell.

I am calm, yet determined, as I kneel next to the boy, and struggle to dislodge the vest, strapped and buckled tightly on his backside. He sobs while I try to set him free. "It's going to be okay," I say again, grappling with great difficulty to get the vest off.

In an instant, I hear a rifle report and the boy's head explodes like a pumpkin being dropped from a second floor balcony. His body droops into my arms and I look down at his lifeless body hanging on mine. I stand, sigh, and wipe something bloody from my hands onto my Army Combat Uniform, ACU's.

The Taliban fighters, screaming like banshees, are almost upon me. They pop off a few rounds, the bullets whizzing past me. I turn and head toward my patrol.

A blast knocks me to the ground.

Small arms fire rattles off from every direction as I high-crawl over to a ditch, a pain stabbing me in my shoulder. I glance over to where the boy had been. He is gone, having blown up anyway. One of the Taliban fighters must have controlled the detonating device, probably a cell phone. What animals, using children like that. No, I can't denigrate animals. Animals are higher species than they are.

I lie there, trapped in the crossfire, my squad engaged in the firefight. With bullets zipping over my head, I'm unable to get over to my squad, so I lay my head on the Afghan dirt and think how these past six months have been nothing more than a vacation in hell. These Taliban just keep coming and coming and coming. This will go on forever until everyone is dead.

I roll over onto my side and notice the boy's brain matter splattered all over my ACU's. The smell makes me nauseous and my hands shake. My clothes are soaked from summer sweat, the pain in my shoulder is intense. I reach up and massage my shoulder only to discover it is leaking blood like a sieve. *I can't* bleed to death here, in a ditch in Afghanistan. I just turned twenty-two.

I glimpse my buddies, Micah, Julio and Aaron engaging the enemy. They are my best friends. We have been together now four and a half years and have been through so much together in combat and back on base.

Then I recall how this day began like any other, routinely trudging along on foot patrol, but realize it will now end in a different way, for me at least. I hope my buddies all make it, even if I don't. Sweat drips from my brow. I lay my head down, close my eyes, and drift off into darkness.

~ * ~

I awake, lift my head and realize I'm sitting at a small table in the corner of a cheap, disheveled and darkened motel room on Bourbon Street early one Sunday morning. I notice dirty clothes and empty beer bottles strewn around.

I can't seem to erase that scene from my mind, or anything about the wars. I can't turn my head off. I think about that event, like it happened yesterday, yet it has now been six months. I'll never forget the terror in that young boy's innocent brown eyes just before he died. I'll forever see that event, as well as the other horrors, play out over and over again. *I've got to make it stop.*

I look down at a handgun on the table in front of me, sigh deeply, then grip a bottle of whiskey, raise it to my lips and guzzle. I slam the bottle onto the table, wipe the dribble from my chin with the back of my hand and pick up the gun, cradling it in my palm. Staring at it for the longest time, I engage its cold steel slide, chambering a round. It reminds me that death is cold, like when, as a child, I kissed my mother in her casket.

"That is how it came to be for me, too," a voice behind me says.

I whip around and face a young man standing behind me dressed in a military uniform. It looks old-fashioned, with a large belt worn over the coat at the waist, and a leather, buckled strap that hangs over the right shoulder and under the left armpit. He steps forward, snatches the gun from me and limps over to the window where he swipes the curtain open with the back of his hand, pulling it apart and peering out. Sunshine streaks into the room. I squint and shield my eyes.

"A cheap motel," he says. "On Bourbon Street. How fitting."

In disbelief, my vision a little blurry, I watch as he ambles back over to me, pries the bottle of whiskey from my hand and helps himself to a nip. "Potent," he says banging the bottle down. "Does the trick." He has a youthful face and a full head of black hair combed over the top.

"What the hell?" I look back at the door. "How did you get in here?"

He studies me a moment and says, "Look kid, the world breaks everyone and afterward many are strong in the broken places."

"What?" I say, my voice agitated.

He drops the magazine from the gun and ejects the round from the chamber. It bounces on the table. He gestures to my shoulder, the one I injured in Afghanistan and says, "The body can heal itself. The mind?" He shakes his head. "Not so easy."

I close my eyes and rub them with my palms. When I open them, he still stands there gazing at me. I look past him, scanning the room.

He finishes another swallow, looks the room over and says, "What the hell you looking for?"

I crinkle my brow. "Did Julio put you up to this?"

"Who's Julio?"

"You an actor? How much did they pay you?" I wrestle my bottle of whiskey out of his grip and swig more.

"Actor?" He snorts. "They're pretentious dandies."

I catch my breath from the whiskey, narrow my eyes and say, "Dandies? What kinda talk is that?"

He smiles. "You're funny, kid."

"Who the hell are you anyway?" I snap. "What's with the old uniform? You in costume for a show?"

He peers down at his uniform, frowns, then takes hold of the whiskey again. "Most call me Hem. You can call me Stein." He takes another pull from the bottle.

I lean forward resting my elbows on the table, close my eyes, and massage the back of my neck with my hands.

"Look, kid," he says, sitting next to me and glancing around the messy room. "You'll never know 'til you have lived through the worst what the best can be."

I look over at him and scowl as he twirls the base of the bottle around on the table by its neck. I look away again, down at the floor, and whisper to myself, "Am I that drunk?"

"Drinking lets you see things you normally can't when you're sober."

I turn back to him, examining his dark brown eyes and mahogany - colored complexion. He spins the gun around on the table like a roulette wheel and says, "You were like all the others. No catalogue of horrors ever kept men from war."

"Yeah. *Now* I get it. I can't go back, yet again."

"*Now* there are things greater than yourself to consider."

I hear someone fumbling to open the door behind me. I turn to look and see my buddies burst into the room. "Let's go, gringo," Julio says.

Micah says, "Yeah, we need to get goin'."

I turn to face the mystery man, but he has disappeared. I look the room over but he is nowhere. Julio slumps onto one of the double beds near the window and Aaron crashes on the other. Micah pulls the drapes open allowing the sun to illuminate the room and stands over me looking at the gun, a nine-millimeter Beretta. "That yours?" he says.

"What? Yeah. Thought about cleaning it just now."

His eyes bore through me. "You shouldn't be carryin' around a concealed weapon. You outta your mind?"

I shrug. "I figure this is the South. Everybody's packing down here."

"Don't mess with the South, mister," he says in his Alabama accent.

"We've all had breakfast," Aaron says. "You hungry?"

I pull myself up from the table, using it to steady me. "No. I just had mine." I motion to the bottle of whiskey.

"Damn," Aaron says peering at me. "You didn't get enough last night?"

"I'm taking a shower." I stagger into the bathroom, drop my boxers and jump in the shower before the water warms up. I rub my face and blow mist onto the shower wall. *What just happened? What was I thinking?* I stand there for the longest time leaning against the shower wall trying to get a grip on reality. *I have to pull myself together.* I have to play it cool. For the guys.

A few minutes later, I drag myself out of the shower and towel off. In the room, Aaron is stuffing clothes in his pack while Julio lies on a bed with his eyes closed. Micah inspects the whiskey bottle and grimaces at me.

"Don't start on me with your bible-thumping," I say drying my buzz-cut head with a hand towel.

"You know I've given up on tryin' to save your soul from eternal damnation," he says.

I drop the towel from around my waist and pull on a pair of boxers. "Stop staring at my ass," I say, throwing the towel at him.

It lands on his head. He pulls it off and throws it back at me. "Your skinny butt?" he says. "I won't ask if you don't tell."

"Funny," I say.

"Girls, stop your quarreling," Julio says. "My head's pounding." Aaron throws a dirty sock at him. It lands on his face. "Hey," Julio says. "That ain't mine." He throws it on the floor.

"Quarreling?" I say. "Where'd an East LA Cholo like you learn to talk like that?" I pull on a pair of shorts.

"Mexican-American is the correct way to address me, Private. Besides, I'm more of a patriotic American than you are. You know my great-grandfather was a decorated World War II soldier in Patton's army."

"Yeah, yeah, yeah. I've heard it all before. Hey, did I ever tell you, you remind me of a young Ricardo Montalban?"

"What? Ricardo Montalban? How old are you?"

"I used to watch old shows on TV Land. *Fantasy Island*? You're the spitting image of him."

"Freak," he says closing his eyes.

I pick up a pair of dirty boxers and drop them on his head. "Dammit, homie," he says, tossing them on the floor. "That's your nasty ass shit."

"What're you guys up so early for anyway?" I pull my socks and shoes on.

"Early?" Aaron says. "While Sleeping Beauty slept the morning away, we've already had breakfast and roamed the streets, fool."

"Stop calling me fool, bro."

"Listen white boy. Just get your drunk ass moving or I'll have to kick it again."

"We're closin' in on checkout time," Micah says. "We need you to pack up so we can get back to Bragg on time."

"Hey," I say, "we should stop at your place in Tuscaloosa. Perhaps Elise or some of Penny's friends would like to see me." I pick up my clothes and stuff them in my pack. I sniff a dirty shirt, shrug, and pull it on over my head.

"I wouldn't let any of them near you," he says.

"If you don't, I'm gonna put a skirt on you, pretty boy. What with those baby blues, blond hair and your rock-solid abs." I try to pinch his cheek, but he slaps my hand away. "You're so sexy."

"Knock it off. You're not my type, scrawny northerner and all. I like a little muscle, you know." He drops the whiskey bottle in the trashcan and shoulders his pack.

I glare at him and stuff the Beretta and the clip in my pack. With the palm of my hand, I slap the sole of Julio's shoe. "Let's go, Amigo."

Julio rises from the bed, moaning. He grabs his pack and heads out behind Micah and Aaron. I lift the bottle from the trashcan and guzzle the rest. *I think I fooled them. I think I got away with it.* I toss the bottle back into the trashcan and follow.

~ * ~

The car pulling over to gas up wakes me. "Get up sleepy head," Aaron says slapping me upside my head.

Swatting at his hand, I say, "Where are we?"

"Just south of Montgomery," Micah says pulling into the gas station. Micah drives, not only because the car is his, but also because he is the only one without a hangover. He doesn't drink. Aaron and I ride in the backseat of his new Dodge Charger, a gift from his father for service to our country. Of course, it helps that his father is a Baptist minister in one of those mega-churches where everyone buys tickets to heaven during the Sunday broadcast.

I'm in luck. There's a liquor store across the street. I bolt from the Charger, run across the street and purchase a bottle of Jim, Kentucky Bourbon. Back in the car, I pop Jim's top and take a hearty swig. Micah, pumping the gas, looks in and frowns.

Aaron plays a hand-held video game next to me in the back seat. Julio returns from the restroom, hopping into the front seat. Micah returns the nozzle to the pump, gets in and turns over the engine. He puts a CD of Lynyrd Skynyrd's *Second Helping* into the car's player and cranks up the volume for *Sweet Home Alabama*. Julio frowns and says, "My head, homie. Really? Redneck music?"

Micah lowers the volume a bit and grins at him. While I stare out the window admiring the beauty of southern, then central Alabama, I think about what happened back there in that Bourbon Street dive. *What was I doing?* I look over at Aaron and up front at Micah and Julio. They are like my brothers, if I had any. We have been through so much together and I can't let them down like that, especially with our third deployment coming, this time back to Iraq.

We're on a four-day pass between deployments. I joined the army right after high school and met these fools in basic training. We all had our reasons. Julio Salas's was to get out of the barrio. Aaron Glover for the same reasons with Southside Chicago, and Micah Reid, well, I haven't really figured him out yet after five years together. He also convinced the rest of us to reenlist. A band of brothers he says, and we all have to stick together. Micah enlisted, putting his football scholarship with the University of Alabama on hold. Go figure. Well, we've survived one tour in Iraq and one in Afghanistan helping one another through the slow and the boring, and the sometimes intense times in combat, as well as drunken escapades off base. Me, Julio, Aaron and some of the others have gotten drunk and laid, but not Micah. He's a good god-fearing boy who won't be with a girl before he's married.

I wrack my numb brain thinking of that strange man back in New Orleans. It's like dreaming about people with whom you've never met. It wasn't a dream. Was it? What was he saying, and what was with the old uniform? It's as if he put on Julio's grandfather's World War II uniform from a trunk in the attic or something, but it didn't look like any WWII uniform I've seen. *I must be out of my damn mind.* In any event, I pull my journal from my pack, tap my pencil against my lips and to the best of my recollection, transcribe what he said to me. From memory, I draw his face. Aaron looks over at the finished sketch. "Your boyfriend?" he says.

"Knock it off." I reach over and pinch his big black nose. We start wrestling but I hold my own and push him off. I open up Jim and take a good gulp. Micah looks back at me in the rearview mirror. "What?" I say, inflecting my voice.

"You're gonna have withdrawals in Iraq, Zach."

I top Jim off, wipe my lips and say, "I've got you, bitch, to hold me through the night."

He shakes his head. I doodle and write some notations in my journal. The journals I use have durable leather covers from an Indian company I found on the Internet, probably someone's incarnated relative. "So just what *do* you write in that diary all the time?" Julio teases looking back at me.

"What idiots you guys are. It's not a diary. It's a journal."

"Ooooh. A journal." He reaches over and grabs it.

"Dammit," I say struggling with him to get it back. He does after I put him in a headlock.

"You fools're gonna get us in an accident," Micah says.

"Look," I say opening to a page. "It has narrative and illustrations of our battles. Okay?"

"Narrative?" Julio says. "Illustrations? Awright, awright, psycho. You need to see a shrink."

"I need to see a shrink? You freaks keep it all bottled up inside. At least I let out."

"We're worried about you," Aaron says. "Let momma take care of you, my sweet boy." He teases me as he strokes my head.

I swipe at his hand, but miss. "Take care of me? You can't take care of yourself."

I stow my journal in my pack and stare out the window as we loop around Atlanta on Interstate 20. We transition to 95 north toward Fayetteville and head for Fort Bragg. I snuggle up with Jim, and while hugging the door, I hope like hell I can hold it together for this deployment, let alone survive it

64065149R00152

Made in the USA
Middletown, DE
09 February 2018